*continued . . .*

# LAST
# HOPE

Jessica Clare
Jen Frederick

BERKLEY BOOKS, NEW YORK

**BERKLEY**

An imprint of Penguin Random House LLC
375 Hudson Street, New York, New York 10014

Copyright © 2015 by Jessica Clare and Jen Frederick.
Penguin supports copyright. Copyright fuels creativity, encourages diverse voices,
promotes free speech, and creates a vibrant culture. Thank you for buying an authorized
edition of this book and for complying with copyright laws by not reproducing, scanning, or
distributing any part of it in any form without permission. You are supporting writers and
allowing Penguin to continue to publish books for every reader.

BERKLEY® and the "B" design are registered trademarks of Penguin Random House LLC.
For more information about the Penguin Group, visit penguin.com.

Library of Congress Cataloging-in-Publication Data

Clare, Jessica.
Last hope / Jessica Clare and Jen Frederick.—Berkley trade paperback edition.
p. cm.
ISBN 978-0-425-28153-6
I. Frederick, Jen.  II. Title.
PS3603.L353L372 2015
813'.6—dc23
2015018839

PUBLISHING HISTORY
Berkley trade paperback edition / September 2015

PRINTED IN THE UNITED STATES OF AMERICA

10  9  8  7  6  5  4  3  2  1

Cover photo by ImageBrief.
Cover design by Meljean Brook.
Interior text design by Kelly Lipovich.

To Mick,

who is the best.

We would be lost without you.

# ACKNOWLEDGMENTS

We want to thank all those bloggers who came together at the last minute and posted about *Last Kiss*. We *heart* you so much.

A Beautiful Book Blog

A Dirty Book Affair

A Love Affair With Books

AalyandTheBooks

All Romance Reviews

Booklover4lifeblog

Ariella's Bookshelf

Book Hooked

Books to Breathe

Charlie & Mel's Book Reviews

Escape Into A Book

Fangirl Moments and My
   Two Cents

I LOVE STORY TIME

Jacqueline's Reads

Lindy Lu Book Review

Maine Book Momma

Nic's Novel Idea

Ogitchida Kwe's Book Blog

Radical Reads Book Blog

Read It Woman

Read-Love-Blog

Reading in Pajamas

Recommended Romance

Seeing Night Book Reviews

She Hearts Books

Sugar & Spice, Smutty & Nice
   Book Reviews

The Book Fairy Reviews

The Book Goddess

The Reading Ruth

Twin Sisters Rockin' Book Reviews

Two Book Pushers

Written Revelry

2 Girls a Book & a Glass of Wine

A Reader Who Reads

Angie's Lil Neck of da Author World

Confessions of a Y.A. and N.A. Book Addict

Ellesea Loves Reading

Erotic Romance Book Blog With Sandy

Four Chicks Flipping Pages

Kimmy Loves to Read

Lina's Reviews: A Book Blog

Naughty Book Eden

Nicely Phrased

Not Another Damn Blog-Blog

Prone to Crushes on Boys in Books

Reading Is Sexy

Red Moon (Silence Is Read)

Reviews by Tammy and Kim

Sassy Moms Say Read Romance

Sinamen Reads Romance

Susan's Books I Like

The Book Blog

The Flare Up Book Blog

Thoughts of an Avid Reader

Treat Yourself with Books

Turner's Antics

Twisted Sisters' Book Reviews

Valley of the Book Doll

The Bad Ass Book Blog

Best of Both Worlds: Books & Naughtiness

BestSellers & BestStellars

Book Loving Pixies

Book Musings & Wine Pairings

ByoBook Club

Cat's Guilty Pleasure

Collector of book boyfriends

Diary of a Book Addict

Fictional Rendezvous Book Blog

Hot Guys in Books

Jo&Isalovebooks

Jodie's W.I.N.E. List

Marebare's Book Shelf

Margay Leah Justice

Momma's Secret Book Obsession

My Favorite Things

Nerdy Chic

Nerdy Soul

Obsessive Reading Disorder

OldVictorianQuill

Reading Drinking and Relaxing

Ripe For Reader

Sexy Bibliophiles

Sexy Vixen Reader

Smut and Bon Bons

Smut Book Junkie Book
Reviews

Sogni di Marzapane

Straight Shootin'
Book Reviews

Sultry, Steamy Reading

Summer's Book Blog

Sweet & Spicy Tales

Tantalizing Reviews

The Ultimate Fan Blog

Travels n Reads

Vera Is Reading

Warrior Woman Winmill

Wicked Women Book Blog

Wild and Dirty Book Blog

Shout-out to the Chroniclers Facebook Group and the Games, Billionaires & More Facebook Group. Thanks for making every day a bright one.

# CHAPTER ONE

RAFAEL

"How come it's always the pretty ones that end up working for these fuckups?" Bennito Vasquez is twenty-five years old. He has a head full of dark curls and no problems with the ladies but he still takes it as a personal insult when there is a beautiful woman out of his reach, and they don't get more inaccessible than Ava Samson.

"Because they're dumb." This conclusion is from Rodrigo. At thirty-two he's practically the old man of our group. But they all look up to me, which makes me feel far older than my thirty-five years of age.

"She's not dumb," Garcia mutters. He's my right-hand man. We've been through hell and more hell together.

Heaven is always two steps ahead of us and just out of reach. Miss Ava is heaven and sex wrapped up into one tempting package. Any man with a pulse has thought about what it would be like to climb into bed with Ava and get lost in her big eyes and tangled up in her dark brown hair.

"If she had any brains, she'd have stayed away from Louis Duval and his crew. Instead, she's sitting in a hotel in Lima with an ugly purse in her lap. That spells dumber than a box of rocks," Bennito declares.

Garcia shakes his head in disagreement. "She's smart. Look at how she acts. She knows she's being watched because she undresses under the covers. She sleeps close to an escape route but has her head toward the door to watch for intruders. Those are better preservation instincts than ninety-five percent of the population."

"Why doesn't she ditch the bag? I'd pitch that sucker and be out of that room in a heartbeat."

"It's clear there's something important there and she can't," Garcia replies with annoyance.

Garcia is right. Ava's smart. When she arrived at the hotel, she looked for listening devices, cameras, sensors. She found a couple of them but not all. Devices are so tiny these days that it takes an electronic sweep to discover all of them and even then some can be missed.

"Still . . . why'd she even come here with Duval?" Bennito asks sourly. He knows it all—or at least thinks he does.

"Because of Rose." I break my silence with a concept that Bennito can understand. "She's there because of her friend . . . her family."

The lightbulb turns on for him. Bennito's research for this current mission resulted in thousands of pictures of Rose Waverly aka Rose Wastkowski. Currently a middle-tier runway model, Rose has social media accounts filled with photos of her lying on the beach, out in nightclubs, and more recently, on the arm of Louis Duval. Duval is a French businessman who makes most of his money on the black market selling information. He has a fondness for blond models and Burgundy wine. His one true love is money.

Of Ava, Bennito found almost nothing. At the age of eighteen, she moved to New York City with Rose. There are no Internet hits with pictures of Ava, and her background check revealed a shared lease with Rose, two credit cards with low balances, and a modest checking account. Her parents are still alive but their connection seems tenuous. There are no phone calls or emails or text messages exchanged between them.

After reading the one-page dossier on Ava that Bennito had compiled, it was clear to me that Rose is not only her friend, but the only person in the world Ava has to call her own.

All of us standing in this room can understand Ava's desire to save her friend because that's why we're here. One of our own is being held as ransom. Our charge is to steal whatever it is that Louis Duval is trying to sell to various criminal factions. If we do that, we get Davidson back. If we fail, Davidson dies.

"Every one of us would strap dynamite to our bodies if we thought it'd save Davidson," I say quietly. "Stupid or not, we'd do it just like Ava's willing to do whatever it takes to keep Rose safe."

Chastened, Bennito returns to his duties. Despite his brash words and lack of thinking, he's a good kid with a gift for coding and computers. He has a feel for it that can't be taught. I pulled him out from under a prosecution in the United States after he'd hacked into a big computer website to impress a girl. Now he does more productive things that are far more dangerous.

But we back him.

Because that's how family works. Bennito is part of our brotherhood, the one Davidson, Garcia, and I formed when we realized that only by relying on each other would we survive the hell that the army was putting us through.

The smart thing for Ava to do would have been to walk away. When she came home with her arms full of groceries and saw Duval and one of his goons sitting in her small apartment instead of Rose, she should have dropped her bags and ran. Instead, she marched in and placed her bags on the counter and demanded to know what was going on.

Duval told her, quietly, that she was to help Rose carry out a task or Rose would be hurt. Ava resisted at first. Which is smart.

But then Duval pulled out his phone, swiped his finger through a few pictures that our secretly placed cameras couldn't pick up, and things got real quiet. Next thing we knew, Duval was telling Ava that she needed to fly to Lima. And Ava?

Ava packed her bag and went.

In the seven days she's been here in Lima, she's had one visitor—Redoine Fouquet. Fouquet is rumored to be Louis Duval's younger brother. Whatever family resemblance there once was has been eliminated by countless plastic surgeries as both Duval and Fouquet attempt to evade the law.

No, Ava wasn't dumb. Whatever her mistakes are, I don't think lack of intelligence is one of them. She's beautiful. That can often be a problem. Maybe she's too trusting or too kind but not dumb.

I walk over to the floor-to-ceiling windows in our hotel and look across the way at Ava's room. Clad in a tank top and yoga pants, she climbs into bed. The other men crowd around the table of monitors to watch. I fist my hands in my pocket.

I hate that they watch her.

I hate that she's in danger.

And most of all I hate that I care.

When Norse, the fifth man of my detail arrives, I tear myself away from the window and from Ava. "What's happening?"

"The object, whatever it is, is up for auction. It will close in forty-eight hours." Norse runs a hand over his shorn hair. It's winter in Lima, which in most places means cold. Here it means wet, humid, and foggy. Norse's cotton shirt is plastered against his chest. As he unbuttons it, Garcia throws him a replacement T-shirt.

Garcia was a sergeant in the army, responsible for making sure that the troops were all properly outfitted and armed. A good sergeant can mean the difference between everyone getting out with all their limbs attached and some newbie losing his toes to gangrene. Garcia was the best that there was. Now he's mine because the army doesn't handle its toys well.

They spend hundreds of thousands of dollars training them, making them into cold, unfeeling machines, but they lose interest in the older soldiers because they have this never-ending flood of new recruits. The nonstop supply makes us all disposable. Use them up and toss them out was the unstated motto. I've been gathering up the army's trash for the last ten years or so. Norse, Garcia, Davidson—all army discards. We take our skills and guns and hire them out. Ironically, the U.S. government is one of our best customers.

Except this time, our payment for a completed mission is Davidson.

"Do we know who the buyers are?"

"Two bids—one from North Korea and one from Libya."

"There'll be more," Garcia says.

I nod. There will be many more because what is being sold are secrets. Secrets big enough that the government felt compelled to kidnap and hold hostage one of my own instead of offering money.

Would we have taken the mission if there was only money on the other end? Probably. The mercenary jobs my men and I carry out are lucrative but not to the tune of hundreds of millions of dollars. That's what Duval's auction will command. It would take us ten years of killing high-priced targets to be able to play in Duval's pool.

"Ava has a visitor!" Bennito calls out.

We all rush to the monitor bank. The left one shows her rising from her bed. She is nearly fully clothed. About the only thing she doesn't wear to bed are her shoes. Sometimes during the day she will wear a belt and before bed will remove it.

She slips on her shoes—another sign of her intelligence. She won't be caught barefoot by a surprise guest. The door opens to reveal Fouquet. He speaks rapidly, backing her into the room and then slamming the door shut behind him. He has a hand around her wrist. Ava shakes her head and gestures at the ever-present purse. Fouquet raises a hand and Ava flinches back.

A low rumble sounds in my throat and I'm halfway to the door when Garcia grabs me. "Don't do it."

"I'm not going to stand here and watch her get beat by that fuckstick Fouquet," I growl.

"And if you go busting over there, then what? What happens to the auction? What happens to *Davidson*?"

Over Garcia's shoulder I see the men all standing and watching. Bennito looks frightened and Norse and Rodrigo resigned as if they knew the life that they were building was too good to be true for men like them. Killers. Forgotten. The refuse of humanity.

I wipe a hand down my face. Responsibility for them all weighs heavily but it's a burden I gladly carry. This is my family now. These men would die for me and I'm not going to put them in harm's way for a woman—not even one as smart, clever, and beautiful as Ava Samson. Because really, what would be the use? My fantasies about Ava are just that—fantasies. No woman would touch me. No woman would have me. Especially not one as fine as her.

And even if she did, I'd have to turn her away.

I give Garcia an abrupt nod and turn away from the door.

"Update?" I ask Bennito.

"Yeah, um, Fouquet left. He didn't hit her . . . hard. It was more like a love tap." He tries to smile but it fades quickly when none of us laugh. No one here is on board with a woman getting struck—ever. "Okay, yeah he hit her like a fucking asshole and she's in the kitchen putting ice on it."

He slumps into his chair. The tension is high in the room as Fouquet is still present. I imagine he was telling her that the sale was going to happen and what her next tasks are.

"We need sound," I say for the hundredth time. Ordinarily we'd get sound but there's a low constant hum that interferes with any vocal noise. Duval has something inside the hotel room that blocks any radio frequency collectors. "Norse, you and Bennito keep track of the bids. Rodrigo and Garcia, I want you to start tailing Fouquet. He's fresh from a two-year prison sentence.

No doubt he's fucking his way across Lima. Since he hasn't raped Ava yet, we can only presume that his brother is keeping him away for some reason."

"What will you be doing?" Garcia asks.

By his grim, unhappy tone, it's clear he already knows but for the benefit of everyone else in the room, I answer. "I'm going to find out what's in that bag of hers."

He follows me out into the hallway. "You like her."

"She's beautiful. Who wouldn't like her?" I walk down the hallway, the dingy wall sconces leaving deep shadows on the purple and green carpet. Garcia follows.

"It is more than that." His dark gaze is searching. I tug my ball cap lower, unwilling to confirm his suspicions. "You think she's brave, loyal."

"And?" My tone is impatient, signaling he should move off this topic.

"Just remember why we are here," he cautions. We stop at the elevator bank and I press the down button.

"I haven't forgotten." Are any of the four elevators going to stop on this floor? I jab the button again. Huffing out a sigh, I respond because Garcia and I go way back and he doesn't deserve a shitty rebuff. "How many people would put themselves in danger for someone else? Even someone that they love? Not everyone. Most people in Ava's situation would get the hell out of Dodge and never look back."

"Most people are smart," he counters. "Fight or flight, most people are choosing the flight option. Those who run today, live to fight again."

"But not Ava," I say quietly. The doors to an elevator slide open. I step in but turn around to face one of my oldest friends.

"I know I'm cursed, but shit man, so long as I don't touch, who the hell is going to blame me for looking?" I give him a crooked smile and as the doors slide shut, I see a reluctant grin break out in return. I don't have any plans to lay my hands on Ava Samson but damn if I'm not going to try to get close enough to see her smile at me.

# CHAPTER **TWO**

### AVA

Lima. The city of contrasts. Golf courses in the middle of the city and businessmen surfing before breakfast.

For me? It's a crapfest city of jerks that like to hit and threaten women.

I rub my jaw, still feeling the sting of the slap. It's not the first hit I've gotten from one of Duval's men, and it won't be the last. I want to fight back. I want to take the small plastic knives in the kitchenette of the hotel room, sharpen one into a shiv, and stab the bastard the next time he touches me.

I won't, of course. But I entertain the thought all the same.

The Louis Vuitton purse on the bed taunts me. It's a really nice purse. Leather, with the brown and gold monogrammed LV logo. I'd have loved to own one, once upon a time. This one was gifted to me, and I wish it wasn't here.

Because what's inside it is incredibly dangerous. I have to take it everywhere with me. It's in the bathroom when I shower. It goes with me when I go down the street for snacks. I can't let it out of my sight, or Rose is dead. That's been hammered into my head over and over again—I must not let the purse out of my sight, or my friend is dead.

Like I'm not already scared out of my mind.

I clutch the purse against my breast and move to one of the windows of the hotel room. I don't open the blinds. For all I know, Duval's got someone watching me out there, and I hate that thought. I do lift one slat with my index finger, just enough to glimpse at the world outside.

People walk the streets, laughing and smiling. I can see their faces even from my vantage point three floors up in the Inka Frog hotel. I see small cars squeezing past the narrow streets, and bicycles weaving between them. I see others shopping down the Calle Enrique Palacios, pausing by the vendor carts that scatter the street. There's a beat-up taxi pulling up to the curb. It's all very normal.

So idyllic. So incredibly misleading.

Maybe a month ago I'd have seen people clutching drinks and chatting on street corners. Moms herding children. Harmless people. Now? I see people lingering, watching passersby. I see men with jackets that could conceal guns. I see too many places that could hide someone waiting to kill me.

Sometimes I think my best friend Rose is the lucky one. She's the reason I'm so mired in this mess.

Rose and I have been friends since childhood. It's Rose that's been at my side since I was a young grade-school misfit. It's Rose that suggested I come to New York with her when I graduated from high school and didn't know what to do with myself. It's Rose that got me work when we both arrived in the city, fresh-faced and eager. She's a regular model; I'm a hand model because my mismatched eyes are pronounced "too weird" and my face isn't quite pretty enough even with contacts in. Rose is stunning, of course. Tall, thin, willowy, she's perfect.

She has shit taste in men, though.

She's been dating some dangerous French guy called Louis Duval for the last few weeks. Every time I went home, he was there, and I don't like the look in his eyes. Rose always laughed at my worries and said that he's harmless for girls like us. There's that whole implication that he's not harmless to other people, and I should have said something about it.

But I didn't. I stuck my head in the sand and went on with my life. And that, it turns out, was a lie. All of Louis Duval's words were lies.

Being a hand (and occasionally foot) model is all about hustling and taking small and strange jobs as they come in. Can I hold this banana for six hours while someone does a time-lapse photo shoot? Sure. Can I get a pedicure on camera for an instructional video? Sure. It's bizarre work but it's interesting, and it pays the bills. Rose does traditional modeling—runway, print work, you name it. She parties with high-end people and lives a faster lifestyle than me.

I just hold a banana for six hours and try not to twitch.

The truth is I'm in this gig because of Rose. It's not like banana holding was my dream career. I do it because it pays money and Rose lines up jobs for me with ease. Rose is always there to make stuff easier for me, and I do my part to make life easier for her. Since I'm not a runway model, I'm the unofficial "den mother" to all these models who are, for the most part, focused on their next job and forget to eat (although that may be on purpose), sleep, and live on cigarettes and rice cakes. Someone needs to buy them tampons, keep track of their schedules, and make sure the apartment's stocked up on coffee and salad.

I enjoy doing that—almost more than I enjoy holding a piece of fruit or rubbing lotion on my hands for five hours.

So Rose and I, we're a matched set, friends despite our differences. Polar opposites, yes, but we get along great. Always have, always will. It doesn't matter that Rose is glamorous and I'm a shut-in. We work, we go to clubs together, we share shoes, accessories, and nail polish. We're closer than sisters. Closer than family.

A week ago, though, Rose's lifestyle caught up with her. I came home to find that Rose wasn't in the apartment. In fact, she wasn't anywhere. Her boyfriend Duval was waiting for me, and he'd taken Rose away.

Turns out he's not a businessman, or at least not a legitimate one, because what legitimate businessman makes a girl courier information? His smooth-talking ways are a lie, and he's a drug runner who's hit a rough patch . . . and he needs help.

Because this time? He's not running drugs, and it seems he's in way over his head.

This is where I come in, he tells me.

My task unfolds. I'm to arrive in Lima at a small, unassuming hotel in the Miraflores District. There, I'm going to meet men. Several men.

My job? Well, I'm going to be a hand model of sorts. I'm going to Vanna White it up around the city. I'll be given a purse full of information that I'm to show the buyers. I'm to chat with them and show them samples of the goods that Duval has for sale. We're going to meet in coffee shops and have a drink like it's no big deal, and then I'm going to walk away, head back to my hotel, and wait for the next buyer.

Once the sale is completed, Rose will be released. We'll be free.

And if I don't do what he says, he's going to kill Rose.

I don't believe him at first. Who would? He's bluffing. Rose is his girlfriend. He wouldn't hurt her.

He must have anticipated my disbelief, because he holds his phone out to me. Puzzled, I take it and swipe my finger over the screen, unlocking it. A photo of Rose, bound and gagged and blindfolded and tied to a bed meets my gaze. I swipe over, horrified, and there are more pictures of her. Her body's covered in bruises, her hands cuffed behind her back.

"She thinks it's love play," he murmurs. "It can change so quickly. You should ask my last girlfriend."

And he nods at the phone again.

A sick roiling in my stomach, I go to the photo albums. I notice the one with Rose is flagged as "yesterday," which makes me sick. Yesterday, I was holding a shoe for a photo shoot and Rose didn't come home. I'd thought she was out partying with some of her runway companions after her last shoot.

I'm a horrible friend.

In a photo album from last month, there are pictures of another girl. Bound. Gagged. Pretty and blond, like Rose.

Then, there are more pictures . . . of her death. Of her sucking on the barrel of a gun and licking a knife. Then, of men doing things to her with the weapons. I suck in a breath, fighting the urge to vomit, and hand the phone back.

I don't want to see any more.

"What do you need me to do?" I tell him, and I'm in. Just like that.

He tells me not to worry. That if we're both "good girls," we'll be set free.

It's bullshit.

I know it's all bullshit and they're probably going to kill both of us, but I don't have options. No one will tell me where Rose is. Louis has her and he won't release her until he's sold that information.

It doesn't matter that Rose has been dating him for the last month. It's just business, he says. He'd hate to do something to her, so I'd better keep in line and do as he asks.

I do ask why me. I don't know anything about information smuggling, or Lima, or heck, I don't even know Louis Duval that well.

That's precisely why he wants me handling it. I alone can be trusted because I have sufficient incentive to keep me in line.

So off I go to Lima, to meet up with a man who might or might not be named Fouquet.

I contemplate going to the police, but I feel trapped. I can tell them that Rose has been dating a guy who is French (except not) named Duval (except probably not) and that she's missing. And by the time someone does something, I'm afraid my trusting, reckless friend will be long dead.

Because I think of the girl in the pictures, the one licking the knife that was later used on her. Did she have a friend that failed?

I won't fail Rose. I can't. And it keeps me in line. It stops me from going to the police, from screaming for help at the airport as I fly from New York City to Lima.

Once in Lima, I get a room at the hotel that Duval directed me to. They're expecting me and have a second-floor room reserved under the name Lucy Wessex. Once I check in, I find someone else has a keycard for Lucy Wessex's hotel room.

It's Fouquet.

I hate the man. He's vulgar and filthy and thinks I'm there in Lima as his plaything. Or at least, he did until he got a good look at my mismatched eyes without my contacts. Then, he changed. Now, I'm a demon, a succubus here to steal his soul.

Whatever, dude. I just want my friend back.

Me being a succubus doesn't mean he's not an asshole, though. He still tries to squeeze my tits and feel my ass, telling me that it's because I'm a succubus and I'm luring him. And when I make it clear I'm not interested in the tit squeezes he keeps trying to give me, he turns to slapping. I'm a hand model, so what's my face matter, right?

Fouquet's the one that shows up with the details of my first job and gives me the handbag, along with instructions to never, ever lose it. Whatever Duval is selling isn't in the purse, of course. Instead, I have folders of information. On each day, I'm to go to a random location in Lima with my purse, meet a man who will tell me a color. I pull out that color folder and hand it over. I wait while they read it and then hand it back to me.

Then, I turn around and walk back to my room and wait for further instructions.

So far, two days have passed. I have five folders. I have met yellow and green, both men with cold, dead eyes. Red, blue, and black are still waiting.

If I do not do as Fouquet asks, I am told that Rose will die, and it won't be quick or pretty.

It's not something I want to call a bluff on. I have to do this. I have to save her. So I'm the good little mule and never say a peep that I'm terrified or want out.

I let the blind fall back down and gaze around the room. As has become my habit, I move to the lamps and run my hand along the underside of the shade. I brush my fingers over the phone, then under it. I unscrew the receiver and put it back together. I drag my fingers over the edges of every hard surface. I'm looking for bugs. Not the kind that crawl (I wish) but the kind that listen in on conversations.

My room isn't safe. I have no hope as long as they can hear everything I say. I have to find all the bugs.

And then I have to find someone to help me. I don't know how that's possible, though, given I can trust no one.

I have to do something, though. I know once this purse is gone and the information sold, I'm dead. I know once the sale has gone through, I'm no longer useful.

I have three days—three colors—to think of something. Two, actually, because I need to go to a café and meet Red today in about an hour.

With a small sigh, I tug my sleeve down over my newest bruises, check my hair in the mirror, and then I'm ready to go.

Almost.

I shut the bathroom door and glance at my watch. They won't let me have a cell phone, so I have to have a way to check time and they gave me a cheap, tacky pink watch. I have an hour and the café is only five minutes away. I have time to burn. So much time. It's driving me crazy, all this time.

I lock the bathroom door and run my fingers all along the sink and under it, then check the lip of the tub and even in the faucets.

I find a tiny listening device hidden under one of the faucets and smash it, then flush it down the toilet. When I don't find any others, I suck in a breath and open the purse.

I'm always a little wigged out at the thought of looking inside the purse. I don't know why. I guess I'm afraid I'll find something worse. Like nuclear missile codes or a murder weapon. Hell, I don't know. I wouldn't put anything past these guys.

Fouquet always comes and checks the purse when he shows up, though. I don't know why, but when he checked it again today, I started to get suspicious. Everything looks as it normally does, though. The five colorful folders are tucked into the center, dotted with sticky notes and tiny flags. A few loose flyers are inside, of local events and printed spreadsheets. Garbage information, all part of my cover. I even have an iPad with Wi-Fi disabled as part of my "businesswoman" shtick. There are lipsticks, pens, and a sanitary pad to make it look legit. I even have a few keys on a key chain, but they don't belong to anything that I know of. I ignore all that shit. Something's nagging me, and I think of the many bugs I've found in the room. I check the purse, pulling the folders out and setting them on the counter. Out go the papers, too. When the bag is empty, I run my fingers over the lining. I might just be paranoid.

I find another listening device, though. Not big. Not thick. Just a small, hard circle stuck in one corner behind the lining that tells me that nothing I say is safe, no matter how many bugs I remove from my room. Shit. I leave it there, so they won't know that I know it's there.

But now, I feel more trapped than ever.

I have to get out. It doesn't matter that I've got an hour before I meet my next contact. The room is stifling and unbearable at the moment, and I just want to get away. I grab the bag and check my wallet. It's got money in it because I am meeting these men at cafés and restaurants and other public places.

I'll go to one by myself. It won't matter because they can hear everything I say, right? A mirthless laugh escapes my throat, choked back by a sob. I want to fling the purse away from me and leave this place.

But since I can't . . . I'll just run from the hotel room instead.


Five minutes later, I'm walking down one of the busy Miraflores streets, looking desperately for a warm, friendly place to go. The district is pretty, but it's also busy. With my halting, barely remembered high school Spanish, I've been able to navigate the area. I'm getting fairly good at miming things such as *eat, money,* and *where's the potty room?*

I pass a café that looks too crowded to be comforting and pause by a street vendor with a bright blue umbrella over his fruits and snacks. Maybe . . . maybe I'll just walk for a bit instead of eating. But Fouquet and Duval are shitty captors and they forget to feed me half the time, and I'm starving.

When I'm not too anxious to eat, that is.

I contemplate a hot churro and pull out my wallet, when a man comes and stands next to me.

There's a saying that shoe salesmen notice everyone else's shoes. I guess I notice everyone else's hands because I'm a hand model. This man has nice hands. He's got a paper cup of coffee, and the fingers gripping it are long, tapered, but strong. Nice knuckles. His nails are well trimmed, too. The men that I have been meeting have bitten nails, short, jagged. Those are the signs of an anxious person. This man is not anxious.

He's safe.

He looks over at me, and gives me a dazzling smile. In perfect unaccented English he says, "Need a recommendation?"

An American! I nearly throw myself at him and not simply because of his smile. He's gorgeous. Thick, black hair, bronzed skin and a grin that could make panties melt from a hundred feet. And he's standing right next to me? At the worst possible moment of my life? I can't decide if this is the worst timing in the world or the best. "Just contemplating what I want to do about lunch," I tell him, my voice breathless. I don't know if it's fear or attraction that's making me all husky and soft-spoken but I don't care.

I clutch the Louis Vuitton bag under my arm tightly as he leans in. "I know a great place around the corner," he tells me. "Want company?"

# CHAPTER **THREE**

**RAFAEL**

She is terrified.

The smile she so desperately tries to project trembles at the corners. And because I'm a sick fuck obsessed with her, I get hard. Granted it's not because she's scared witless, but because she's standing so close I could touch her. If I were her lover, I'd wrap my hand around her waist. I would tug her close, grip her shirt, and tongue her so deep she'd feel it in her toes. And since this is clearly a fantasy, the cars around us would keep moving past, the pedestrians would circle around us like an iceberg in the waters, and life would carry on uninterrupted.

It is only for me that the world would stop.

I shouldn't be here. I'm interrupting our task but I can't stand that she's afraid or that the asshole Fouquet has laid his hands on her.

"Company?" she repeats in an uncertain tone. "I don't know. I really shouldn't." Her soft lips have turned down and worry has crept into her eyes.

And what eyes. They are different colored—one deep brown and one brilliant green. With her pale perfect skin and her unique eyes, she's stunning to look at. It takes my breath away just to meet her gaze.

"Just for an hour? For a poor, lonely fellow American?" I give her my most winning smile.

Her own is shy, and some of the fear goes away. I'm glad to see that. She glances around weighing safety against her need to escape, her need for company. I worry she's going to decline, but she looks at me again, then nods. "Got a place in mind?"

I gesture at the café I just came out of. It's a French-style place but it serves food as well as coffee. As a bonus for Ava, the waiters are bilingual. "This one's nice and not too noisy."

She nods and ducks her head, stepping forward to go inside. I notice her grip on her bag is white-knuckled and tight. I move ahead to open the door for her, and she passes me as we go inside.

We grab a table at the back of the place, where it's quieter. I gesture for one of the waiters to come over and take our order.

She wilts into the chair beside me and pulls the purse into her lap. "Thanks. So you're American, huh?" She tilts her pretty head and the sun shines down on her makeup-covered bruise. She's done a good job covering it up but it's still visible. Under the table my hand clenches into a fist. At some point I'm going to take Fouquet into a private room and beat him until his teeth are falling out and he's crying for his mother. "What are you doing here in Lima?"

"Visiting family," I lie. "You?"

She blinks, as if taken aback. Maybe she doesn't have a lie prepared. "Um, vacation." Her hands clutch her purse. "Where are you from? Midwest?"

"Arizona." Does it matter that she knows the truth of where I grew up? It's not where I live now and I haven't been back to that town since I left for the army at age eighteen.

"I'm from Ohio. A—I mean, Lucy Wessex." She holds out her hand, the other clutched to her bag.

"Rafael Mendoza." I always use my real name. There are those who believe aliases are necessary in this business, but a great deal of my success rests upon the fear that my name raises in the stomachs of my opponents. That fear often buys me precious seconds of hesitation. But it's clear she's never heard of me. And why would she? Before she fell into Duval's grip, she was a model—although none of our research revealed any print or digital ads, unlike that of her roommate, Rose, who walks the runways in Paris, Milan, and New York.

I can't figure out why anyone would find Ava's creamy beauty lacking. Maybe Ava's lush rack and bubble butt prevent her from being the clothes hanger that fashion demands. Whatever the case may be, Ava is starring in all my fantasies now. It's Ava's hot ass that I'm palming as I drill into her and it's her dark hair that I have clenched in my hand as I pillage her body.

"Coffee?" I raise my hand to get the attention of a waiter again but it's unnecessary.

A dark-haired, skinny man-child appears at her elbow and bends low because he's been admiring what I can't stop thinking about. "What would the lady like to drink?"

"Coffee is fine." She gives him a brief flick of a smile.

"Nothing else?" he queries.

"You should eat," I say gruffly. She hasn't eaten much over the last two days. Fouquet is responsible for bringing her things, and other than the purse and one small bag of food, she's been largely without.

"I'm not hungry," she says, but an unladylike rumble betrays her.

"We'll have a charcuterie plate," I order. I hold up my hands about two feet apart. "A big one. You guys have that, right?"

The waiter scuttles with the order, leaving Ava alone with me.

She bites her plump lip and gives me a hesitant look. "Thanks for the food, but you shouldn't have done that."

Is she worried about the money? Duval probably hasn't given her a dime. "I would've ordered it anyway. The serving portions here wouldn't keep a bird alive."

She smiles, a quick twist of her lips, as if she knows that there's nothing good about her current circumstances but still can't keep her humor to herself. Every part of my body responds to hers so if she smiles, then I'm smiling, too, even though she's neck deep in Duval's plans to auction off information that could put an entire country at his disposal and I'm here to steal that information.

"You look bigger than a bird."

I suppress the instinct to flex but it's an effort. She speaks and I want to know how high I should jump and whom I should pound on the way down to make her life easier.

"Hence the big board of food."

"Can I make a confession?"

Yes, please. Her soft-voiced question strikes me low and, predictably, I react. At least I'm sitting down and the table is covering my growing wood. "Sure."

"I don't like Peruvian food." She grimaces. "I can't recognize half of it."

"I'll eat all the weird-looking shit for you."

She grins wide and I'm slayed. Holy fucking shit. There's the smile I knew she was capable of. That smile is enough to power the entire city for one friggin' night.

"No rain today," she says lifting her head.

"Yes, it's beautiful." We both know I'm not talking about the weather.

She gives me a wry look. "That's kind of cliché, isn't it? Something a guy would say to a girl in a Nicholas Sparks movie?"

"I wouldn't know. Haven't seen a movie of his but this is Lima. It's not exactly Paris."

Her smile turns wistful. "I kind of wish I was in Paris."

"I'll take you," I volunteer immediately. "Say the word and I'll have you riding the elevator at the Eiffel Tower. You just tell me when."

Those round cheeks of hers pinken, and it makes her strangely colored eyes even brighter. "Mr. Mendoza—"

"Call me Rafe."

"Rafe," she says, and my dick gets hard just the way she rolls my name around on her tongue. "I appreciate the offer but . . . now is really not a good time for me. Personally. Please don't be offended."

She's trying to let me down gently. The look on her face is troubled and sad. And just like that, I go from giddy with lust to sober again. She's not here for fucking fun. She's here because she's in danger and I'm distracting her, like a dick.

I need to get my business concluded. I tug my ball cap down and shift slightly away. I wonder what the keywords are, the secret mission code words to get her to open her purse and show me the sample.

"Why did you say you were in Lima again, Lucy Wessex?" That's a shit fake name. She doesn't look anything like a Lucy Wessex, which brings to mind a perky blonde from Connecticut whose daddy runs a hedge fund and whose mom, Muffin, bangs the tennis pro.

"I'm, ah, on vacation."

"Been to the beach?" I'm picturing her lush figure in a tiny bikini.

"Not yet." She looks sad. "Been too busy. I do love the beach, though."

"I'd love to take you."

She shifts uncomfortably. "Maybe I should go."

Shit. I've been too forward. My hand shoots out to grasp hers. "No," I practically shout at her. I take a deep breath and then manage to blurt out a few words to make me sound less like a madman. "No, please stay. I'm enjoying the company."

Her skin feels like silk under mine. I'll dream about this tonight. It's not lust that I feel for her. I know what lust is. I've felt it every day since my cock hardened as a boy and I spilled into my sheets. This is fever, burning, life-changing mania. I want her more than I have wanted anything in my life. But that want will never be satisfied. I know this and still I linger over her skin. And worse? Worse, she allows it. I withdraw slowly, stealing one more moment of pleasure.

I hear a tiny hitch in her breath as I withdraw, as if she liked my touch, but since I'm a big, scary motherfucker with calluses on my hands, I know I've dreamt that sound up. But I pack it away with my other memories. I've gotten a good close look at her. I know what she sounds like—husky and warm. I've inhaled her clean scent and touched her satin-smooth skin.

It's not much for other men, but for me? It's more than enough.

"I have to go somewhere soon," she admits. Her hand pulls from mine and goes protectively to the purse in her lap. I've seen her take that damn thing everywhere, even into the bathroom in her hotel room. It's clear that's the information she's supposed to share. It's clear I should be thinking about it and how to get it from her.

But all I can think about are her soft hands. "At least stay to help me eat the mammoth pile of food I just ordered."

Her grin flashes again, and a small chuckle escapes her throat. "Can we eat fast?"

"We will throw down," I promise. "Like wild animals."

## AVA

Rafael Mendoza is utterly charming. God, I wish I were here in Lima on vacation, like I said. I wish I were a carefree model that could pick up a beautiful man on a street corner and think this could go somewhere.

But I keep thinking about the meeting that's going to take place shortly. I check my watch. In a half hour, I have to be at an entirely different café, meeting an entirely different man. The man the red folder is for.

I'm a little too fascinated by Rafael Mendoza, though. His manner throws me off. It's the cagey way he answers my setup questions, like he's more interested in watching me than what I'm going to say. That should worry me right there, but for some reason, it makes me feel . . . I don't know. Protected? Maybe it's because of his hands. It's those nice fingers, and the calluses on his palms. I actually don't mind calluses on a man's hands, because they tell me a lot about a guy. They tell me he's used to working with his hands. That he's not afraid of getting dirty. That there aren't the accompanying rings of dirt under those well-trimmed nails tells me that he's also fastidious.

He's also devouring me with his eyes, like watching me is more filling than eating that plate of meats and cheeses in front of us.

He watches me eat a few slices of meat and cheese, and then that grin tugs across his face again as I lick my lips. For a moment he looks rakish and utterly sinful. "Tell me about yourself, Lucy Wessex?"

I'm utterly flustered at that. What can I tell him that is safe? Private? "Oh, I'm pretty boring."

"I shouldn't think so." He nudges the cheese knife at his side toward me.

I blink and look at the charcuterie plate in front of us. I'm eating, wolfing down food, but he's not touching it. Didn't he say he was hungry? Why is he not eating? He's just . . . watching me. Like a hawk. Or a predator.

This is starting to feel like a trap. My heart pounds. "I . . . I think I need to leave."

Again, his hand touches mine. "Stay. Please." He gestures at the food. "You've hardly touched it."

My stomach is rumbling, but I'm no longer hungry. There's something off about this. Something too watchful about Rafael Mendoza. He's giving me mixed vibes and I don't know what to think. "I really do need to go."

"Will I see you here again?" he asks. Again, he nudges the knife toward me.

His question flusters me even more. I shake my head, heft my purse under my arm, and then stand. "I'm leaving for home soon."

"Be safe," he tells me. He doesn't get up. Instead, he picks up a piece of cheese from the plate and eats it, as casual as could be.

I watch him for a moment longer, my head whirling and full of confused thoughts. "Thanks for the food. I really do have to go."

Then, I rush out the front of the shop and across the street, trying to keep my steps hurried but casual.

I pause to look back once I cross the street, to see if he's still in the café. The table is empty. I glance around to see if he's following me, but there is no one near, no one on the street other than a couple laughing and talking in soft voices under a nearby awning.

Rattled and not entirely sure why, I head down the street for the reveal.

An hour later, the show-and-tell is done and I head back to my hotel room.

I don't relax until the door is locked and I sit back down on the edge of my bed. I'm trembling. The luxury purse feels like a ball and chain, and I wish to God I could pitch it out the window. I give it an angry toss onto the bed, feeling frustrated and unsettled.

I was so calm when I met the clients. Said my piece. Gave them the information. Sipped my drink. Left.

And yet I meet one handsome stranger in Lima and I'm all rattled. What is it about this guy that throws me off? Is it because, for the first time, I felt like someone actually saw me instead of Rose's friend? Is it that I'm attracted to him and the timing is incredibly lousy? The thought unsettles me. I can't afford to be distracted.

He . . . wasn't after the information, was he? Was he using me to get what I carried? He hadn't shown interest in the purse, but I don't trust anyone anymore.

On a whim, I shift on the edge of the bed and open the purse. I pull out the red folder and flip through the sheaves of xeroxed copies inside. Some of them are of receipts. Some are of emails to a government agency. It looks legitimate, but what do I know? There are thin sticky notes highlighting passages that are inane, and the flags are placed at random spots. This one has a sticky flag by a request to purchase a stapler. I guess *stapler* must be code for something.

There's a quick knock at the door, and then I hear the doorknob rattle. I shove the folders back into the purse, my heart pounding.

Fouquet storms into the room, his too-plastic face furious, his eyes wild. I instinctively draw back a little, and when his gaze lights on me, his nostrils flare with anger.

"You stupid bitch," he snarls and advances toward me.

I get up from the bed and retreat, holding the case in front of me like a shield. "What did I do?"

"You met a man at the café!" He pulls back as if to backhand me.

I flinch away, holding the purse in front of my face. "What? Yes I did! He was nice and bought me lunch. I didn't say anything! I wouldn't do that. I wouldn't risk Rose!"

"You met Rafe Mendoza. Do you know who he is? How dangerous he is?" He pushes at the purse clutched in my arms, slamming me into the wall.

"No!" I cry out. Rafe Mendoza is a name that means nothing to me. "Of course not. Who is he?"

"A hit man," he hisses. "You flirted with the enemy. Are you too stupid to do this job? Shall I find another mule?"

"No," I say quickly, ducking out of the way before his swinging fists can hit me again. "I can do this. I can." Rose is depending on me. I have to do this.

"You might have cost us a buyer. The Turkish buyer is pulling out now that Rafe Mendoza is here." He grabs at the purse and tosses it toward the bed. I immediately lunge to catch it, and he slams me backward onto the bed. I immediately scramble to get up, because on my back with this man? Not where I want to be.

He grabs my ankle and I kick at him, panicked. "This is not part of the deal!"

Fouquet laughs. "I do not want you, idiot girl. Not with your ugly eyes." He drags me back down onto the bed and his hand goes to my throat, pinning me. "Now. Tell me what Rafe Mendoza said to you."

I stare into his pale eyes and for a moment, I'm hit with a surge of hate so strong that I'm tempted to shuck all responsibility and tell him to go fuck himself. I think longingly of the knife back at the café that Mr. Mendoza nudged toward me. I should have slipped it into my case.

But my best friend, the person I love most in this world and owe everything to, is being held by killers.

So I swallow my anger. "He said his name was Rafael Mendoza. He's American. From Arizona." I detail our conversation as best I can. I want to point out that they have me bugged and they could hear everything, but it'll sound bitchy and confrontational. I need to be nice, sweet Ava so they don't take their anger out on Rose.

Fouquet's face tightens as I speak, and the hand on my throat grows punishing. His thumb is right over my windpipe, and for a moment, I wonder if he's going to choke me. "If you kill me, you have to mule your own purse," I tell him in a raspy voice.

The hand loosens. "Did he say anything about the bag? The buy?"

"No."

"You're sure?"

Did he think I got some sort of silent signal? The only thing he did was nudge a knife toward me. "I told you everything."

Those pale eyes narrow again. Fouquet delivers another ringing slap to the side of my face. This one smacks my teeth against my lip, and I feel it split, taste my blood in my mouth. "If I look like shit, people are going to notice," I warn him.

He narrows his eyes at me and grips my chin, puffing my cheeks like a chipmunk's. Then he says, "You had best clean yourself up nicely, then." And he releases me and crawls off the bed.

I sit up and scramble backward, ignoring my aching wrist and my throbbing face. "What now?"

Fouquet straightens his jacket. "Now I must go apologize to the Turkish buyer. I will try to convince him he is still interested." He glances back at me. "You will see me again when decisions have been made."

I slide to the corner of the bed. "Can you send up some food?" I'm starving. "And a first aid kit for my face?"

"Later," he says dismissively. He shuts the door behind him and then I'm in the room alone again.

I exhale in relief. Touch my throbbing lip. The longer I'm here, the more Fouquet hits me. By the time I've met with all the buyers, I'm going to be a freaking bloody pulp. It just reminds me that I'm expendable to these men. I have to be more careful.

I get up from the bed and begin my regular check for bugs

and listening devices, running my free hand along windowsills and lampshades. As I do, I think about Mr. Mendoza. I think about him nudging the knife toward me. Was it a signal I somehow missed?

Is he on my side? Or just using me because I am a tool to be used?

Either way, he might be my only hope.

# CHAPTER **FOUR**

## RAFAEL

On the way back to the hotel I stop by and pick up some soft bread, cheese, and sliced salami. She probably doesn't have a knife in that room. I'll leave it outside her door. She can think it was Fouquet who left it for her or that it was dropped by some other resident. I don't care. I just want to get some food inside her before she collapses from hunger. I add a box of macaroons. She was eyeing the table next to us who had an order of them.

When I arrive at the hotel, Fouquet is climbing into his black Audi. A quick detour down an alley yields the employee entrance. I pass by a few who say hello to me, and then quickly disappear into the stairwell.

I wait in the stairwell for a few minutes. Not because I'm worried I'll get caught. Fouquet has left. Outside her room there is no guard, but I don't make the mistake of thinking there aren't eyes on her at all times. I wait because I need to get myself under control. A great stupid portion of me wants to charge down the hall, kick down her door, and drag her into the bedroom. She will, of course, be willing. She claws at my clothes, ripping them off and then falling to her knees. In porn, that's what the women do. They fall to their knees, jerk out the big cock and swallow it whole, looking at the camera the whole time as if cock is the best fucking meal in the world to them.

Ah, how porn has steered so many men wrong.

No one has ever had their mouth around my cock and no one has looked at me worshipfully. With fear. With anger. With a hell of a lot of pain, but no worship.

It's a stupid, foolish game I'm playing with myself.

The fuck of it is, I don't need her to suck my cock. I'd rather be facedown on her pussy, inhaling her musk and drowning in her juice. So instead of her falling to her knees, I'd push her on the bed and I'd rip her pants off and bury my tongue inside her until she's crying out for God or Buddha or whatever greater entity she thinks is bringing her glory.

That would be me. Rafe Mendoza. I laugh and the bitter sound bounces off the walls so I can hear the echo of my own mocking. The cement wall is a good place to bang some sense into myself.

A sharp knock to the head brings clarity. I've never brought a woman glory, only pain. No doubt it would be the same for Ava. Even if I had a chance, which I don't because snowballs in the Amazon have a better likelihood of survival than I have of ever laying my tongue on Ava, I wouldn't allow myself to touch her. My mother told me I was cursed in the womb. I lived to prove her wrong, but each successive year of my life revealed the truth.

I hurt those I touch. I kill those I love.

Deprivation isn't all that bad, not when the alternative means hurting an innocent woman.

I tuck my chin against my chest and step out into the hallway. A door next to Ava's room opens and a heavily armed man about six feet tall steps out. He straddles the entrance, watching me carefully. So Fouquet isn't the only one within arm's reach of Ava. Out of my periphery, I glance into the bedroom. There's another man inside, seated with a long gun over his knee. I could take the two of them out, grab Ava, and have her on our way to the island in about thirty minutes.

But if I do that, I'm signing Davidson's death warrant and he's too good a man to leave behind. Besides, what would I do with Ava if I had her? Stare her into an orgasm? Stroke her hand until she whimpers with pleasure?

*Fool*, I curse myself. But I'm still here like a jackass standing with my pitiful offering of food.

I walk on past, gripping the bag, and then stop at the far end of the hall. The room is silent, unlike a couple of the others that had television sounds. I lift my phone to it and open an application. The lock snicks open in seconds. As I open the door, the thug retreats into his room. I wait for a count of ten, walk back down, drop the bag and then hustle to the elevator. I'm just another tourist who forgot something.

When I get back to the base, Bennito gives me an update.

"Fouquet was back. He slapped her a couple of times and I think she told him about you."

"He hit her?" I growl.

"Yeah, man, across the face this time."

I've got my hand on the doorknob before I come to my senses.

Squeezing the metal until the round ball starts bruising the skin, I strive for calm. "Place a call to her room and tell her that there's a meal for her outside her door."

"Didn't feed her? What kind of date are you?" he jokes as he punches in a few keys on his computer.

"A shitty one."

I force myself to walk back to the monitors, and we watch as she turns away from running her fingers over the lamp to eye the phone with suspicion. She lifts the receiver. Bennito adopts a Peruvian accent even though he is from West Texas. "Senhora, there is a package at your door."

"Um, okay. Can I ask who brought it?"

"Your white knight."

I cuff him on the back of his head and he hangs up. "What? You're the good guy in this situation. I was smoothing the way for you in case you hook up with her later. I see how you watch her."

I imagine shoving my fist into his toothy grin. "Don't fuck around. This isn't a game."

"Yeah. Yeah." He holds up his hands in surrender. "No more jokes, but you know, I'd have thought that you'd be swimming in pussy. If I had my own private island and a boatload of cash, I'd be Leo fucking DiCaprio with my harem of supermodels to feed me grapes and rub my feet. But you, I never see you with a broad. Never. There are plenty of hot *mamacitas* on the island and they'd all open their legs for you in a heartbeat, but you don't even look twice at them."

"Rub your feet, Bennito?" Garcia has crept in behind us. "You have a dozen supermodels and you think only of food and feet?"

Garcia's gentle mocking has the intended effect. Bennito flushes but doesn't bring up my near-monkhood status again. He changes the subject. "I saw a picture of Leo the other day. What the hell do those women see in him?"

"Money. Fame. Power." I tick them off.

"All of the above," Garcia adds.

Bennito harrumphs. "You've got all that."

A warning look from Garcia shuts him up, but I don't care that Bennito believes I abstain. It's a good lesson for him—to go without builds character. And the longer you go without, the more that you forget what you are missing. At least that is the lie I tell myself.

Across the street, Ava peeks out her peephole and then opens the door. She looks around and then at the floor. Her hand reaches out, snatches the bag, and drags it in quickly. Slamming the door shut, she leans against the wood slab and peeks inside the bag. Then she lifts it to her nose.

Damn straight it smells good. Fresh from the bakery. She hurries over to the counter and unpacks everything.

"Shit, did you buy out the entire store?" Bennito mumbles around a chip.

It does seem like a lot of food now that it is spread out. There are honey butter rolls along with fresh cheeses and meats. A couple of fruits roll precariously to the edge. There is jam along with chocolates and the macaroons.

"She didn't eat enough," I remind him.

"Right. So is the stuff Duval selling legit?"

She breaks apart the roll and shoves half of it in her mouth. Her head drops back and even though I can't hear her, I know she is moaning. God, I want to hear that sound. Is it soft? Is it a short sigh or a long, extended low note that would make my cock shiver in response?

"I assume it is or we wouldn't all be here."

"What happens next?" Garcia leans a hip against the edge of the desk.

"From the surveillance, she has five folders in her bag. She's presented the yellow to the buyer from North Korea. The green went to the Libya. Once all the buyers have their chance to look at it, then the auction goes down. We wait for the exchange, fuck that up, and make off with the package."

"And if we don't get it?" Bennito asks. "What happens then?"

"That's not an option." Garcia cuffs Bennito again.

"What the hell? It was just a question," Bennito complains.

I place a pacifying hand between them. "You are new, but the vow you made when you came was to protect everyone at the Tears of God as if they matter more to you than your mother. We leave no man behind. It does not matter if God himself holds one of us hostage. A man or woman of the Tears of God knows to wait, for his family will come and save him. Isn't that why you are with us, Bennito?"

He has the grace to look ashamed but with the exuberance of youth rallies immediately. "Well that and the women."

Garcia slaps him across the top of his head but it's light this time. Almost affectionate, but Bennito's head will ache tonight from all the strikes; maybe it will drum some sense into him. As we all laugh, the monitors flash.

The door to Ava's apartment bursts open. Fouquet is at the door. He is motioning to two others behind him. Ava has the second half of the roll halfway in her mouth when the man I saw in the hallway pulls her to her feet. They drag her out and the door slams shut behind her.

"Fuck." I jump to my feet. "They must be moving her."

Garcia shoves a bag in my hands—the one we laughingly call the Boy Scout bag. "I double-checked the emergency kit this morning. Go!"

I grab my two Glocks and shove them into a dual shoulder holster. I sling the leather over my shoulders and catch the jacket that Garcia tosses at me. And then I run. I don't even know if I'm running to save Ava or the package at this point; I just know I can't let her out of my sight.

# CHAPTER **FIVE**

## AVA

"Where are we going now?" I ask for the tenth time in the last ten minutes. There is a man on each side of me in the car, and the purse is in my lap. My wrist feels sore from where Fouquet has grabbed me, over and over again.

No one answers me. Of course they don't. I don't matter to them. I get my answer soon enough, though, when the car pulls up to the airport and parks in the fire lane.

The airport?

I'm frowning in surprise when the man on my right—Afonso—grabs my hand again. I hiss in pain when his fingers dig into my wrist, and his mouth curls into a sneer. "Don't get too excited, little one. This is only temporary."

Excited? At his bruising hands? I jerk my hand out of his grip. "Don't touch me."

"You will be with me, Daughter," Afonso says, and holds up his passport. Afonso Wessex, it says. Ugh. He then hands me mine as "Lucy Wessex."

"Great," I say, my voice lacking enthusiasm.

"Try anything and your friend Rose will die," Fouquet calls from the front seat. "And it will not be a quick, painless death."

*You guys are dicks*, I think, but I don't say it aloud. I just say, "I know. I'm not going to do anything."

Because Rose is depending on me to be the good, sweet mule. And that's who I'm going to be.

I look over at Afonso, and he's peering down the front of my blouse. What a classy "dad." I hitch it higher instinctively. "May I use my plastic gloves and hand lotion while we're here?"

They're used to my weird issues with my hands. I'm a hand model, which they know, and so I'm constantly lotioning my hands and putting on plastic gloves to protect them from any sorts of environmental mishaps. I bought them one day after I'd met the first buyer and have used them religiously since, even though Fouquet looks at me as if I'm up to something. I've told them it's because I want to go back to work as if nothing has happened once this is all done. And they allow it, which might be some kind of psychological torture, but the plastic and lotion are a comfort.

The gloves serve a second purpose in that they're going to keep my fingerprints off any of this shit. Mule or not, I'll still go to prison if the kind of information I'm carrying gets out and has my name attached. It's Snowden levels of information from what I can tell, and the thought terrifies me.

"Put those in your bag for now. It will give you an excuse to keep your carry-on with you." Fouquet tosses the box of disposable gloves that were in my luggage in my direction. I catch them and am startled by the dark ring around my right hand. My wrist is ugly and bruised, and I wince at the sight of it. I pack the gloves and the lotion into my case.

I go into the airport with my "dad" Afonso and Fouquet flanking me. We don't even look casual, not in the slightest, but no one notices. Maybe it's because we're in Lima and no one gives a crap about this sort of thing?

We get to the check-in counter, go through security, and head to the waiting area. It's all very low-key and I want to scream at the people wandering past, lost in their own thoughts. Can't they see I don't want to be here with these two men?

But everything is normal, and I hand my ticket to the girl moments before getting on the flight. "Enjoy your stay in Pucallpa," she tells me with a smile.

Is that where we're going? Never heard of it. I smile back, because what else can I do?


"Pick a card," Afonso tells me for the hundredth time, leaning in too close to my seat. "Any card."

Oh God, I hate this flight so much. Fouquet received a phone call at the moment of boarding and told us we'd meet in Pucallpa so it is just my "dad" and me.

I glare at my captor, who's getting more drunk by the minute, thanks to harassing the flight attendant. I should have more patience. He hasn't hit me once, and if he smells of whisky and hair product, that's better than a punch to the mouth.

But I swear, if he looks down the front of my blouse one more time, I'm going to lose it.

"Come on," Afonso says, waving the deck at me. "Pick a card."

He keeps trying to do magic tricks. I'm not sure if it's a euphemism for something or if this is more of the daddy-daughter shtick, but it's creeping me out.

For what feels like the millionth time in a row, I pick a card. The plastic gloves on my hands make it difficult to pull one out, but I manage. Two of clubs.

He shuffles the deck and gives me an exaggerated wink, then slaps a card against his forehead. "Is this your suit?"

It's a diamond. "No."

He frowns and looks down at his card. "Eh?"

I show him mine. "Maybe I jinxed it." I'm pretty damn unlucky.

"No, it just needs the touch of a real hand," he says, nodding at my gloves. "Those are messing up the flow. They, like me, need the touch of a real woman." And he gives me what I suppose is a lady-killer wink.

Gross. I smile politely and wiggle my gloved fingers at him. "I'm sorry. I'm going to keep wearing these. My hands are my livelihood."

He snorts.

Lightning flashes out the window, and I nervously peek out again. The clouds below us are an angry, thunderous shade of black, and I can see lightning flashing. We've been in the air for less than an hour, and it feels as if all of Peru is covered in storms. It makes me nervous. "I'm a hand model," I tell Afonso for the millionth time. "Hand and foot, but mostly hand."

"You're protecting them from sunlight, yes?"

"Sunlight, other people, you name it," I agree. Right now, my gloves are full of shea butter. I'm moisturizing up since we're on the flight and I've got nowhere else to go for the next few hours. Plus, it sounds weird but moisturizing relaxes me. It's part of my routine and it's soothing, and lately I've needed a hell of a lot of soothing.

Afonso now gives me an assessing look. "Your hands, they are soft, eh?"

My creepster meter goes through the roof. "Yep," I say flatly, and turn back to my window. It's a cue for him to leave me alone, and I wish I had one of those eye masks so I could put it on and pretend like my "dad" isn't here.

The tiny plane has two rows of seats on one side, and one solitary seat on the other. I've got the misfortune to be in the center of the plane with Afonso. What's weird is that there are a ton of seats open. The plane seats thirty or so, I'm guessing, but other than the stewardess and three men in the back, there's no one else on board. Pucallpa must not be a hot Sunday flight spot.

I'm the only one with a seatmate, too. Lucky, lucky me.

Afonso could easily take an empty seat in a nearby row, but he's content to bother me and spend the flight time peering down my shirt.

Claustrophobia hits me and I feel sick to my stomach. In my hotel room, I was alone for the most part. Here? Afonso is in my space and he won't go away. His hand grazes my thigh, and my stomach clenches nervously. Rape hasn't been on the table yet, but suddenly, I'm not ruling it out.

And that frightens the hell out of me.

I need to get away for a few minutes, if only for a breather. Thunder rumbles outside of the plane. "I need to use the restroom, Afonso. If you'll let me out—"

"Don't be in such a rush," he tells me, and gives me what I assume is supposed to be a sexy grin.

"Really must go," I say, standing up in my seat. "Stomach upset."

And I groan emphatically, my gloved hands squishing as I fist them tightly and press them to my stomach.

He frowns and gets up to let me out, though I'm pretty sure I feel his fingers drag over my shoulder and down my thigh as I shimmy past. Shuddering, I make my way down the aisle to the plane's small bathroom at the back of the passenger compartment. The purse is slung over my arm, and I enter the tiny cubby sideways to ensure I don't smack it against the door. Once inside, I lock the door behind me, put the lid down, and sit down on the toilet.

I don't have to pee. I just need to breathe.

I practice deep breathing for a few minutes, trying to calm the panic rising in my throat. They're moving me to a new city. Fouquet is getting rougher, and Afonso is getting more forward by the hour. If ever my life felt like it was hanging by a thread, it's now. I think of Rose. Poor, poor Rose. What are they doing to her? Is she safe?

*I'm trying, Rosie. I'm trying so freaking hard.*

My hands tremble for long minutes and I stay in the bathroom until I'm completely calm once more. When I finally open the door again, one of the men in the back immediately stands up to go to the bathroom.

His gaze meets mine, and I freeze.

It's a handsome man with familiar piercing eyes. Mendoza. He's *here.* As I watch, he lifts a finger to his lips, indicating silence.

And he smiles.

# CHAPTER SIX

**RAFAEL**

Ava is startled by my presence but hope streaks across her face. She thinks I'm here to save her. Unfortunately the most I can offer at this point is that I won't rape and harm her, but I need the information she has. In this controlled setting with only the small dark-haired man watching her, I can easily make the switch. Five different-colored folders with only a few pieces of paper. Our duplicate isn't perfect because we haven't been able to get close up. The best we've got are telephoto shots of the papers, which reveal what appears to be intercepted emails and transcripts of telephone calls. We aren't sure.

Bennito made up a dummy replacement in about an hour. The matching purse was purchased by Norse the day before at a local high-end shop.

I pick up the decoy purse, setting it on the seat behind me so Ava doesn't see it.

"Sorry." The turbulence of the plane dislodges her footing and she falls into me, her handbag tumbling to the ground.

Instinctively I wrap my arm around her waist to steady her but the action only brings her closer to me. The smell of scented lotion and woman invades my lungs. I close my eyes and take a deep breath so that I can imprint her in my mind.

There's the plush feel of her tits against my hard chest. Her small hands grip my forearms, and one of her legs has settled between my thighs. Shit, a little adjustment and I could be rubbing my increasingly hard cock against her cloth-covered pussy.

But there's no time for that. I use the jostling of the body of the plane to cover up the switch. With my arms around her middle, I quickly push her purse under a seat and then hand her the dummy.

She doesn't notice the switch. Her eyes widen, taking in my face, visible beneath the low brim of my cap. The swift intake of breath is surprise and recognition. "Are you that guy? The one they're afraid of?"

"Shhh." I place a finger over my lips and tip my head toward Afonso. She snaps her mouth shut but her eyes are pleading with me to help her. "Who is with you?" I jerk my head toward the front.

Her eyes fill with tears. "His name is Afonso. Are you from the U.S. government? Who sent you?"

The plane makes another bounce and I take advantage of the moment to reposition us. Her hand goes to my chest.

I shake my head. "Do you have the package with you?"

Disappointment sets in. "Go to hell," she spits. She struggles in my grasp and I let her go.

"*Filha*, come here," Afonso orders. His daughter? My ass.

"Be strong," I murmur and release her, shoving her hard down the tiny aisle. I shut out her stricken face and get the purse—the correct one—out from under the seats and then slam the lav door closed. Whatever hope she had that I am here to save her is now dead. I have my orders. Steal the information, intercept the buy, free my man.

Nowhere in the plan did it allow for rescuing a sinfully soft body and a pair of gorgeous mismatched eyes. I don't look at the mirror, because I can't face myself right now. I place the stolen purse on the toilet lid and unzip it. Inside are the folders, complete with tabs and sticky notes. I pull those out and take snapshots of each. I dig through the cosmetics and the useless key ring, then shove the folders back inside. *Fuck*.

The information isn't here. It's somewhere else. The only thing the buyers are getting is a bunch of paperwork. I should have known that Fouquet would set up a two-part sale. By selling the information in parts, the buyers are kept from taking the information and running without payment. But that complicates my plans by a hell of a lot.

I pull a small black nylon bag from my back pocket and wrap it around the purse to disguise it, and then exit the lav. The plane is bouncing like a carnival ride. The two men in the back are breathing into puke bags.

Over the top of the seats, only Ava's head is visible. Afonso is missing, probably using the forward lav. I settle into a seat two back from Ava. She doesn't turn around but the plane is noisy. Or maybe she hates me now and wishes the bottom of the plane would open up and the sky would suck me out.

I shove the stolen purse under my seat and reach for the in-flight magazine. Outside the sky is nearly pitch black despite it being early afternoon. The wings are lit up, in part from the onboard lighting and in part from the lightning.

Ava's head bobs and weaves and then dips forward. She must be getting sick. Afonso staggers out of the lav and drops into one of the front seats, away from Ava but close to the bathroom.

The plane feels as sturdy as a tin can held together by twine. The seat belt light is blinking furiously. Overhead the speakers turn on and a strained pilot reports the obvious.

"This is the captain speaking. We are experiencing some unexpected turbulence. Please stay in your seats with your seat belts fastened until further notice."

If I lean out of my seat, I can see Ava white-knuckling the armrest. If I thought for a second that she'd welcome my comfort, I'd crawl up to her row and hold her hand or finger or toe or whatever body part she'd allow me to touch.

Lightning flashes again and the plane rumbles with the thunder, the vibrations shaking the fuselage. Another flash, and an even louder clap of noise echoes through the body of the plane. The men in the back start yelling in panic.

"Oh my God! The wing is on fire!" Ava screams. She points and even Afonso notices. Across the small aisle we watch in horror as the engine explodes and the wing shears away. The plane tips violently to the left. Overhead, the luggage racks open and the oxygen masks drop out. The stupid purse rolls my way. Ava yelps and reaches down to grab it, unbuckling her belt.

The fucking plane is falling out of the sky and she's worried about the goddamned purse. Worse, it's the fake one that I traded out. She's not risking her life for that. I grab the stolen bag and rip the nylon cover off of it.

"Ava, climb into a seat and buckle in. Got me?" I yell at her.

"I need that bag," she cries.

"I have it." I pick it up and despite the tilt of the plane manage to make my way to her seat. "Here." I hand her the real bag. She hugs it to her body and releases a sob of relief.

"How do you know my name?" Ava blurts out.

"What?" I answer her distractedly. I'm not looking in her direction.

Afonso has my attention now. He's somehow found a parachute. I lean across Ava and see the limp arm of the stewardess nearly brushing the floor of the plane. Fuck. That goddamned asshole shot the stewardess to get access to the emergency chute. Her dead body sprawls in a nearby seat.

I glance back at Afonso and the parachute. Ava and I need that chute. Afonso turns to the exit door and starts tugging. Dumbass. He's never going to get the door open. Cabin doors can't be opened when the landing gear is up but he apparently doesn't know that. He struggles with the door, pulling hard on the handle.

How long would it take me to get to him? I unbuckle my belt and press my finger to my lips so Ava won't give me away. Inching forward, I creep toward Afonso but he hears me and pulls his gun from his waistband and shoots.

I duck back but a sting hits my eye. I brush it and realize that his bullet must have caught part of the metal of the seat, which ricocheted and struck me in the face. I blink rapidly and brush away the blood. He must have caught a vein over my eye. Those wounds bleed profusely. Shit.

"Stay here," I shout to Ava. The rattling of the plane has reached epic levels.

"I'm not going anywhere, asshole," she snaps back.

I can't stop the grin from spreading. That she's chippy is a good sign. We'll need attitude to survive this.

I push off with my legs and launch myself toward Afonso. He brings his gun up and shoots again but the plane pulls to the right suddenly. We go flying, my body slams against the seats, and Afonso crashes into the opposite exit door. Near Afonso lies my emergency kit. I reach for it.

"Mendoza, the wing. The wing is gone," Ava screams. I right myself and look out the window. She's right. I abandon the stolen bag, Afonso, the parachute, the Boy Scout pack. My only chance of making it out is to belt in and hope that the seats break our fall into the Amazon. Afonso grins wildly and grabs the purse, looping it over his arm. When we land, I'm finding him and gutting him.

With both wings gone, the plane starts a free fall. The rumble inside the tube is deafening. Hand over hand, I climb back toward Ava's seat and manage to fling myself into the seat. She reaches over and helps me buckle in.

"Your eye," she gasps. "You're bleeding like—like—"

"Like I've been stabbed in the eye?" I finish. Now that I'm upright and can feel my laceration-free forehead, I realize that the shard must have pierced my eyeball. The hazy vision in my left side isn't due to blood but because I got a piece of metal in my eye. I turn to her. "Is it bad?"

"I don't see anything," she frets. Her hands pat my face and even though we are hurtling toward our death in a metal can, I can't help but think of how soft her hands feel. They're like flower petals or silk sheets. They are the softest goddamned things in the world, and the last thought in my head before I black out is I wonder how they'd feel on my dick.

# CHAPTER SEVEN

## AVA

I wake up with my face pressed against a warm, broad chest and my legs tangled in the leaves of a tree. Somewhere close by, I hear birds chirping. There's sunlight dappling my face and everything feels damp.

Everything also hurts.

I'm dazed and my head is ringing with pain, and the sun is beaming right into my eyes, which is freaking annoying as hell. I rub a hand across my face and it takes me a few moments to realize that I shouldn't see the sun at all if I'm inside an airplane.

Then I remember the storm. The thunderous boom as the plane was hit by lightning. Screams. The wing catching fire. The chaos of Afonso with his gun. Free-falling through the cabin, my grip on the seats the only thing keeping me from flying through six thousand feet of empty air.

Mendoza's hand ripping out of mine when the cabin depressurized. The screams of people going silent.

Mendoza.

I remember him, too.

A noise from somewhere nearby catches my attention. It sounds like heavy breathing. I open my eyes and look around.

I'm still strapped to my seat. There's a portion of the plane underneath me, and the two seats Mendoza and I buckled into are still together.

He's next to me, the broad chest I'm currently draped across. His eyes are closed, dried, crusted blood around the injured one. He's got an enormous bruise on his forehead and his arms are around me, as if he was trying to protect me even as we fell.

"Mendoza?" I ask, sitting upright and pulling out of his arms. Sitting up makes everything in my body scream with pain. My ankles hurt, but I don't know if it's because they're seriously injured or because they were tucked under the seat in front of me, which is also still attached. I test my legs, untangling them from his longer ones, and wince at the pain shooting through my body. It feels like I've been trampled in my sleep. My ribs hurt, and my right arm radiates agony.

But . . . I'm alive. I sit up a bit straighter and look at my right arm. The purse I've carried for days is gone. The skin is puffy and turning purple. When I flex my fingers, the pain brings tears to my eyes. I look away from it, faint and sick to my stomach at the sight. It's not just the pain but what it represents. I'm a hand model. I can't do a thing if my hands are jacked up.

Not that it matters right now.

"Mendoza," I say again, because I'm about to panic, and panic hard. "Wake up. Please."

He doesn't stir.

Fear clutches me, and I grab his shirt with my good hand and give him a shake. "Mendoza?"

That doesn't wake him, either. I press my cheek to his chest and listen for a heartbeat.

It's slow and steady. Whew. I sit up and examine him again. The knot on his forehead is huge. Maybe he just got knocked out. I'll have to figure out how to wake him up once I figure out where we are. It looks like our section of the plane somehow separated from the rest of the wreckage, which is why we're alive and not a skidmark on the ground.

I shift in my seat and the world tilts. My eyes go wide and I freeze in place, then look around.

I can see trees overhead, and sunshine, but it's just now occurred to me that we're not on the ground. The chairs are tilted and everything shakes when I move.

I'm pretty sure we're in a tree. Clutching at the arm of the chair, I sit up carefully and look around.

I see nothing but air and leaves, green vines and dappled shadows. In the distance, I hear the sound like heavy breathing again. I look at Mendoza, but it's not him. Oh God. Is it Afonso? Is he still here? Biting my lip, I crane my neck and try to peer down below. We're at least twenty feet off the ground.

It's like the wreckage has been swallowed up by a wall of green. Green and wet. On the jungle floor, there's more greenery and what looks like smoking wreckage. Pieces of the plane are scattered all over the forest floor, along with a few scattered suitcases. In the distance I see another row of chairs, this one face-down in the dirt. The heavy breathing starts again, and this time I see the source: a jaguar, stalking through the wreckage.

My eyes widen and I go very still.

A heavy rain begins to fall, spattering me from above. I don't move. My gaze is on that jungle cat as it sniffs through things. If it notices us, I don't know what we'll do. Mendoza is unconscious and if I try to move him, we might both fall out of the tree . . . and land right in front of the cat.

The situation hits me and I start to cry. I'm alone. I'm really fucking alone. I've never camped a day in my life, much less been in a jungle. I look down at my hands. They're my livelihood. My way to earn a living. My income depends on them being soft and perfect, my nails elegant ovals.

I have a long gouge down the back of one hand, and my pinky is bruised and swollen. My wrist looks like an elephant's leg, if elephants were black and blue. Not gonna be hand modeling for a long while after I get out of here.

If I get out of here.

*I'm sorry, Rose. I'm trying. I'm trying so hard.* I shudder back a sob as the cat slinks into the underbrush, something dangling and arm-sized in its mouth. I'm in the jungle with a busted hand and a stranger that just wants the information I'm carrying . . .

And I don't even have the information anymore. The purse is gone. I sniff hard, trying to fight back another sob that's threatening to break free.

"Don't cry," a voice says softly.

I turn and look at Mendoza. His shirt is sticking to his big body, wet raindrops splatting down his face. He looks at me and smiles crookedly, and lifts a hand to try to touch my face. "Don't cry."

I'm so relieved to see another person that I fling my arms around him and start weeping again. It sends a shockwave of pain up my arm, but I ignore it. Mendoza is awake and I'm not in the jungle alone.

"You're alive," I wail at him.

"Easy, easy," he says, prying my arms off his neck. Our movements cause our perch in the trees to shake again, and we both go still. My body's pressed against his with rain pouring down. Neither of us moves a muscle. Then, Mendoza looks up at my face, his inches from mine. "Are you all right?"

"I'm okay," I tell him. I hurt like fuck all over, but that'll wait for another time. "We're in the tree. I think it cushioned our fall. We're in the jungle. I don't know where everyone else is. There's a jaguar down there, though. And I'm missing the purse and the folders." The words tumble out of me in a rush. It's like I want to get all the bad news out of the way before he has time to process it.

His fingers push a damp lock of hair off my forehead and he studies my face with his good eye. The other is swollen shut and crusted with blood. "But you are all right?"

Was he hit on the head harder than I thought? I contemplate reminding him that I've lost the purse, but maybe that isn't the smartest idea. "I'm all right," I say again. I touch his forehead gently. "You've got a huge bruise, though. Are you okay?"

"Well enough," he agrees, and tries to shift in his seat. As he does, the entire chunk of plane groans and shifts a few inches.

"We should get down from here," I tell him, still clinging to his shirt. It's kind of helpless and overly girly of me, but I am just so stinking glad that I'm not here alone. "But there's jaguars down below."

"They won't bother us as long as we don't seem too weak. They're opportunistic predators," he tells me, and glances down at my body.

"Oh," I say. Should I try to seem less wimpy? I look and I'm still clinging to Mendoza's front, and my breasts are pushed against his chest. And he's looking, too. Right. I sit up slowly and glance around. "Afonso had a gun. Think we can find it?"

"If we can find Afonso," Mendoza agrees. "Or what's left of him."

That sounds pretty grim. I feel bad, too, because I prefer the "what's left of him" part of the scenario. I shouldn't wish it on anyone, but life will be so much easier for me if Afonso is dead.

But then what happens to Rose?

I squelch the terrible thought and examine the tree. There's a limb not too far below us. "Shall we get down and assess our surroundings?"

Little by little, we manage to get out of the wreckage and the tree. It involves a lot of crawling downward, testing branches, and clinging to tree bark. Mendoza's steps seem to miss a lot, and I realize he's misjudging distance because he can't see out of his bad eye. There's also a deep cut on my leg that I didn't see before, and I wonder how many other "surprise" injuries we're going to find.

By the time we make it out of the tree, my wrist is throbbing painfully and the rain has stopped. Mendoza stands next to me, and then wobbles on his feet. I grab a handful of his shirt just as he totters. "Whoa!"

He catches himself, and gives his head a little shake, as if to wake up. "I think I need to sit down."

"You sit," I tell him, pointing at the base of the tree. "I'm going to see if I can find the snack cart from the plane. We need to clean and bandage that eye of yours. It looks pretty bad."

"I can help you look," he says, ignoring my order to sit.

"No, you can't," I say, and tap his chest with my index finger.

"If you topple over and hurt yourself, I can't pick you up. Sit down and I'll check the area. I won't go far."

Again, his mouth curves in a half smile. "You're very bossy."

I snort. "It's because you're a terrible listener. Now sit." I wait, a stern look on my face until he throws his hands up and sits down, heavily, at the base of the tree. I point at it, then him. "If I come back and you've moved from this spot, I'm going to give you hell."

"Yes, ma'am," he says, and rubs his head. I can hear the tease in his voice, though.

Once I'm satisfied that Mendoza won't try to hurt himself further by "helping" me, I start picking through all the fallen debris. There are bits of unidentifiable parts everywhere, but I do manage to find a bag with some Hawaiian shirts. Under a nearby fern, there's a battered water bottle, its contents intact. The drink cart might be somewhere around here. That's good news, since I have no desire to venture into the jungle.

I take my findings and limp back over to Mendoza. He's got his head tilted back against the tree, and manages a smile for me when I sit down on the ground next to him. "I saw your wrist," he says. "It looks bad."

"It's not good," I agree. "But I'm more worried about your eye." I hold up the water bottle and give it a little shake. "This is the cleanest water for miles around, I'm thinking. We should use it to wash out your eye and bandage it."

"It's only swollen; it'll be fine tomorrow. Are you thirsty?" he asks. "Maybe you should drink it."

He's watching me with that curiously intense gaze I remember from the lunch together. It makes me want to blush under his scrutiny, but now's not the time to be prissy. I'm thirsty, too, but I'm also practical. I have no idea how to survive in the jungle. If

Mendoza knows even rudimentary camping shit, he's leagues ahead of me. He's my ticket out of here, and so he's going to get the clean water for his eye. "Wounds first," I tell him. "Then we'll see what we have left over."

"I was right," he says with a chuckle. "You are bossy."

"No," I tease back. "You're just a bad listener. Now tilt your head back and let me look at your eye."

After a few minutes of examining, I have come to a single medical conclusion about Mendoza's eye: it's gross. I dribble clean water into it to try to flush out some of the crusty stuff, but I'm not sure what else to do other than bandage it and keep it clean. So that's what we do. With the clothing from the bag, I pack a clean white undershirt against his eye and then hold it in place with strips of the Hawaiian shirt. It might be the only extra clothing we find in the jungle, and it might be a bad idea to destroy it, but to me, losing an eye seems worse.

I tie the knot behind Mendoza's head and try to ignore that my movements are pushing my breasts into his face and he's probably getting an eyeful of tit meat. "There," I tell him. "That should at least keep bugs and things out of it until we get out of here."

"Thank you, Ava," he says in that low, soft voice. It sounds like a caress when he says my name.

"You didn't tell me how you know my name," I point out.

"I'm Rafael," he tells me. "Before when we spoke, I gave you my real name."

"And you totally just avoided my question," I reply pertly. "So unless you want to lose that other eye, you should answer me."

Instead of being threatened by my cruel words, he just grins at me like he's proud.

# CHAPTER **EIGHT**

## RAFAEL

The ricochet of the bullet has swollen my eye shut. I might be slightly concussed from the free fall from six thousand feet into the jungle. I've no clue where we are and we have no supplies, but I've never been happier than when Ava stuck her tits in my face. Those babies felt like the softest pillows ever created and I would've been happy to suffocate in the damp valley of cleavage. Maybe I'd even get the chance to lick her sweat away.

I might have groaned and pretended my injury was worse to lengthen the moment. Her delicate hands smoothed over my forehead and, it may have been my imagination, but it seemed liked she might've lingered over my hair. *Dig in*, I want to grunt.

"What the heck is that sound?" Ava clutches me to her.

If I don't answer, does that mean I can stay in this position forever? Because I want to. Actually, no, I'd like to move over and suck one fat tit into my mouth until it's hard as a diamond. Then I'd like to slide down until my mouth is level with her pussy and see how salty sweet she tastes between her legs. The beast between my legs roars to life and it's a good thing that the monkeys above us scream again, causing her to jump and strike my good eye with her elbow. The pain serves as a reminder of where we are, who I am, and what the fuck I should be paying attention to.

"It's the howler monkey. They sound like humans screaming or sometimes like the jaguar. They're kind of dumb and if we found Afonso's gun, we'd be able to kill one and have meat every night for a week."

She shudders. "I don't want to eat monkey."

The jungle is hot and wet during the day and cold at night. If the mosquitos don't eat you alive, the jaguars and anacondas might. Not very many people can crash-land into the middle of the Amazon and make it out alive, but I'm upping our odds from around 20 percent to 50 percent based on Ava's positive attitude. Unless my eye heals up, I'm not giving us more than that. If we could find the Boy Scout bag, though, we could bring our odds up significantly.

"There's plenty of food in the Amazon from plantains to fish, so if you don't like monkey, we won't eat it."

She shudders again. "Thank you."

"You a vegetarian?"

No, that couldn't be right. Didn't she eat some prosciutto at the café? But I want to hear it from her. I want to know everything about her.

"No, but for some reason eating something that screams like a human freaks me out."

"Monkey is off the menu," I say, making no attempt to move away from her rack. "I have a knife in my belt."

"Do you have anything else besides the knife?" she asks. Her tone is accusatory like I'm holding out on her.

"No," I say slowly. "Just the knife."

She narrows her eyes and then reaches out with her good hand and pokes my waistline. "What about that?"

"My pants? I don't think that they'd fit you or they'd be a good weapon. Besides, I'd rather my legs didn't get eaten by mosquitos."

"Look, if you just plan on leaving me behind, then do it now. Don't string me along."

"I have no idea what you're talking about." Just my luck to perv on a crazy woman.

"That!" she spits out, and this time her finger jabs lower, right into the meat of my dick. I flinch back. "I can tell you're packing something. What's that thing in your pocket?"

"None of your fucking business," I growl out, my happy feeling sucked away. I can feel the heat rising in my face that has nothing to do with the humidity. I will my erection to subside but as she stares at it, it does nothing but grow.

"Oh my god. Is that a . . . that's not a gun, is it?" Her lips part in shock.

"No." The erection isn't going to go down anytime soon. Not with her eyes wide with wonder. She raises her gaze to me and then drops back down again, and hell if she doesn't lick her fucking lips. I turn away, unzip, and then pull the shaft straight up behind the waistband of my cargo pants. I fasten the zipper, carefully, and then pull my T-shirt down over the top. It hides most of the problem. "Let's go."

"I'm sorry," she mumbles.

I surge to my feet, catching her off guard. She stumbles back and thankfully stops staring at my junk. "Enough," I growl more roughly than I intend. "We have important things to concentrate on, like where are we going to sleep for the night."

She looks stricken and nods in agreement. "Sorry, I just was taken by surprise. You don't have to tell me what's in your pocket if you don't want to. But I need to remind you that we're in this together."

I feel like an ass. I don't know whether to laugh or cry that she thinks my dick is fake. That's a new one. Most chicks scream in terror. Time for a change in subject, because even her laughing mention of the man downstairs is making it excited. My loose-fitting pants are never loose enough when the beast is roused, and since I laid eyes on Ava, I've been thinking about little else but her, a flat surface, and mind-blowing orgasms.

I change topics. "If we find water, we'll follow it downstream until we find a village. Problem solved. We're saved." Why that makes me disappointed, I don't think I should examine.

But before we reach civilization, I need an explanation from Ava about the stuff she was carrying in the purse. It's important enough that Afonso tried to take it, but it'd be nice to know exactly what I'm dealing with.

I survey the scene. The seats that saved us are sitting in the canopy above. Around us are bits of metal and plastic, but the foliage is like a dense wall. We'll need to go into the foliage to see if there's anything we can salvage.

"How do you know my name?" she repeats.

"Because I've been watching you for several days. You're passing out information to potential buyers for Louis Duval. His brother Redoine Fouquet is your keeper, and although he didn't rape you, he did hit you." I reach up and lightly trace over the bruise on her upper cheek. Ironically, that was the result of Fouquet's fist, not the plane crash.

She jerks her face away from my touch and I fist my fingers into my hand. Of course she doesn't want me to touch her. Why would she? A pretty woman like Ava has men at her feet constantly. It is her beauty combined with her unusual eyes that made Fouquet fear her. The devil wears many faces, including my own.

"I'm not going to hurt you. I just need to know what was in the purse. What were you selling?"

"I don't know," she cries. "And if we don't find it and get it back to Duval, my best friend is going to get killed!"

"Who's that? Rose Waverly? She's a model like you, right?"

"Not like me. Rose Waverly is a runway model—a famous one."

I shrug at this meaningless factoid. "But you're a model, too, right?" At least that's what we concluded based on Bennito's research.

"A hand model!" She shoves her injured hand toward me. "That's all I've ever done, but I may not be able to get another job now."

"Huh, I guess that's why we never found pictures of your face." It also explains why her hands feel petal soft.

"Who's we? And how much did you investigate? Who are you working for? Who are you?" She places a hand on her hips and looks like she's not moving until I give a full debriefing.

"I'm a mercenary. I take jobs from different people for different things, and one of those things happens to deal with Duval."

"That answers nothing."

That's all I'm giving out. I reach up to rub my skull, and all my muscles in my shoulder scream in protest. We're both going to feel like a piece of crap tomorrow. "I'd love to stand and talk all day, but we need to move. There are only a few hours of daylight left, and we need shelter before the sun goes down."

"I'm not moving an inch until you give me more answers."

I stare at her, and after a few heartbeats of silence, she throws up her good hand. "Oh, what am I even talking about? I may not even get out of this place alive."

"Yeah we will." I look around for a stick. Bamboo would be good. "We're going to look for some weapons—anything that could be made into a spear, like a shard of metal we can wrap to the end of a stick. There's a black nylon pack with reflective tape on the bottom. It's indestructible and if we find it, it has everything we need—tent, sleep blanket, mosquito repellant, water purification tablets, flint, lighters."

"It's like a survival bag?"

"It's not *like*. It is," I say smugly.

"All right. I don't trust you, though, and I'm keeping my eyes on you."

As if that bothers me. I pick up the half-empty water bottle. There must be more where these came from, although water is the least of our worries. With a leaf and a little sand, we can collect dew and rainwater. We need dry clothes and shelter.

It's hard to see the sun because of the dense canopy of leaves, but the moss on the tree indicates we are standing north.

"You camp before, Ava?"

"No. Never." She claps her hand to her neck where a mosquito had just settled.

"Get a malaria shot before you came down to Lima?" One of the biggest dangers came from the mosquito bites.

"No, but Rose did a shoot in Tahiti a couple of months ago and I went with her. We got a number of shots then."

"Here's our plan. We need to find long-sleeve shirts and pants. That'll help protect us from the bites. If we can't find that, we're going to cover our exposed parts in mud. The dried mud will protect us from bites. We also need a large tarp or poncho that we can use as our shelter."

"But if we find your pack, then everything will be okay, right?" She sounds so hopeful I don't have the heart to tell her that the bag doesn't have anything bigger than a paring knife disguised in the lining of a water bottle, which is fine for making fishing poles from bamboo but not great for fending off the predators of the jungle. The faint amount of sunlight that is breaking through the trees indicates it's probably midafternoon. We have only a few hours before dusk sets in, and we need to be somewhere safe before then.

"Right. Let's go." I pull off my belt and withdraw the knife hidden inside the buckle and attach it to the end of the leather. Handing the bottle to Ava to hold, I wrap the belt around my free hand. After I have the weapons secured, I pluck the bottle out of her hands and chuck it into the dense foliage to the south.

"What are you doing?" she cries. "That was our only bottle of water."

"I'm trying to flush out any animals like sleeping snakes and other bugs. There are about two hundred things in the jungle that can kill you, and most of them you can't see until you're on top of them."

"What if we don't find your bag?" Her tone is a little quavery.

"Then we use what we do have." I grab her hand and tuck it into the waistband of my pants. "Hang on. Step where I step and watch out for anything that moves."

She plasters herself to my back and like the sick man that I am, I enjoy the hell out of it.

We move forward and find nothing but the water bottle. After about thirty minutes of searching, I'm drenched with sweat from the heat and the humidity. Ava is panting lightly from the exertion. I mark a rubber tree with my knife. If I have to, we can use the latex the tree produces for protection but at this point, I don't have anything to collect the liquid in other than the water bottle, and we'll need that to store water.

"What do you think will happen to Rose when I don't make it to Pucallpa?" she asks as we cut through another tangle of vines and dense underbrush.

"At some point the plane will be reported missing and a search team will be sent out. The plane's black box has enough battery to release a signal for about thirty days. We'll be out of this place by then." I answer confidently, although my belief in our successful evacuation from the jungle is diminishing. There is absolutely no evidence of the crash—at least not south. "Duval needs you and the buy will take place later. Rose will be freed then." This is all a lie. I have no fucking clue what will happen to Rose. Most likely they'll rape and kill her but I'm not telling Ava that. She somehow believes that Rose is still alive. "Let's go east and then north and see if we can't make a wide circle of where we landed. There's got to be something."

"Like what?" She sounds tired. "There were only a few people on the plane, so there can't be much luggage or food."

"You found a few things, so that means there are more."

"Do you think anyone made it out alive?"

"Not really. I think we were damn lucky to have survived the fall." I decide not to tell her that I think Afonso might have killed the pilot and flight attendant before the plane went down. Maybe one of the passengers in the back of the plane survived. "The likelihood that anyone else did is low." Except Afonso, who had a parachute that was half attached to him as well as the purse with the stolen goods and my Boy Scout pack. If he made it out alive, I'll have the pleasure of killing him. That makes me pretty happy, and I forge forward.

# CHAPTER **NINE**

## AVA

My head is whirling with information as we trek through the jungle.

This Mendoza guy has been watching me.

He says he's only after the information Duval has for sale, but I think there might be more to things. After all, I know how men treat a woman when she doesn't matter. When she's less than nothing to them. That's exactly how Fouquet treated me, and so did Afonso. Like I was an object with tits. I've caught Mendoza staring, but not in a bad way. Just in an interested, appreciative sort of way.

He remembers that Fouquet struck me. His touches have been gentle. Considerate.

He stares at me when he thinks I'm not looking.

All of this makes me wonder how much of his story is surface and if I'm reading more into his behavior than I should. I've dated guys in the past, of course. I'm not dating anyone right now, but I know the signals. It's obvious that Mendoza's into me.

Which is . . . not the worst. If he's into me, he'll keep me safe. I wouldn't be the first woman in the world to trade attention to a man for safety. I've just got to take this one day at a time. Right now, I need to focus on getting out of the jungle alive. I can worry about Rose when I'm back in the city and the deal is back on. They can't carry forward on the deal without Afonso and without me.

At least, I hope they can't.

*One thing at a time, Ava*, I tell myself.

Mendoza pauses and looks around the jungle thoughtfully.

I brush a wet lock of hair off my forehead and peer at the ferns and trees myself. I don't see anything other than more jungle. "Why are we stopping?"

"I'm thinking."

"Okay. Well, what do we do now?" I'm not a camper in the slightest, so I'll follow his lead. Right now I'm just grateful I have someone with me. I try not to think about what this would have been like if I was alone. If he wants to stop in the middle of nowhere, I trust him.

He squints up at the sky with his one good eye. "I think we've got about an hour before we lose daylight. We should finish checking the area to make sure there's no predators and set up camp." He turns and points at a large tree nearby. "Maybe at the base of that tree there."

"Shelter is good," I agree. I'm tired of wandering through the jungle. It's hot, muggy, rains on us every hour, and bugs are crawling all over the place. I hate it. If this is what camping involves, I don't want it. I will happily be a city girl for the rest of my days.

He turns and looks back at me. "How are you?"

I give him a thin smile. "I'm pretty miserable at the moment but I'm standing. How about you?"

"Not nearly so miserable as you," he says, and the man almost sounds cheerful. He takes the lead again, and we approach our chosen tree that will be the shelter for the evening.

A closer inspection of it is disappointing. It's . . . well, it's a tree. I'm disappointed that it doesn't have a ton of low-hanging branches or anything that looks shelter-like. The roots are enormous and widespread, and there's a cradle-like spot between two on the far side that Mendoza points out. "We can get some leaves and make a blanket of some kind to cover the ground so we're not rolling in the mud. Maybe we can cut a few more to make a canopy. And we need to find some dry wood for a fire."

I stare at him blankly. "Dry wood? It's been raining constantly."

"I didn't say that we would find it, just that we need it for a fire." He gives me another crooked smile. "We might be without one tonight."

My heart sinks at the thought. "Let's not think about that for now. Tell me what to do to get started."

We divide up chores. Since Mendoza has our only knife, he's going to cut fronds and make our tiny shelter. I carry a lightweight stick as a club, and I have the water bottle with me. My job is to search the immediate area for wood, debris, and anything we might be able to use.

I head off to work, making sure to keep the sound of Mendoza's whistling near as he cuts branches and palm fronds. I move slowly, tossing the water bottle into the brush each time to flush out anything. Whenever my bruised hand brushes a leaf, I get a throbbing pain.

Occasionally I hear something slither away, but all I find is mud and bugs and leaves. As for firewood, I find a few sticks here and there, but everything is soaked. I keep my bad arm pressed against my chest and cradle the pitiful amount of wood against it there, along with my club. It might be firewood tonight if this keeps up.

I'm nearing the edge of how far out I dare go; Mendoza is barely audible in the distance. The brush is thicker here, but there's a break in the tree canopy overhead, which is a good sign. I toss my water bottle—and it thunks against something.

I freeze in place, waiting for a pissed-off jaguar to come roaring out of the ferns. When nothing does, I step forward, my curiosity getting the better of me. A hint of navy blue appears, and then it becomes a square, boxy form of some kind that is out of place in the wild jungle. I see a brown loafer sticking into the air, and I stare at the entire thing for a moment before I realize that I've found one of the missing passengers, still strapped into his chair. He's not facing me, but the portion of him I can see is entirely too short, which means a lot of him . . . compacted when it hit the ground. The bit of skin I can see between ankle and sock is swelling, bloated, and purple. As I watch, a fly lands on it.

A strangled cry escapes my throat.

Two seconds later, Mendoza is there, his hand on my shoulder. "Ava? What is it?"

I turn and bury my face against his chest.

I don't want to be here anymore. I don't want to process this.

I know I'm being childish, but I don't want to be strong right now. So I push my head against his neck and let him wrap his arms around me, stroking my back.

Soothing me.

I close my eyes and breathe deeply of Mendoza's scent. He smells like sweat and mud and rain. It's a good scent, though, and I take deep lungfuls of it.

He makes a soft noise in his throat, comforting me, and his hand slides down my back again, even as rain starts to pour down once more. A normal guy would probably want to get out of the rain, or tease me for being a baby at finding a dead guy.

Mendoza just holds me like there's no place he'd rather be.

And as I'm pressed against him, ignoring the throb in my bad arm, I feel something pressing against my lower belly that's not a hand. Mendoza's aroused at my wet body pushing against his. Okay, that's probably my fault. I'm fine with that.

But it reminds me just how freaking *big* his equipment is. It's not something I should be noticing in a life-or-death situation. It's not. But when a guy's got something like a Maglite stuffed down his pants?

You sort of freaking notice, no matter the situation.

Actually, Maglite might not be big enough. More like wine bottle. Jesus.

A guy with an inappropriate boner? It happens. I can get past it. A guy with an inappropriate boner that's bigger than any log I've been able to find in the rainforest? A lot less okay. Actually a little frightening.

Mendoza trails his hand down my back again. "You all right, Ava?"

I must be tensing up. I pull away. "Yeah, I'm good. It . . . just startled me." *And I'm not talking about the dead body.*

"Is it the pilot?"

I make a choked sound, focusing on the dead body again. "The pilot? Um, I didn't check."

He pats my shoulder and releases me. "I'll check. Don't look."

As he moves away, I busy myself with picking up the wood I discarded as I pushed my body against his. My puffy wrist is sending a distress signal all the way up my arm, and it's going to have to be looked at soon, but there's time for that later. Right now fire—and okay, getting away from the dead guy—is a priority.

"Pilot," Mendoza says after a minute. "If it makes you feel better, he was dead before he hit the ground. Head's cracked open. He probably lost consciousness and never woke up."

Strangely enough, that does make me feel a bit better. I swallow hard. "Does he have anything on him we can use?"

"You want his jacket?"

"Oh God. I really don't." Just the thought makes me nauseous again.

"You might get cold tonight."

"Then we'll just snuggle," I say desperately. I really, really don't want to take a jacket off a dead guy and wear it. That's inviting all sorts of horrible karma, and I can't even handle all the bad karma I've got already. "All right?"

"All right," he says in a curiously blank voice. "Give me a few minutes and I'm going to drag this away from camp so no predators come this direction. Why don't you head back to the tree?"

I nod and head back to our makeshift camp. It feels cowardly to run away, but I don't care. I go to our nest in the trees and I'm not entirely surprised to see that Mendoza's been super busy while I've been in the bushes, exploring the area. There's a nest of leaves as a makeshift bed, and he's started a lean-to that's lashed with a few leaves and more vines. For a guy with one eye, he's pretty handy. So what if the dick in his pants is bigger than the snakes in the jungle? I set the wood down on the leafy bed and work on the A-frame for a bit. I may be pretty helpless, but I know how to tie a knot or two, and I'm left handed, so that means I can just use my right arm as support.

I work on this for a bit to take my mind off the dead guy . . . and the very-much-alive guy. By the time Mendoza comes back, twilight is arriving, I've slapped a hundred mosquitos off my skin, and the lean-to is mostly done. I had to guess at how things worked, but Mendoza gives me an impressed look when he returns. "Good job," he says.

"If I did it wrong, I'm sorry. I just—"

"No, you did great, Ava. Really." He moves to my side and pats my shoulder, then awkwardly removes his hand again. "I left the body on the riverbank. Figured some predator will get it by morning and won't come this way looking for it."

"Okay."

He squats near my pathetic bundle of firewood and I flinch, expecting him to give me shit for not finding more. He picks one piece up, squeezes it, and then shakes his head. "Too wet for a fire tonight. If we cover it and keep it in a safe spot, maybe it'll be dry by morning."

I swallow hard and slap at another mosquito. "Will we be okay?"

"As long as no big predators come looking for us, yes."

"That's not very comforting."

Mendoza turns to look at me and reaches into his shirt. "I'm not a fan of making promises I can't keep." He pulls out a pair of small bags and smiles. "I did find this, though."

Pretzels. "You found the drink cart?" My stomach growls hungrily, and I want to rip both bags out of his hand and scarf the contents down.

"Part of it. There were a lot of smashed cans and these two bags. I'm hoping we can scout for a bit longer tomorrow and find the rest of it."

"No more water, though?" I'm really thirsty and the sips we've been taking from our bottle haven't been doing it.

He shakes his head. "We'll refill it when it rains again with a leaf, just like we did earlier." As we'd walked, he'd taken a big leaf from a tree and held it, making a funnel while the rain poured, and I held the bottle. It had provided us some water, but I felt as if I could drink an entire jug.

"And no sign of your Boy Scout bag?" I ask.

Another grim shake of his head. "Or Afonso. If that bastard got away . . ."

"It won't do him any good. If we can't get out of here, he can't either, right?"

He rubs a hand over his wet hair, careful not to touch the bandages on his face. A rueful smile crosses his face. "Right."

Rain starts to spatter once more, and I want to scream when the first droplets hit my skin. It has rained off and on all day, and just when I start to get dry, it starts again. I'm not looking forward to sleeping wet in the dark jungle, and Mendoza just shakes his head and moves to the firewood, bundling leaves around it and tucking it against the tree trunk. He then moves the lean-to over one side of the trunk and gestures that I should join him. "We'll have pretzels for dinner, unless you object."

"And here I was hoping we'd dine on bugs," I say lightly, and step in.

"That's breakfast," he teases back.

It's so ridiculous that I laugh, and he smiles at me in the twilight.

We scarf down a bag of pretzels each, wash it down with a few mouthfuls of water, and then try to get comfortable. There's not a lot of room in our tiny, half-assed shelter. Water still drips down, but it's protecting us from some of the worst of the rainfall, so there's that. Mendoza moves to the outside, and I realize he's doing that so I can be in the most sheltered part of the lean-to, where the least rain will hit.

That's . . . sweet.

"There's room for both of us," I tell him as a fat raindrop plops on his head, right where his bandage is. I gesture at the covering over his eye. "You need to keep that dry."

He shifts uncomfortably and doesn't move toward me. "I'm fine."

I roll my eyes and lie down, scrunching my body against the interior. "Get in here. I don't bite." I know why he's reluctant. It's that monster in his pants that I've pointed out like some sort of blushing virgin. Hell, I don't blame him for that. "Monster in his pants" might be putting it mildly. Too mildly.

I've dated guys of all shapes and sizes. I'm no stranger to sex, and I've seen my share of ugly penises. Circumcised, low hanging balls, I've seen it all. However, I've never seen a dick that's quite as big as Mendoza's. He's gone past the whole "lucky guy" category and straight into the "what the ever-loving fuck" category. The "don't get that thing near me" category. The one that makes my legs tighten and want to clamp together at the thought. I haven't seen him naked, but if what is outlined in his pants is legit, he's abnormally huge. To think I mistook it for a weapon earlier is laughable.

No handgun is *that* big.

Thing is, I don't care about the size of his dick. I mean, not as more than a conversational sort of topic, like my heterochromatic eyes. But I know Mendoza's a guy, and if we snuggle—based on his reaction to me before—he's going to get wood. That will make things super awkward.

But if we don't snuggle, he sits in the rain and we lose out on body heat. That puts things decidedly in the "snuggle" column. I cradle my bad arm against my chest and pat the palm fronds on the ground, avoiding any misgivings I might have about this. "Come on."

Mendoza moves in next to me, though I can tell he plainly doesn't want to. All right. I'm going to have to make the first move if we're going to get past all this awkwardness. I wait until he stretches his long legs out and then I move a little closer to him, tucking my head against his shoulder again and pressing up against him. Not in a sexual way, just in an innocent sort of cuddle.

He hesitates for a moment, and then puts a hand around my shoulders.

"Watch the wrist," I say, gesturing at my bad arm.

"I should look at it."

"In the morning," I say, because it's getting so dark I can barely make out Mendoza. I actually don't want anyone to touch my wrist right now, including myself. It hurts too much. I lean against him, and he's warm like my own personal radiator. That's really nice. I almost don't mind that it's raining and getting cold and dark.

Almost.

It's silent in the jungle as it gets dark. Too silent. I hate it, so I speak again. "Maybe we should play a game."

"Hmm?"

"Yeah. You tell me one thing about you that I don't know, and I tell you one thing about me that you don't know. Each night. By the time we get out of here, maybe we'll come out of here as friends." I nudge him with my good elbow. "Though I'm gonna be real honest and say I'd prefer we left as strangers because we get rescued so fast."

He chuckles.

"I'll start," I say. "My eyes are two different colors."

"I knew that." His voice is soft in the darkness.

For some reason, I feel a blush creeping over my cheeks. "Okay. I told you that I'm a hand model, right?"

"You did. Keep going."

"Okay." I try to think of a different fact for my game. "Here's one. I lost my virginity when I was fourteen. Camp. He was a counselor and all of fifteen. It was all very glamorous when I was a kid, but looking back, I guess it's pretty stupid." I smile faintly at the memory of what a dumb, rebellious teen I was. "He had such smooth moves, though. Even sang me a Justin Timberlake song. I was hooked after that."

He snorts. I can't tell if he's amused by my anecdote or grossed out. I guess I wouldn't blame him for either.

"Your turn," I say.

Mendoza's quiet for such a long time that I start to wonder if he's going to play our game or not.

I drum my fingers on his chest, waiting. "Well?"

He stiffens against me. After a long, tense moment, he says, almost grudgingly, "My friends call me Rafe."

I roll my eyes. This is what I'm getting from him? "Gee, what a secret," I say dryly.

He doesn't respond. Against my shoulder, he's all tense again. Uncomfortable. I wonder if he has another erection.

I wonder if he's going to spend the next few days—God, please let it be only a few days!—awkward around me. I guess we need to get things out in the open. "Maybe we should talk about it, Rafe."

"It?"

"You know. Godzilla."

# CHAPTER **TEN**

## RAFAEL

I wonder how long it takes to drown yourself in a rainfall. Or at least kill an erection permanently. If I believed in a higher being, I would suspect that I was being punished for some bad deed I've done in the past. I've done a lot of them, so I guess this is karma shitting itself all over my head. It's the only way I can explain how I am stuck in the jungle with the hottest piece of ass in all of humanity.

Unfortunately that hot-ass woman is looking at me like I'm a freak—which I am—and that I could hurt her—which I could but have no intention of doing.

"Godzilla?" I try to muster a smirk but from her confused look, it probably appears like I need to take a shit. "You have an imagination."

She wanted to play some game like "Never Have I Ever" in

the jungle? I could top her stories on the first try. I've never sucked spider venom out of my own leg. Drink. I've never tracked a murderous Chinese thief into Saint Petersburg and killed him. Drink. I've never killed a Columbian drug dealer inside his fortified compound. That one was particularly sweet. Drain the cup.

"Oookay," she says, and it's evident she doesn't believe me. "Look I'm not afraid you're going to rape me. After all, you say you've been watching me, so I presume you've had plenty of opportunities and just aren't into that. Which is good. Very good."

She pauses and it's clearly my turn to talk now.

"Right. I'm not into that. The rape thing," I clarify.

"Good to know."

I shift slightly away but her body follows mine, and despite the awkwardness of the conversation and her obvious distaste for what's in my pants, I get hard . . . again. I rub the back of my head against the tree as if the sharp bark can pierce my thick skull.

I'm in the fucking jungle. My eye may be permanently damaged. I have to get one hand model and myself out of this place before Duval and his little army descend on us and decide to kill us in the middle of the Amazon rainforest.

I should be focused on getting what sleep I can so that tomorrow I can find enough supplies to help us make it to a village, which may be ten miles downstream or a hundred. Instead I keep thinking about how soft her fucking hands are and how, despite the fact that it's 2,000 percent humidity and we both sweated like dogs earlier, she still smells *good*—womanly and delicate, which isn't possible.

My nonstop erections around her defy explanation, too. Sure, I've gotten hard before but not from just *looking* at a woman. Not since I was a perpetually horny teenager and even the local department store circular could raise a half chub. But since then I've spent a lot of time putting sex and women out of my mind. There's little point when I can't do anything about it.

My dear sainted mother dubbed me a killer before I could spell the words. I was the result of the most vile experience a woman could suffer. I ate my twin sister in the womb. Nearly killed my mom on my way out of the birth canal. My giant dick was the evidence of my cursed existence.

I should never have been born, she hissed at me repeatedly.

She's probably right but not much she could do about it when abortion went against her religion. So I lived, but not a day went by without her reminder that I was a monster created by the devil. I existed only to hurt women, and the very evidence of that hung between my legs. From before I could form words, I knew that my own body was a weapon fashioned to harm, maim, and kill.

I tried. Fuck I tried to make my mother happy. I tried to ignore what was happening in my pants. I tried and failed and proved her right. I existed to hurt women. So I stayed far away from them.

And that's where I've gone wrong, I conclude. I spend too much time with Garcia and the men. That's the only rational conclusion. Somewhere along the line, I started avoiding women and now the first isolated exposure to one is sending me reeling. If I were home, I could remedy this by taking myself in hand—literally—but I know better than to stand outside of our shelter in the pitch black of night with my dick in hand jerking it while a dozen predators lie in wait.

She shifts again and I bite the inside of my mouth to keep from moaning out loud.

"So who are these friends that call you Rafe?" she asks.

"Aren't you tired? Because I'm bushed." I make a big show of stretching my arms, almost knocking some of the leaves off our shelter.

Maybe if she sleeps then I can sleep. I was in the military. We were taught to sleep anywhere in any conditions no matter how hot or cold or how many enemy artillery shells were flying over our heads. I can sleep through this torture, too.

"I'm kind of cold." She burrows even closer and I swear to fucking God her hand brushed against *Godzilla*. He roars to life and the blood flow that rushes into my groin is so swift I nearly pass out.

I jump up before I do something insane like grab her hand and press it even tighter against me. "I'm going to find you a blanket."

She grabs my leg. "You said that we shouldn't go out in the dark—that it's too dangerous. It's pitch black out there. You can't leave."

She was right but I had to do something. "I'm going to take a piss."

"Can I at least have your knife?" Hurt and fear war for supremacy in her voice.

I rub a hand down the side of my face. My five-o'clock shadow is going to be a full-on beard if we don't get out of here soon. "Sure." I pull off my belt and reattach the knife to the buckle. "Don't kill me when I get back."

"Don't act like a predator," she retorts.

Too late for that.

I retrace our steps from earlier today. The pilot is going to get eaten tonight. It's just a fact of life. We might as well salvage what we can from him. I locate him easily and strip off his clothes. The white dress shirt is a lost cause soaked with blood. The suit coat isn't much better but it's made out of decent enough wool. I can take a knife to it and make strips that we can wrap around Ava's wrist if she needs a splint, although from my cursory look, the hand and wrist look more bruised than anything. Still probably hurts like a motherfucker but if she had broken anything she wouldn't be able to take a step without the pain overcoming her.

In the pilot's pockets he has two energy bars and a pack of gum. I ball up his socks that are still mostly dry and stick them in my pockets. The one shoe that Ava nearly stubbed her toe on was too soft of a leather and worn to be a decent weapon. The clothes she might not like but we could use them for bedding.

I find nothing else, not even his pilot's pistol. Maybe he didn't carry one. I walk a little ways away and take out my dick and piss. The dead pilot has done a good job of deflating my erection. I rub my hands in the soil and then find a wet leaf to wash the debris off. I roll up the clothing, pull out the socks, and stuff those in the roll of clothes.

"It's me," I call out as I approach.

She moves inside the shelter and I duck inside, tucking the roll of the pilot's clothing to my left so she doesn't see it. No sense in having her worry about it tonight.

"Did you find anything out there?"

"A couple of health bars. Want one?"

I feel her shake her head. "No." She hesitates. "Did you get that from the pilot?"

"Yeah. Better that we have it than one of the jungle dwellers."

"What's going to happen to him tonight?" From the sound of her voice she knows exactly what is going to happen.

"He's dead and he won't feel anything."

She shudders. Her fear generates an itch at the back of my neck, and as she sits huddled beside me, I realize I'd rather have an excruciatingly painful erection and solid blue balls for days than have her be this upset. This woman's a trooper. She hasn't cried except for that one time when she realized she was sitting in the middle of a tree. I think those were actually tears of relief and gratefulness.

She hasn't complained. She hasn't done anything but try her damnedest to survive. And I've been taking shots at her for trying to be friendly and stave off her terror. I stretch out my legs and then pick her up.

She yelps.

"For warmth," I mutter.

"Yes," she breathes out. "You feel like a radiator."

In spite of all her curves she weighs less than a few banana leaves. Or maybe I'm just distracted by all that plump flesh in my grip. I settle her between my outstretched legs and wrap both arms around her. I try to position them low so I'm not crushing her tits. *Oh shit, she feels good.* She feels like ice cream on the hottest day in August or sunshine on a cold spring day. She feels like a shower after a long day of manual labor. She feels *so damn good.*

"Sorry." My dick presses into her thigh. Lying down, I feel like the circulation in my leg is getting cut off but I make no move to readjust. Being uncomfortable, painfully so, may be the only thing that gets me through the night.

"I'm sorry if I hurt your feelings by calling it Godzilla. I guess I figured guys just love to brag about their penis size and that it would be funny, but it wasn't and I'm sorry."

"Guys don't get hurt feelings," I reply.

"Oh really?" She twists to look at me, and her tits brush up against my chest. Marshmallow soft and just as tasty I bet. I grind my teeth a little.

"No, just tired. Really, really tired. I'm exhausted in fact." I lean my head back and close my eyes, but immediately I conjure up a picture of her, sweaty and nude with her breasts swaying in my face.

"Well, I'm sorry for making you *tired*, then," she jokes.

"You're forgiven." I snap open my eyes and stare out into the night. Maybe a jaguar will attack us and I'll have to leap from our hideout and wrestle him into submission. No, because then I'll have a post-adrenaline erection.

"You do have to admit it's rather large."

"Ava," I bite out.

"Yes?" She doesn't sound at all cowed. In fact, I think she's trying to hold back giggles. Although those could be fear giggles. Bennito laughs like a schoolboy when he's nervous.

I should just confront the issue head-on. It is the elephant in the room and it's not going to get any smaller with her sitting in my lap. "I have a large dick and obviously I'm very attracted to you, but nothing is going to happen. I promise. I would never hurt you."

"Sex done right never hurts. Unless of course that's what you're into, which is perfectly fine but not for me."

"Ava, can you not talk about sex right now?"

"Oh God, of course. I'm so sorry."

I take a deep breath and close my eyes.

She shifts, trying to find a comfortable place among the branches and hard soil. She shifts and every fucking time, she rubs against me.

"Ava, you need to stop moving," I rasp out hoarsely.

She stills immediately. "Sorry," she says quietly. She leans her head back against my chest and I hear her taking long, concentrated breaths as she tries to find peace in her mind. Enough so that she can fall asleep.

I concentrate on moving the blood from my dick into other areas of my body.

There's one easy way to get Ava out of my mind, and that's to think about the first time a girl saw my dick. She pointed and then screamed, stumbling up from the sofa where we'd been making out. Her father had burst down the stairs to find out what was wrong. We'd made up some story about seeing a mouse. She broke up with me the next day. Then there was the girl who thought she could give me a blow job, only she tried to go too fast and ended up puking all over me.

One by one I bring up all my teenage catastrophes until the throbbing in my cock subsides. I even pull out the worst of my memories—the one I keep locked away behind a concrete wall of shame and horror. The one where my attempt at sex ends in blood, pain, tears, and retribution.

My stomach churns as the screams of the girl and my mother mix together in an unholy chorus. *You're an animal. A curse. You should have died in the womb. You are my cross, my penance.*

No, I'd never subject Ava to that.

# CHAPTER ELEVEN

## AVA

"I think I just saw a spider eat a bird," I tell Rafe as I come back from the bushes after taking a pee. "Did I mention I hate the Amazon?"

He chuckles and hands me the water bottle. "I'm not a fan of it at the moment, either."

I eye the water bottle. My mouth is dry, but the water isn't super clear. It's rainwater, which means it's only as clean as whatever it fell on before landing in our bottle. Ugh. I try not to think about the things I'm ingesting as I swallow a mouthful.

"Drink more than that," Rafe commands. "You need to stay hydrated."

"You're joking, right?" I peel a portion of my wet shirt away from my skin. "Every ounce of me is freaking hydrated at the moment because it won't stop raining."

"Drink it," he says again, in a tone that brooks no argument.

*Prick*, I almost call him, but I choke back the word a moment later, conscious of our conversation last night. "Jerk," I say instead, and he simply grins at me.

Rafe's a bit sensitive about his big equipment. It's a little surprising to me. Most guys with that big of a dick would probably relish the opportunity to whip it out and impress people. Rafe acts all scandalized at the thought of me even noticing it's there.

And really, I'm good at tuning things out . . . but I'm not that good. It's like a python lying in wait, and clearly visible through his wet pants no matter how much he adjusts himself or tugs his shirt down. I felt it against me last night while I tried to sleep.

Thing is, I'm probably exaggerating its size because his clothing is probably making things seem bigger than they are. Maybe that's why I'm so fascinated and terrified at the same time. It's like in horror movies, where they delay the reveal because the reality isn't as scary as our imaginations.

Right now, my imagination is having Rafe walking around with a two-foot club between his legs. Which seems ridiculous, because—

"Here," Rafe says, appearing out of the corner of my eye.

I jump a little, startled out of my thoughts. A hot blush steals over my cheeks as he holds a health bar out to me.

"Eat this," he says.

*Is that a health bar in your pocket or are you just glad to see me?* I stifle my insane laughter and take the bar from him. "It's from a dead guy," I say, pointing out the obvious. "Do I have to?"

"It might be the only food we have for the next week."

Well, that answers it. I guess I have to. I unwrap it and when Rafe makes no move to eat the second one himself, I snap it in half and offer him one portion. "I need you to stay strong, too, just in case someone needs to wrestle a gator."

A ghost of a smile touches his face. "Alligators are shyer than you think."

They weren't the only ones. I take a bite of the bar and gag on the flavor. Peanut butter granola. Dry. Stale. Terrible. I eat every bite, though, and lick the crumbs off my filthy fingers. Rafe does the same, and then we wash it down with more rainwater.

"Breakfast of champions," I say dryly. "Nummy."

He brushes off his long fingers and I think for a hungry moment that he should have let me lick them clean. That's the stomach talking, though. He's probably touched all kinds of unsavory stuff out here in the jungle.

*Like his penis.*

Okay, I really need to get his dick out of my head. *Focus, Ava. Focus.* "So what do we do now?" I ask Mendoza, and then slap at my cheek, where a bug lands. Then I scratch my arm, because I'm covered in bug bites. I'm trying not to notice them but I feel bitten and itchy all over.

They seem to like my paler, softer skin to Mendoza's bronzed tan. Bastard. I swat at another.

He approaches me as I slap the bugs, and then he holds his hand out. "Give me your arm."

I do, curious, and he examines my wrist and upraised welts. I've clawed at the bites all night and a few of them look pretty rough. "You haven't broken anything. We could wrap it up, just to keep you from hitting things, but the swelling should go down. As for the bites . . . you're going to tear yourself up, Ava," he says. "We should mud up."

"Mud . . . up?" I laugh. "What, because we're not dirty enough?"

"To cover our exposed skin. Keep us from getting bitten even more."

I don't like the thought of voluntarily getting even filthier, but just then another bug lands on me. I swat it away. "Let's do it."

"Come on," he tells me. "Let's head for the river."

We pack up our small amount of things. Mendoza's got our tiny bundle of firewood wrapped in the pilot's old jacket and he's used one sleeve with a knot at the end to hold our supplies. In it goes the extra clothing, the water bottle, and some halfway-wet wood. I hope it dries up tonight enough for a fire. I don't think I can take another night in the cold, wet rainforest.

The other sleeve he's cut and torn into strips that he uses to create a sling for my arm. He lets me decide when to use it. When we walk, I find it helps to cut down on the jarring.

I let Mendoza take the lead and I fall in behind him. He's all peppy and full of energy this morning, and I am definitely . . . not. It was the worst night of sleep I've ever had. First, I was cold and sore. Then, Mendoza pulled me against him, and that fixed the cold thing. But every time I moved a muscle, he snapped at me. I spent most of the night afraid to move, his enormous dick pressed against my side. Snuggling for warmth should have been more pleasant than it was.

And then, of course, there was the rain and the bugs and by the time dawn rolled around, I wanted to cry from sheer exhaustion.

I don't, of course. I'm stuck here and I have to save Rose. Crying won't get me out of the jungle or stop the bugs from biting. So I'll just have to suck it up and keep going.

Rafe moves through the bushes, using a long pole to swat and skim at the ground, trying to flush out anything that bites. It makes moving slow, but safe. It also gives me a lot of time to study his back. And his backside. When his legs move, I can see a heavy bulge resting on one side of his pants leg, telling me that I need to change my initial speculation from "club" to "baseball bat."

God, I am such a pervert for creeping on a dude that's trying to save my ass. I'm not a size queen, but I'm morbidly fascinated by a guy with such enormous equipment. I mean, if I had the world's biggest tits, I guess I'd expect him to stare at those, right? Or ask questions? I think it's only reasonable.

I still feel like a jerk for thinking about it, though, so I try to think of something else. Anything. And my mind goes to Rose. My sweet, gullible friend with such a trusting nature and such shitty taste in men. I picture her pretty face, and the way she was tied up in those photos on Duval's phone, and now I want to cry. I clear my throat and blink back tears. "So, hey, Rafe?"

"Yeah?" he says, pushing aside a big leaf so I can walk under it.

"You think Rose is still alive?"

"I don't know," he says bluntly. "They might kill her, or they might keep her alive if she has use to them."

I wince. "Thanks for softening the blow."

He glances back at me and then grimaces. "Sorry. The truth is always best, even if it stings. False expectations only lead to dashed hopes."

Well, he's got a point there. I go back to ogling his butt (because really, it's a nice one) and nearly run into his back when he stops abruptly.

"Caiman," he tells me. "Don't move."

*Caiman?* I squeak and hide behind him, since he's the one with the knife. "Like a *crocodile* caiman?"

"Two different things," he says in a calm, low voice, eyes scanning the distance. "Just stay still."

"Okay," I say, and press my body up against his back, because I'm terrified. I slip my hand out of the sling and wrap my arms around his waist. His back is broad enough that if I hunch down, maybe hungry caimans won't notice me. I press my cheek to his spine and close my eyes.

Minutes pass. Long, long freaking minutes. I get nervous, because I hear splashing, but we're still not budging. Under my cheek, I hear Rafe's heart racing, but he's not moved a muscle. I open my eyes again and try to peer over his shoulder. "Are they gone?"

"Soon," he says, and his voice is a bit strangled.

"Can I see?" I whisper in his ear. "Is it safe?"

"Shh," he says, and quietly removes my arms from his waist, careful not to touch my bruised hand and wrist. He's pulling me away from him, and I can guess the reason why. Hands at his belt are too close to *below* the belt.

For some reason, that annoys me. Not again. Are we going to have to go through this constantly? Pussyfooting around the fact that he's got a big dick and he's attracted to me?

Can't a girl climb on a man in terror without him getting wood?

We need to get past this. I refuse to sleep another night afraid to move a muscle because Mendoza gets a stiffy the size of a rowboat. Something has to change. We have to become more comfortable with each other if we're going to survive. It's stressing me out and I feel stressed enough as it is.

"It's gone," Mendoza says after a long moment. I'm still stewing, so I don't respond. He prods the ground in front of him and then gestures for me to follow. "Come on."

I make a face at his back, but I follow.

I've heard the river in the background all night, but this is my first chance to see it. Churning brown water filled with logs and debris meets my eyes. It's wide and looks deep, and trees overhang on both sides. The banks are muddy and steep. It looks rather forbidding. "Please tell me we're not going swimming in that," I say faintly.

"Can't," he says. "Piranhas."

"Oh good," I say sarcastically. "Thank God there are man-eating fish in the closest body of water. That sure makes me feel safe."

"Stay here," he says, and moves toward the riverbank. "It's steep so I'll get the mud for us."

"Not moving," I say, hugging my arms to my chest. Piranhas, caimans, bugs, and bird-eating spiders. Boy, camping sure is fun. Boy, I never want to leave the city ever again.

Rafe slides a leg toward the steep riverbank, using his walking stick to brace himself on the side of the bank. He gets a handful of mud and then climbs back toward me. "Here, I'll do you."

"Please do." Damn it, even that sounds ridiculously oversexed. I turn my back and lift my hair, and he slathers wet mud on my neck. And I can't help it. I squeal and shudder a bit.

I hear him inhale sharply. He pauses, and then his hand brushes across my shoulders brusquely. "Hang on," he says in a flat voice. "I'll get more mud."

I turn and look as he heads back to the river, and sure enough, he's sporting another erection. This can't continue. We need to be a team. And not in a sexual way. Just comfortable with each other if nothing else, and it isn't going to work if he's constantly worried about touching me. Right now? He could grope my tits and if it was for my safety, I wouldn't care. It wouldn't be a turn-on, but I wouldn't lose my shit.

I'm not so sure about Mendoza.

Another thought occurs to me as he returns to my side and slathers more mud across my shoulders and down my good arm. What if the erections are a reaction to discomfort at being around me? I make him uncomfortable and his body responds in an embarrassing way? Kind of like dick Tourette's? I feel a stab of sympathy for him. He's so big and tough in every other way that I can't imagine him being so uncomfortable around me.

An idea flashes in my head.

I'm a firm believer in taking this sort of thing head-on. So once he finishes smoothing the mud down my arm, I turn around and start to remove my shirt.

"Ava? What are you doing?"

"I'll show you mine if you show me yours," I tell him, hauling off my shirt. "Let's get it all out in the open, okay?" No more wondering, no more speculating. I'll see his dick will be normal-sized and I can stop staring at it. He'll see me naked and realize that I should lose about fifteen to twenty pounds. Plus, I'm covered in bug bites.

We'll have a good laugh at each other's parts and then we'll be comfortable around each other. End of story.

# CHAPTER **TWELVE**

RAFAEL

She's taking off her shirt. Holy mother of God. Her tits are barely covered by some lace that is almost the same color as her skin. She's got nipples the size of erasers that are barely covered by a seam in the fabric, and the juicy flesh looks like it is ready to burst out of its restraints. As all the blood in my body drains south, I sway like a puppet whose strings have just been cut. I can't walk or speak. I can only stare.

My pants are so tight I'm afraid I'm going to pass out from blood loss.

I lick my very dry lips, imagining what it would be like to take one of those fat nipples in my mouth and run my tongue around the dusky areola. My hands itch to cup the abundant breasts and see if they overflow my own big hands.

I swipe the back of my hand across my mouth, forgetting I'm

coated in Amazon mud. As the slimy, gritty sand coats my lips and tongue, I'm roused from my lust-induced trance. I conjure up the image of the last woman I laid hands on. See her blood, hear her screams. Remember the horror and fear and disgust that everyone around me wore. Spitting the sand to the ground, I snatch up her shirt and shove it to her. "What the fuck are you doing? Put this on."

"No, we're having it out right here." She jerks away and the motion makes her breasts jiggle.

If possible, *Godzilla* swells even larger. A menacing rumble echoes between us. Her eyes widen when she realizes it's from me. I shake the shirt in front of her. My desire for her is overriding all the shame and self-loathing I can muster.

"Put this on." I enunciate each word so she can't mistake my meaning.

"No."

"Yes."

"Rafe, you are acting like a maiden aunt who's never had sex before," she jokes.

I freeze, just for a second, but she sees it. She sees my hesitation and I know the minute that she connects all the dots because her eyes widen and her mouth forms this perfect fuckable circle. Not one that I could get my dick into.

"Holy shit," she breathes. "How is that possible? Look at you? You're gorgeous. I mean, surely you've had offers? Is it a religious reason? Are you a monk? Like a warrior monk?"

I lunge at her but with my jacked-up eye and a forgotten pool of mud that I was using to cover her at my feet, I misjudge the distance and slip. She grabs for me but she loses her balance, too. I clutch her to me and twist so that her fragile, unprotected, *naked* skin isn't touched by the dirt or rocks or branches. When her legs fall around my waist and she places her hands on my chest to push upright, I nearly come.

I'm dry tinder in the middle of the desert at noon and she's the spark. My whole frame is seized with lust and my judgment is choked to death by desire. That's the only explanation I have for digging my mud-caked hand in her dark hair and pulling her roughly against me.

She yelps in surprise when her mouth meets mine, but her lips part and her tongue darts out to lick the seam of my lips. I open under her assault. And then I can't remember who started what, only that her mouth is wet and hot and her tongue is aggressive.

I open my mouth wide as if by doing so I can suck every ounce of pleasure out of her. I trace each lip with my tongue and then delve inside to stroke the insides of her cheeks, the roof of her mouth. I drag my tongue across the surface of hers as if I could tattoo my taste buds with her flavor.

And she kisses me back.

I drive my tongue into her mouth again and again. She curls her little tongue around mine, licking me with each stroke. I grab her ass and move her until her pussy is riding my cock. I know it's huge. I know I could cleave her in two by trying to shove inside her body, but God I want to.

More than anything I want to rip down her pants, spread her legs, and plunge inside what I presume will be the hottest, tightest, wettest snatch in mankind.

*Get off her*, I yell at myself, but my mind isn't in control right now. All thoughts of the curse, of the pain I inflicted in the past, of the warnings of my mother, of the beatings that she inflicted to make me learn my lessons, are subsumed by the blood that pounds heavily in my veins.

My cock strains against the zipper and she writhes against me. I don't let her go for a minute because I know if I do, she'll jump away from me and look at me as if I'm a freak. Even though I'm dying to tongue her nipples, which have hardened into tight points that are drilling themselves into my chest. Even though I would like nothing more than for her to sit her bare cunt on my face so I can eat her out. Despite all this, I won't stop. For some reason she's in her own lust fugue state and I'm keeping her there.

She moans against my mouth, and the vibrations she sets off inside my body are indescribable. My toes actually curl and my legs tense up. I've jacked off enough to recognize the signs of an impending orgasm but fuck if I know much about women. I can't tell by her moan how ready she is.

I've watched porn. I've seen chicks squirt all over the camera but I know that shit is fake. Faker than a hooker's love. I don't have enough fucking experience to know if she's going to fucking come.

My impending failure at pleasing her brings a clarity that I didn't have before and that I don't much appreciate. Why don't I just put my knife into her heart? It would be an easier way for her to die than with the devil in my body. I loosen my grip on her hair but to my surprise she doesn't climb off or move away from my embrace.

"Touch me," she says. Her voice is hoarse. "I'll die if you don't."

Conflict wars inside me. Does she really need me that badly? I place my hand on her back.

"No, here." She grabs my hand and places it at her waistband.

I may be inexperienced but I'm not dumb. Trembling, I wipe the mud off on my cargo pants. Her skin feels exceptionally soft and very *bare*. "Keep going," she whispers as I halt at the place where ordinarily there's hair on a woman. Instead I encounter no resistance; no soft nest, just bare, bare skin.

Maybe I'm in a porno. Maybe I'm back on the island and I'm having a really intense dream about spy games and planes blowing up and a gorgeous woman wanting me to finger her. At least that's what this dream girl is indicating. This has to be a dream. Has to. Because it's too goddamned good.

I close my eyes then so I can keep dreaming, so I can forget, and I let myself slide my fingers lower and then curve them between her soft thighs. She's sopping wet under the cotton and it's so easy to press one finger inside her.

We both suck in a sharp breath when I ease my long finger inside her. And then we groan as it is sucked in.

"Another," she pants.

I slide another finger into her wet, hot depths, and then when she nods, I use one more. The third meets resistance but she bears down and her walls soften to accept me. I brace the heel of my hand against her clit and then slowly thrust my fingers inside. She moans and shivers and whispers encouragement.

It's just my fingers. I'll just touch her with my fingers. Nothing else and she'll be safe.

"Yes, right there. Oh, Rafe, that feels so good." I curl up and mouth her jawline and then her long, elegant neck down to the erotic curve where the neck becomes shoulder. I can feel her walls tighten and pulse against my fingers. Her own dig into my pectorals, which is its own kind of pleasure.

I move back up to lick the hidden space behind her ear, and her breath hitches and her cunt walls squeeze my fingers tight.

"Faster, Rafe. Harder," she instructs.

I obey. I plunge my fingers inside hard and fast, setting up a fierce rhythm. She bucks against me, her hips moving rapidly in time with my fingers.

A stronger man than me, one with more experience or maybe just one who had more control, may have been able to withstand all that rubbing and moaning, or the slick feel of her cunt walls squeezing my fingers so tight I wonder if they'll break off. Then again, if they do, then they've been sacrificed at a worthy altar because, Christ, she feels like heaven. And I can't take it anymore.

I plant my feet flat on the ground and thrust upward, completely out of control. She rides me and my fingers like we're a bucking bronco ride at the seediest cowboy bar in the most remote part of West Texas.

As my hot seed jets out of me, I throw back my head and roar. Around me her entire body contracts—the thin walls of her cunt, her thighs around my hips, her fingers on my chest. I jerk upright and hold her tight against my body with my one hand and continue jacking her hard and fast, just as she'd asked. Another orgasm rips through her body and she shouts my damn *name* out louder than the stupid monkeys in the trees.

"Rafe, my God, Rafe!" The echoes of her screams will haunt me and please me in alternating modes for the rest of my life. Her smell is baked into my nose and whenever I'm alone, my fingers will curl in the memory of her smooth cunt and her tight, wet walls. I both hate myself and am ridiculously pleased.

She shudders against me, twitching when I withdraw from her

clearly sensitive skin. The desire to throw her down on the ground and bury my face between her legs is overwhelming. I'm tense with the repercussions of what just happened because instead of wanting her less, my cock is immediately hard and wanting more.

The orgasm I just experienced doesn't leave relief. Oh no. I'm greedy. Fucking her with my tongue would be a good start. Bending her over a rock and pounding her with my cock would be even better.

Roughly I push away and draw a trembling hand down my face. "We'd better get going. Why don't you wear the jacket until we can mud you up some more."

"Oh, okay," she says in a quiet voice.

I've hurt her somehow and that makes me feel like shit, but maybe that's what's going to get us through this without me throwing her against the first semi-flat surface I can find and fucking her to death. Literally.

I make an impatient movement and she gets the hint and hops off my lap. My shorts are uncomfortable so I tell her to wait while I stumble down the hill again, ostensibly for more mud. But before I slather up, I undo my pants and pull off my shorts to wash in the water. I pull the pants back on and tuck the water-rinsed shorts into my back pocket. I slather up my arms, neck, and face and then return with a handful for Ava.

"I'm sorry about the maiden aunt remark," she says as I rub the mud on her exposed skin.

I shrug. The less I say to her the better. Every time she's kind, she makes me think of things that I can't have.

My sole mission right now is to get us out of the jungle and return the information to the U.S. so I can get Davidson and go back to my island.

I should have told her I was a monk when she suggested it, but my dick was too inflated to let me think rationally.

"I didn't mean it as an insult."

"It's fine," I grunt. "We've got supplies to look for." I hand her the health bar. "Eat this."

"But I ate the other one," she protests.

"Eat the damn bar, Ava."

Her hurt morphs into anger, but she grabs the bar from me because she can clearly read my intent. Eat the bar or else.

As she eats, I gulp down water, leaving her about a quarter of it.

Her deliberate bites and overobvious chewing end with a very fake smile. "There, happy?"

"No," I respond gruffly and hand her the water bottle. She makes a show of wiping the opening before lifting her mouth to it.

I have to look away because everything about her mouth is sexual now. Everything. Even when she is glaring and her lips are pursed in an unhappy expression. That face just makes me want to kiss her until she's slack with lust.

"Let's go." I don't wait for her to agree but just turn east. I pull out my knife, attach it to the buckle, and wrap the whole thing around my palm. Over by a small clearing, I spot two good broken bamboo branches to use as a walking sticks. I hand one to Ava, which she accepts with narrowed eyes, and keep the other for myself.

"Why are you so angry? I thought orgasms made men happy. Is it the V thing? Because I don't really care about that."

I turn to her and she steps back when she sees the fire in my eyes. She has no idea how hot it burns, how long it has been banked, and how it could consume us both.

"I'm angry because now I want to fuck you."

"And you think I'm going to protest?" She threw her hand back toward the matted grass where I came in my pants while I fingered her. "I was totally with you. I came hard with just your fingers. It was great. Really great." Those last words sound a bit confused, as if she's surprised at how much pleasure it brought her.

Let her be confused. Let her want. Better than the alternative.

I turn and storm off into the jungle instead of responding to her.

# CHAPTER **THIRTEEN**

## AVA

Well, that escalated quickly.

Here I wanted to see a little dick, get everything out in the open, and the next thing I know, Rafe and I are tongue-fucking and he's fingering me until I come. And while it's crazy good, and the release is wonderful and just what I needed to ease some of the tension in my body . . . I still haven't seen his dick.

He's a virgin. That explains a lot, and it also adds a hell of a lot more questions. The virginity explains why he gets weird when I mention his dick. It explains why he stiffens up when I touch him. It explains why he sucks at playing a game about secrets.

It doesn't explain why a man as sexy as he is hasn't had sex before. I mean, Jesus. The man has a mouth that makes me wet just looking at it. He's got scars on his chest, but I'm like most girls in that I find scars more sexy than frightening. He's got a tight body that ripples with muscles, and combined with that big package? As long as it's not *too* big, I'm down with some straight-up nasty Amazon sex.

But . . . he's a virgin.

I admit this has me a bit stymied. There has to be a reason behind it. I ponder this as we trek through the jungle, slapping more mud on our bare skin when the rain washes it away. He's silent as we walk, the only sound the movement of leaves, the wildlife around us, and our walking sticks smacking into the earth. I don't know if he's pissy because he fingerbanged me or if he's pleased about it. He's not speaking to me at all.

It makes the jungle trek shittier than usual. Combined with the bugs and the mud and the rain that constantly seems to be pissing on us? I'm more convinced than ever that I'm never leaving the city again.

I'm lost in my dire thoughts when Mendoza stops abruptly in front of me. I pause just before I run into his back. I know from my experience earlier that he's not a fan of that. "What is it?"

"I see something up ahead," he says, voice low.

I drop my own voice, too, worried. "More wreckage?" Dear God, I hope not.

"Stay here," he says, not answering me. He pushes ahead and disappears between a pair of bushy ferns.

Stay here? I look around. There's nothing that differentiates this part of the jungle from any other part of the jungle, and I hear Mendoza's footsteps moving farther and farther away. Screw this. I'm not getting left behind. I push ahead after him. I've already seen one dead body. More won't gross me out too much. Hopefully.

Ahead, Mendoza's squatting at the base of a tree, examining something. I move to his side. "What is it?"

He looks up at me and scowls. "I thought I told you to stay put?"

"I thought I told you to whip your dick out earlier? Seems like neither of us is good at listening, huh?"

Rafe gives me another black look and then wipes mud off something that looks like my purse, except there's a piece of tape on the bottom. I hug my chest, the sodden jacket sticking to my skin. My wrist hurts but I ignore it. "Should I point out the obvious? That looks like my purse."

"Except for this part right here, yes," he says, indicating the tape on the bottom. "The idea was to switch it with your bag and steal the information."

I stare at the back of his head. "That is an incredibly dick move. My best friend's life is at stake—"

"Hers isn't the only one," Rafe says abruptly. He shoves his stick at another bag, this one made out of black nylon—the kind you find in stores that involve the outdoors. I only know this because Rose did a shoot with Tumi once and the on-set manufacturer's rep showed her how indestructible it was. He picks it up and starts rifling through it, completely ignoring me.

"So it's my fucking friend for yours?" I bellow at him. When he doesn't look back at me, I swat his ass with the end of my walking stick. "That is bullshit!"

He stands up now, eyes narrowed. "I'm not working with a lot of choices right now, Ava. I have to do what's best for my men."

"What about what's best for me? Did you ever stop to think that if you stole that information, you're totally screwing me over?"

"You weren't part of the equation . . . before." His voice drops.

"And now?" I choke out.

His gaze flicks to my mouth, and I know Mendoza's thinking about our kiss earlier. About his hand sliding between my legs and getting me off. About his big cock grinding between my legs as he came.

My breath pants in quick, shallow gasps, and now I'm thinking of it, too, even though I'm enraged.

"Now things are . . . different," he says, and turns away. "I don't know what I'd do."

For some reason, that softens my anger. I never wanted to be a mule, myself, but circumstances forced me to. Maybe he doesn't want to dick me over, either. "Fair enough," I say shakily. "We can argue about the bags when we get rescued."

He looks back and flashes a grateful grin in my direction. "Deal."

That grin makes me weak in the knees all over again. I feel like a stupid, giggly teenager that just got told by a cute boy that he likes her. Ugh. What is wrong with me?

*A lot,* my brain chimes in. *Hot guy that hits all your buttons + big dick + virgin + Stockholm syndrome = Ava fascination.* Right. Thanks, brain. Thanks for nothing. Maybe Rose isn't the only one that has poor taste in men.

"Is that your bag?" I say after a moment. He nods. "So we're going to be okay, right, it has everything we need to survive?"

"It did," he agrees flatly. He flicks it open a moment later and displays the empty contents. "Someone got here before us."

I stiffen, glancing around in the jungle. "Someone else is here with us?"

"Someone else survived, yes. And since Afonso was the last

one near the bag, odds are it's him. Or it could be anyone else. Or it could have been raided by natives."

"Natives?" I ask. "There are natives living here in the jungle?" It seems like the most miserable place on Earth to me. Why anyone would want to live here in the bugs and the mud, I have no clue.

"Yes, and not all of them are friendly."

"Well, shit."

"My thoughts exactly." Rafe stuffs his sleeve bag into the nylon sack and starts walking. "Which means we should keep moving."

That afternoon, there's a complete and utter downpour that saps my will to live. The jungle's pretty shitty on a regular basis, but throw in a skin-drenching soaker and I'm ready to hang up my towel and call it a day. My wrist aches even more than before. The layers of clothing I wear aren't staying dry, and they stick to my wet skin and make me prune up. Even the mud can't stick to my skin, and after an hour or two of the constant downpour, I'm clean and fresh as a daisy. I'm also miserable as hell, and my teeth chatter despite the humidity.

I'm hungry, but we're filling up on rainwater at least. Our bottle fills over and over again due to the drenching rainfall, and so we're not thirsty. There are no bugs, which is a small blessing. Very small.

But by the time the sun starts to set and the temperature drops, the rain hasn't let up a bit. I might be sniveling quietly out of sheer misery, but I'm still moving because Mendoza keeps powering through the jungle like a one-man crusade. If he's tired, cold, hungry, or scared like me, he's not showing it.

One of my flimsy shoes squelches in the mud and gets sucked off my foot. I stagger backward and move to retrieve it. As I do, Mendoza doesn't stop. He just keeps plowing forward.

"Wait," I call to him. "My shoe."

He pauses, and I backtrack to the muddy glop where my flat is now making its home. Not that it's much use against a jungle, but it's all I've got. I stick my hand in and retrieve it, and it's positively slimy. And because I have no other shoes, I have to stick this stinking thing on my foot. I resist the urge to cry, though my face scrunches up as I slide it back on.

"Got it," I say faintly. "Thanks."

Maybe Rafe notices that my stiff upper lip is now soggy with misery. He comes to my side and rubs my arm to encourage me. "You okay, Ava?"

I nod. I'm not okay. I want to throw my shit down and flop on the ground and wait for a rescue, but I can't, because there isn't one. We're in the middle of nowhere, and the only people that might come looking for us are the bad guys. So I suck it up. "I'm fine."

"Not too much longer, and we'll find a place to stop for the night, all right?"

I nod, my head bent so he won't see my red-rimmed eyes and know I've been blubbering. I don't want him to think I'm weak, so I save my sniffle until he turns away. He's the one with the eye patch, after all. I've got two good eyes. If anyone should be weeping about their fate, maybe it should be him.

We trek for maybe a half hour longer before Mendoza raises a hand in the air, scanning the brush. "Wait here."

"Why?" I ask wearily. My teeth have started to chatter again.

"Just trust me, okay?" He pulls out his knife and disappears into the brush.

I panic for a moment because the downpour is muffling his footsteps. "Say something if you're not okay," I call after him.

There's no answer. Just when I start to panic, I hear a crashing through the leaves and a curse word. "Rafe?" I cry out, clutching my walking stick. "If you don't answer me in two seconds—"

He appears triumphantly through the bushes a moment later, holding out a limp snake as long as I am tall. There's a grin on his rugged face and I swallow my cry of alarm. "How do you feel about snake for dinner?"

Probably the same way I feel about the jungle. But my stomach growls, reminding me that we don't have any other food. So I eye the snake. "It's really freaking big."

"It is," he says proudly. "Almost lost him." He points at his eye patch. "This is fucking with my depth perception." Rafe grins and then gestures behind him. "You should see what else I found."

"If it's another snake, you'll have to forgive me if I scream and don't sound excited," I say, following close behind him.

He laughs. "No, this you'll like."

I sidestep as Rafe slings the headless snake over his shoulder. "After you."

He steps forward, pointing ahead with his now-dirty knife. "I was hoping that would turn out to be what I thought it was, and I was right." He pushes through the underbrush to a small cliff overhanging with tree roots and half-exposed rocks. Ahead, there's a break in the cliff wall.

A cave.

I gasp. "Please tell me that's not inhabited by lions and tigers and bears, oh my."

"Not from what I can tell, but if you can hold a few things, I'll check it out again." He holds the snake out to me.

I stare at him, then at the snake, and gingerly take it in hand. "You're lucky I've already rumbled with a bigger python in this jungle," I tease him. When I get nervous, I fall back to cracking jokes, and it seems that Rafe's going to be the recipient of my humor.

He gives me a weird look, then hands me the bag of wood and clothing and disappears into the cave.

*Way to go, Ava*, I tell myself. *Just can't help it with the dick jokes, can you?*

I sigh at my inappropriate humor and hold the snake, and it's so big the weight of it hurts my bad hand. How on earth did he kill this with his tiny freaking knife? He's a badass. That he found me dinner and a cave makes him ten times sexier than if he was the most gorgeous, most normally hung guy in the universe. If he can cook this for me, I'd happily show my appreciation with a bit more hanky-panky.

Then again, I'd probably hanky-panky with him again anyhow. Last time was pretty intense. I squeeze my thighs together at the memory of him, his fingers inside me. If the rain wasn't so miserable—

"It's safe," Mendoza calls, jogging back out to see me. He takes the snake from my hands, and as he does, I notice that he's affected by my earlier words, too. Godzilla's making his presence known.

Of course he is. I'm such a jerk, teasing the virgin. I feel guilty as I follow Mendoza into the cave.

The interior's not anything to write home about. It's about twenty feet deep and not all that wide. There's a lot of debris and dried leaves in the cave, but it's big enough for the two of us to lie down inside with room to spare, and it's dry from the endless rainfall outside, which automatically makes it a win.

Mendoza points at the piles of leaves around the edges of the tiny cave. "We can gather that up and use it as tinder for the fire. If our wood's even halfway dry we might be able to get something going. Just check for scorpions before you stick your hand in. I'm going to gather some leaves to make a bed."

I don't point out that everything in the jungle is soaked. That's obvious. If he's getting leaves, maybe he has a plan to dry them. "Tinder. No scorpions. Check."

He dumps the dead snake near the entrance and then disappears off into the jungle. I unsling the bundle of wood and check it. It's a little damp but hopefully usable. I concentrate on prodding my walking stick into all the piles of leaves, and then when I'm convinced there's no creepy-crawlies, rake it into a pile off to one side of the cave.

Rafe brings massive palm fronds and long, leafy ferns, stacking them at the front of the cave while the rain just pours and pours. Then, he moves to a section of the cave, unbundles the wood, and covers it with tinder, then starts striking his knife against a stone. "Works in the movies," he tells me. I can't tell if he's joking or not.

I watch him for a few minutes, but as the sun goes down, it's getting colder and colder, and I'm shivering in my clothing. It's not keeping me warm at all. In fact, I might be warmer without it. So while he tries to get the fire started, I strip off my layers. Since it's raining, there are no bugs, and the mud has long since washed away. I peel off the jacket and my T-shirt, and then I pull off my pants and my shoes. It takes longer with one hand but I'm afraid to use my bruised wrist even though Rafe is convinced nothing is broken. It doesn't matter if it's not broken; it still hurts like the dickens. I'm in my panties and my bra, and while I'm chilly, the wet clothing isn't sucking my will to live.

"Got it," Rafe says quietly, and he picks up a bundle of tinder and begins to blow on it.

"Fire?" I say, breathless with excitement. I move in close to him to see.

His eyes go wide at the sight of me in just my bra and panties. "Ava," he says, strangled, his gaze on me. Meanwhile, the flame starts to go out.

"The fire," I remind him, and he immediately starts to blow on it again. "And I took my clothes off because they were making me cold. Once we get the fire going, you should take yours off, too."

He shakes his head and doesn't look in my direction. I glance down and yup, Godzilla has appeared once more. For some reason, this gives me a twinge of sympathy. This has to be difficult for Mendoza, because I'm getting naked around him and grabbing him and he probably has real, legit reasons for being a virgin at his age.

So I say nothing else, just squeeze my sodden clothing free of water and then lay them flat so they can dry. It's not as effective with one hand, but it gives me something to do. Mendoza gets the fire going decently, and it's so warm and wonderful I want to cry. He feeds more tinder to it even as the wood underneath hisses. "I don't know how long it'll last," he tells me. "So we'd better cut up the snake now and cook it while we can."

"Sounds good," I tell him and to my surprise, it does sound

good. I guess two granola bars in as many days is what it takes for me to enjoy the idea of eating snake. "Want me to cut it?"

"I've got the knife," he says, getting up abruptly. "Just watch the fire and I'll handle it."

I feed twigs and dried leaves to the fire as he cuts up the snake, and then spits it on twigs. We cut up even more to cook and then dry for walking rations tomorrow, which sounds horrific but beats an empty belly. And while we wait on the food, Mendoza gets rid of the entrails and the skin by leaving the cave again, even though it's dark outside and it's not smart.

It's clear he's avoiding me. It's also clear he's not about to take his clothes off. When he returns to the cave, he rinses his hands with the runoff at the cave lip, then toys with the leaves near the entrance to the cave. "These aren't quite dry yet."

"Then come sit with me." I pat the stone floor next to me. "Please."

He does, his gaze carefully on the fire.

"We've got a few minutes before the food's ready," I tell him. "Don't you want to get out of those wet clothes?" And because that sounds horribly porny, I add quickly, "They'll dry faster and you'll be warmer."

He shakes his head. "This is fine."

I sigh and move toward him. "Can we be practical for a moment? This isn't about getting sexy. This is about staying dry. I've been covered in mud all day, and bugs, and I'm about to eat snake. I haven't seen a hairbrush in forever. I've never felt less sexy in my life. But I know I'm warmer with my wet clothes off, and you will be, too. And since we don't have blankets, you're my biggest source of heat, okay?"

Rafe tosses another twig on the fire, ignoring me.

I can't believe I'm having to convince a guy to get naked with me. "I know you're a virgin. I know you have a huge dick. I promise you I won't be weird about either one, okay? Whatever your reason for celibacy, I respect it. I'm not going to mess with you. I promise."

That gets a response from him. Astonishment. "You think I want to be celibate?"

Now it's my turn to be confused. "Why else would you be a virgin?" But then I think back to earlier today, when he slid his fingers inside me and rubbed his cock against my panties. There wasn't shame in his body, like he was doing something forbidden. There was hunger, dark and intense.

Hunger like there was in his eyes right now. "You don't understand," he says in a low growl.

"Try me."

"I killed a woman during sex."

I blink. "How?"

His lip curls at my stupid question. "How do you think?"

"Asphyxiation? I mean, some people get off on that, but . . ." Maybe he asphyxiated her with his cock? If ever there was one to choke a girl to death, it's that one.

He gives a sharp shake of his head and stares into the fire. "No. You misunderstand. I tried to put my cock inside her and she died. End of story."

I'm a little aghast at this. I mean, his cock is big, but I didn't realize it was killer big. I can't help but glance down at his pants again. He's not erect, I don't think, but he's still bigger than most guys, which is pretty staggering.

"And that was your only time?" I ask softly.

He rubs his unshaven jaw and stares into the fire.

"Have you ever had any sex that didn't end with . . . anything like that?"

Rafe looks at me, and then his gaze flicks to my near-naked body. He's probably thinking about this morning, when I rode his hand and screamed his name.

Was that the only time anyone's touched him sexually and didn't freak out on him? I don't know what to make of this information. The more I see Mendoza's monster dick outlined in his pants, the more I get used to seeing it. It's huge. Scary huge, and not in a sexy way. I think most size queens would even get a bit alarmed at the sight.

But I also feel sympathy for the big guy. He's sexy and muscular, and most girls would give their right hand to be able to touch him. The fact that he's never had a great sexual encounter other than this morning?

It makes me want to give him more. I'm attracted to him despite our predicament, and I want to show him that sex can be good, even if it doesn't have a dick inside a vagina.

So I sidle closer to him. Put a hand on the buttons at the top of his shirt and begin to slowly undo them with my good hand.

He freezes. His breath is rasping hard in his throat. "Ava, don't—"

"Shh," I tell him. "We should get these cold, wet things off of you." I wish my hand was better so I could make this sexier. For now, he has to settle with me fumbling with his hem. I manage to free a patch of skin and then give up. "Do me a favor and take your shirt off, will you?" I ask, holding up my bad hand. "This is working against me."

"What are you going to do?" he asks.

"Get you naked so you can dry off," I say. "Then I'm going to rub up against you for a bit and touch you, if you're okay with that." I lean in. "I'd volunteer to kiss you but my breath probably isn't minty fresh."

"I don't fucking care," he says, and his gaze goes to my mouth. There's the hungry, intense look again. Like he's going to die if he doesn't eat me alive.

I shiver, and I feel my nipples responding, getting hard. My pulse throbs between my legs, too. "I'll kiss you if you take off your shirt, then," I tell him. I wonder for a moment if he's going to take it off, but he doesn't hesitate. Off it goes, and onto the floor in a wet, sodden heap.

And now I get to gaze at Mendoza's male beauty. He's got a few scars here and there, carved among his muscles. He's got a sprinkling of chest hair, and his skin is a dark, rich, warm brown that speaks of long days in the sun and his Hispanic heritage. He's also mouthwateringly gorgeous, a few tattoos on his arms interrupting the otherwise perfect sculpture of him. There's a happy trail near his belly button that disappears into his pants, and I run a finger over it, fascinated. "Man, I should not like looking at you so much," I sigh.

He stiffens.

I quickly feel the need to qualify my words. "It's distracting," I say, running my finger up his chest. He relaxes. Lord, there's a six pack, complete with ridges. This man must not have an ounce of fat on his body. God, I bet his ass is incredible, too. And his thighs. "Pants off?"

"I'm fine," he says in a voice that is stern, gruff.

I ignore it. I don't like taking no for an answer. So I lean against him and put my good hand on his cock, keeping the throaty purr in my voice as I raise my mouth to his. "Pants off?"

Rafe groans and captures my mouth with his. His kiss is rough, wild, hungry, and intense, and it affects me more than I thought it would. All the while, my good hand grips his cock and I try to not think about how what I'm holding feels like gripping the wrong end of a baseball bat and that it's not going anywhere near my girl parts without a metric ton of lube. Probably not even then, considering he's killed someone with it. Can that even happen? I wish he had been more explicit, but I could tell that he'd rather die than speak another word about that incident. *I* don't think he snuffed out anyone with his dick, but he does and it's clearly scarred him, so much so that this big, strong male is afraid of *me.*

But I can stroke him and pet him and show him that it's pleasurable to be him.

I break the kiss and nibble lightly at his open mouth, even as my hand rubs over his cock again, and then I go for the buttons on his cargo pants. "Undo this for me."

He rips at the fabric, his breathing harsh, and then he's free and that enormous cock is pressing against my hand once more. I can feel heat radiating from his skin, and he's rising tall and proud. He's enormous. Has to be nearly a foot long, and thick as my wrist.

Jesus.

But his pants are open and he's looking at me with wild, ravenous eyes, and I feel . . . oddly special. Like this is a big moment and it means something. My heart gives another painful squeeze that this gorgeous man is so starved for touch. I've been careless with my body over the years, having one-night stands and pointless relationships. I've probably slept with more guys than I should admit. But I doubt this matters to a guy like Rafe, because he's looking at me like I'm the most beautiful, perfect girl on Earth because I dare to put my hand on Godzilla. I'm not the plain friend with the weird eyes and the kooky job. I'm Ava, and I'm gorgeous to him.

So I slide my hand forward and grip him, palm to flesh.

The breath shudders from his lungs. He groans low, and I stroke carefully. Hand jobs are tricky, because hands can be really damn dry. Mine are soft from the rain and because I'm fervent about lotioning them, but he still needs more lubrication. I think about letting him lick my hand to wet it, but there's a better, slicker lube I can use. I rest my swollen wrist against his hard shaft, and I shove my good hand into my panties. His eyes widen and his breath hisses out as I glide my fingers through my folds. I'm wet at touching him, monster cock or not, and I'm loving his reactions. "Hang tight," I tell him, and lean in to kiss his parted mouth again, my tongue flicking against his. He groans again, and that makes me even wetter. When my hand is good and slick, I pull it back out of my panties and place it on his cock, and then gently stroke.

Rafe's head falls back, and his hand clenches over mine. "Ava, no—"

"Going to come?" I ask, my voice gentle. I give him another tiny stroke, more of a jiggle, really, and kiss his mouth. He's got a hair trigger, but that can be worked on. "Do it," I say in my naughtiest voice. "Come all over my hand." And I stroke him carefully again, tightening my fingers around that beast of a cock.

Rafe growls, the sound feral and wild, and his hand clenches over mine. A hot spurt of liquid slaps against my arm, and then he's coming even more. His fist works over mine, helping me milk his orgasm, until both his hand and mine are covered in his come, and he's breathing hard, exhausted, and beautiful to look at.

The look in his eyes is dazed. "Why did you do that?" he asks.

I lick my lips and then taste a drop of his come, beaded on the tip of my thumb. "Because I wanted to, and because you're sexy." I shrug. "Do we need more of a reason?"

# CHAPTER **FOURTEEN**

## RAFAEL

I wish she was less beautiful—that she wasn't so round and luscious like a ripe jungle fruit dangling in front of a starving man. I stare at her mouth, the one that has curved round her thumb and licked off a dewdrop's worth of come. The rest of it—the shit not in her mouth—covers her hand. It's like a silky rope, weaving in and around her fingers.

Godzilla, as she calls it, lies against my leg, the upper half curled to the left. I'm still half aroused. I force myself to think of snakes slithering in a mass orgiastic pile at the bottom of the cave like in the Indiana Jones movie. And nuns. No, nuns can be sexy. Ava in a nun costume would make me come in a nanosecond.

And then I'm hard. Again.

When she sucks in her breath, I jerk the corner of my pants over to cover up the new erection, but the fabric does little to disguise it. I move into a crouching position and ignore the pain that shoots from my cock up my spine. Hopefully the pain will make my arousal die off. I grab sand from the bottom of the cave and rub it over my dick until the come is off along with some of my skin. I'll have to be more gentle with Ava.

How can I stop wanting her? This must be hell—to have the very thing that you desire but cannot have dangled in front of you unceasingly. The need to protect her and keep her safe is warring against the need to possess her. Under my skin, those two violent desires are battling and I'm afraid of the victor. Afraid for both of us.

"Don't do it again," I growl and ignore the dark desires that course through me as she warily eyes my advance. Her eyes flick to the side, signaling her desire to escape, but before she can run to another part of the cave I grab her hand and rub dirt over it, scraping off the evidence of my weakness until all that is left is her soft flesh.

"It's just a hand job," she says, slightly defensive, slightly confused. I don't clear up the issue for her.

I'm a razor-thin thread away from taking the club between my legs and shoving it in one of her hot wet holes. How many times does she think she can touch me, or how many times does she think can shove her fat tits into my face before I throw her down on the nearest surface and break her in two?

"Get some sleep," I order.

"I thought orgasms were supposed to mellow people out. Not make them into bigger assholes." She jerks out of my grip and stomps to the other side of the fire. I try not to watch her but my traitorous eyes follow every movement. The firelight makes everything more erotic. When she bends over, the light highlights the swells of her breasts and creates shadows in the deep valley between them.

I brace myself for the onslaught of tears but I get nothing except her quiet breath and small movements as she tries to find some comfort on the stone and dirt. Somehow her quiet acceptance of my shitty behavior is worse. If she cries then I would have an excuse to go to her and sweep her up in my arms under the guise of comforting her.

But her silence is far more effective punishment. She shuts me out and I have no reason to go to her. The fire will keep her warm. The cavern will keep her dry. She has water and food. Tonight I am merely a nuisance, and an ungrateful one at that.

As penance I force myself to stay awake all night to feed the fire.

In the flickering firelight, she looks angelic. Her hair pillows around her face. The flames cast a golden glow over her normally pale skin. Her lips are red, her cheeks rosy. The heat of the fire gives her a healthy glow.

I can almost convince myself I'm not in the jungle and that Ava and I are camping out in the desert. Outside the monkeys scream at each other, the pumas howl, and the snakes slither around on the ground. In here, it's warm and dry.

I watch the fire so long I imagine myself in another place, with Ava. This time we're on the beach. She's got some tiny white bikini stretched across her ass and when she walks, the drums start playing. I'm lying on a lounger, one of those wooden things with a cushion so my ass doesn't get sore from sitting on it so long.

She stops at the edge of the water and the ocean waves lap at her feet, giving her tiny caresses. For some reason, because this is my fantasy and her ass is like a minor miracle, she begins to do toe touches and every time she bends over, the white spandex rides a little higher until it's bunched between her cheeks.

She casts a coy look over her shoulder and then runs her fingers along the elastic edge of those bikini bottoms and pulls the excess fabric from her crack. She tugs the white bottom down so far I can see the crease between her cheeks. She purses her lips together and winks. Then the bottoms go down so far she's mooning me.

I shoot up from the lounger and am on her in a half second. Maybe less. Rockets move slower than me.

I shove the white bottoms down around her thighs and then push her into the sand. I spread her cheeks and see her outer lips are swollen and wet and her dark eye winks at me. I lean forward and bury my face in her ass, licking everywhere, sucking everything. I'm the parched guy in the desert and her cunt is the only font of water available. *That's* how hard I am on her, how far my tongue is up her pussy.

When she's panting and crying and begging every known deity for mercy, I take my dick in hand and press it against her opening. She's sopping wet and my dick slides in like there's two gallons of lube spilled between us. Her cunt walls grip me tight but I don't shoot my load immediately.

Nope. I savor it. I draw out to my tip and then push back in so slow that ants crawling at a picnic have time to eat the entire pie. She continues to drench my cock with her come and I hear the slap and suck of our bodies as she arches into my every thrust. I slap her ass and watch the bubble of flesh jiggle erotically. I slap her again and she mewls for more. I tap those mounds a few more times until she goes wild on my cock.

*You're so big*, she screams. *I want more.*

I give up the spanking because I need both hands to hold her hips for my furious rutting. I pant and grip tighter. I wrench her body flush against mine and she rides me, reverse-cowboy-style. The ocean water tickles our knees, and I have one hand feverishly working her clit while the other clamps her torso to me.

Her head twists around and we kiss in a savage meeting of teeth and tongues. I work her harder and she creams all over me again and again.

My breath comes out in tiny irregular gasps and the thick head of my cock pulses beneath my hand.

A scratch against the rock has me flicking my eyes open.

She's awake and her big eyes are round with emotion. Wonder? Disgust? Confusion?

I can't read it because lust has clouded my vision. I don't close my eyes, though, and recapture the beach, her ass, her screams because real Ava is better than dream Ava even if she's across the fire from me. Even if she's fucking terrified of my beast.

Shit, who can blame her? I'd be terrified if I was a girl, even a big-hipped beauty like Ava.

She can't take me. No one can.

I rub myself roughly knowing that this is the only pleasure I'll know, other than a one-time hand job that might come my way if I open my wallet. I can pay for that. I can pay for a mouth or even two. But I'll never feel anyone's cunt walls around my cock, especially not the angel across from me.

But I use her anyway. She stares at me and I stare right back, rubbing and tugging and imagining her rising from her bed and coming over to me and taking me all in from tip to root.

"It's just a hand job," I grit out in a perverse echo of her earlier words.

Her tongue flicks out to wet her lips. "Why don't you let me help you?"

"Because I want it too much." I can't keep the honesty back, not when her luminous eyes follow my every movement. And then as the orgasm winds all my nerves and tendons tight, I close my eyes and explode in my hands. For all the buildup, the release is less than satisfying.

When I look across the fire, she's on her knees. A chill hits me.

Now that she's had me in her hands, this half-baked satisfaction is all that's left for me. Anger fills me up and then drains away as quickly as it came. How is this her fault? It's a curse.

My *madre* told me this when I was ten and my cock was the size of a beer bottle. I was given a girl breaker. That's what she called it because I only lived to hurt women. I was the devil's spawn, she said. My mother was violated and she became pregnant but the baby girl was eaten by the baby boy in the womb. When I grew older, I was the image of her rapist and my cock was the instrument of the devil.

She tried to beat the demon out of me but it didn't work. I had to take a life before I believed.

"How'd you kill the girl?" she asks, breaking into my reverie.

I use the sand again to clean myself up and shove my used cock down my pants in hopes that it will forget about sex.

"You're pretty hard up if you want to hear snuff stories before you go to bed," I mock.

Instead of getting upset, she tilts her head and inspects me. "You're pretty hot when you're angry."

Whether she said it to cool my jets or make me laugh, I'm not sure, but it works. I start laughing and she cracks a smile in response. Jesus, this girl.

I suppose she deserves an answer. It could even serve as a warning and then maybe she'd stop looking at me like I had something worthwhile to give her. Public service announcement: Big dick can kill. Also, I'm an asshole.

I lean back on my not very comfortable rock and start talking. "When I was fifteen, an older girl asked me to prom. I was stoked. She had heard a rumor about my size and wanted to find out if it was true. I'd only made out with a couple other girls and both had run away when we got to the heavy petting stage, but this girl had experience and was tired of her pencil-dick teenage lovers."

"Her words or yours?"

"Hers. That's how she asked me out. 'Hey, Rafael, the word on the street is you have a monster in your pants. How about you let me pop your cherry after prom. The pencil dicks I've been dating couldn't find the G-spot if it was a map in Quake.' Prom was three weeks away and I followed her like a puppy. We made out a few times leading up to the event and so she felt me up under my pants, under my shorts. She knew what she was getting into and I figured—given her experience—that she'd know if I was too big. When she didn't call off the date, I figured we were good to go. Prom night comes. It's pretty much a blur because I'm just a walking hard-on at this point."

Ava laughs. "I can't believe she made such a production out of this."

I shrug. "I rented a hotel room, we took our clothes off, and Godzilla pops out. When she sees it, her excitement level drops to about a five and she's at maybe two when I get the condom on. But she wasn't going big game hunting in the north without returning with her bagged and tagged trophy, so she opened her legs and told me to put it in."

"For an experienced girl, it doesn't sound like either of you did much prep," she observed.

"I was fifteen and a virgin. I didn't know what foreplay was. I figured that was feeling her up under her clothes, which I had done. And she seemed excited enough."

"So did you pull out a knife and stab her? Shoot her in the head when she didn't come? I mean, how do you get from prom night to morgue?"

"I breached her. She died. End of story."

She makes a face. She wants more. She wants to hear the whole gory thing. About the fountain of blood. The way her brothers mutilated me in retaliation for touching their sister. The way that my mother viewed me as a curse and crossed herself a dozen times whenever I came near. But all she needs to know is that the only way I can protect her is to keep my fucking hands off her.

"Breached? Like you didn't even go all the way in?" I nod. "I don't think you can kill someone with your penis," she frowns. "She died right there? Right in front of you?"

I grimace. "No, she died two days later. But there was a lot of blood." I close my eyes trying to forget, but the vision of that girl and the blood between her legs and around my dick is painted on the back of my lids. I pop my eyes open and stare at her. Better. Much better.

"Was she having her period?"

"Can we stop talking about it?"

"I guess, but I still don't think you killed her." I open my mouth to recite the facts again but she holds up her good hand. "No, I get that you believe you did. I doubt medical science would back you up."

"I tried to have sex with her. She bled horribly. She died two days later." Her brothers took me out and beat me within an inch of my life and I was grateful for each blow. "Those are the facts."

She reaches out and her hand lands on my knee. I jump because I didn't realize she was so close. "Is celibacy your atonement? Because I'm sure you didn't kill that girl."

I turn on my side, away from her sympathy and the soft light in her eyes. I can't have that. "I'm sure I did."

# CHAPTER **FIFTEEN**

## RAFAEL

It takes a long time to get to sleep but eventually I will myself into some sort of suspended consciousness. The next morning, the jungle wakes at dawn as the night predators give way to the day ones.

Ava is sleeping. Half her body is coated with mud. Her hand and wrist are still swollen and there are scratches and insect bites on much of her exposed skin. Her hair is matted and wound together in such a state that there could be birds nesting in there. I've never seen anyone so fucking beautiful, so fucking desirable.

I want to scoop her up and bathe her in the warm rain until she is nothing but milk white skin highlighted by rosy flashes of arousal. My pants are tight but I've resigned myself to the fact that I will always be aroused when she's near. Hell, when she leaves I'll probably be aroused by the thought of her.

Outside I gather more kindling and throw it at the mouth of the cave. If we have to, we'll return here, but staying another night would mean that we've made no progress getting out of the jungle. And we need to go. Ava's hand needs medical attention and I need to figure out how I'm going to negotiate with Uncle Sam to get Davidson back without the information.

Placing the water bottle along with two pieces of grilled snake meat on a rock near the fire, I head north to see if I can find any more pieces of wreckage. The first twenty minutes yield nothing but pupunha fruit. We could roast these tonight. The sweetness of the fruit would be tasty after the dry, rubbery snake. I fill my pockets and move on.

To the left there's a gap in the foliage, as if someone or something jumped into the middle and didn't leave. I poke around with my bamboo stick but nothing moves. A machete would be good about now.

A busy brown and gold pattern not known to be found in the Amazon catches my eye. With slow and measured movements, I gently push the brush aside. Under a branch, the purse lies looking almost showroom perfect. The branch undulates and the green markings of an emerald tree boa appear.

He's not going to like me disturbing his resting spot. It's possible I can tug the purse out from under the branch without disturbing the boa. Possible, but not likely.

What the hell, nothing ventured, nothing gained. I bring my bamboo stick down slowly until the brush falls back into place. The leather handle of the purse is still visible through the palm fronds and ferns. Like it's a game of Operation, I slide the stick forward until it just kisses the edge of the loop. A few flicks and I have the handle caught on the end. The bag scratches on the ground but the branch above it doesn't budge.

"You'll thank me for this later," I tell the snake. His tongue comes out in disagreement, but he makes no moves from his resting spot. I inch the purse out one agonizing tug at a time until it's finally at my feet. I pick it up and flip it over. The bottom is bare. This is the real deal, not the fake we'd mocked up.

The sun's position indicates I've been gone for about forty minutes. That's too long to leave Ava alone. Sticking the bag under my arm, I hurry back. I find her crouching behind a rock about thirty feet from the entrance.

"What's wrong?" I whisper, hunkering down by her side.

Her tense muscles relax slightly but she remains alert. "Some guy went into the cave while I was using the facilities."

"Pissing?"

She frowns but nods her head. Apparently we can be in the jungle but we can't talk about shitting and pissing.

I reach down and tug on the leather belt she has wrapped around her wrist. Smart girl. Always so smart. Reluctantly she releases the buckle and I take up the knife. We both know I'm better with it but even beyond that I get anxious without a weapon. I hate not having a gun or a bigger blade than one that fits inside my belt. Still, I can gut someone with this.

Placing the bag between us, I tap the top, motioning for Ava to sit down.

"What's he look like? Native? Other?"

"Other. I think . . . I think it might be Afonso. He had a gun and big knife." She stretches her hands about three feet apart.

"A fair fight, then." I tighten the belt around my hand.

"What about that?" She points upward. Sitting on top of the mouth of the cave is a puma and she looks hungry. "If someone is in there, why not just let the cat eat him?"

"Bloodthirsty, I like it." I nod in approval. "But if we want anything on him, like his gun or his knife, the puma might take it into the tree with her and then we have to kill the puma. We don't want to do that."

"No, no." She looks horrified. "No killing the puma."

I don't tell her that it's more likely the puma kills us than we kill the puma with my three-inch blade and a handbag.

First things first. Afonso and the puma can wait.

I reach in and pull out the folders.

"How long did you watch me?" she asks as I scan the contents.

"A while."

"And in hired gun terms, what does that equal?"

"Long enough to know your favorite morning drink is milk and sugar with two drops of coffee. Is that like flavored milk?"

She punches me lightly on the arm.

The folders reveal nothing. It *is* just a bunch of emails and transcriptions of phone calls. It's innocuous stuff but I can see that it implies that there's more and *better* or more dangerous shit where this came from.

Behind me, the puma shifts. She hears something. We'll have to think about this later. I flip the folders shut and pull the pupunha fruit from my pocket. The small plum-sized fruits are hard and perfect for throwing. I rise and whip three in quick succession across into the jungle underbrush. A bird flies out and the puma leaps forward to investigate.

As the puma leaves, I take off at a run, ordering Ava to stay by the bag. The resulting noise has the intended effect and Afonso sticks his neck out of the cave. I launch myself forward straight into his chest. He flies back with a thud.

I have the element of surprise on my side and I'm able to knock one weapon out of his hands. The gun goes skittering to the side.

His other hand grips a machete tight. He must have found that in the plane wreckage. One of the businessmen must have been preparing for a jungle jaunt and packed it in his stored luggage. I want it.

A fist hits me in the damaged eye, and my vision blurs enough so that I almost don't see the blade slicing toward my face.

I kick out blindly and hear a grunt. There's a crack and then a cry of pain.

I roll to the left and the blade crashes into the dirt.

"Where is it?" Afonso snarls.

I stay low to the ground, crouching as he circles me.

"Outside." There's no point in pretending I don't have it. His eyes flicker toward the opening and I use that minute distraction to leap forward. My momentum drives us backward. He slices down with the blade and I feel it cut into my skin but I don't stop. I keep moving until his back slams into the rock wall of the cavern. If I die in here, Ava won't make it. Afonso will find her. He'll rape her and then he'll leave her broken body to the animals.

I fall back and drive him forward again. The blade cuts deeper. I feel the warm river of blood spilling down the valley of my spine.

I have little time. If the blade hits a spinal nerve, I'm done for. I power forward, driving my shoulder under his blade hand.

He cries out and with my free hand, I bring up my belt knife and stab it forward and twist. The scream of pain he releases could be heard at the basin of the Amazon. I pull out the knife and drive it again, just to get him to shut the hell up.

His body goes limp beneath mine. Taking two steps back, I fall on my knees. My vision is blurred but his face is a macabre mask. Where his eye once sat, there is only a bloody hole. Beneath it is another stab mark, jagged and round where I turned the knife as hard as I could. I shove his face into the dirt and yell for Ava.

My back feels like it's on fire but I ignore it as I pat Afonso's pockets. He's got a ton of shit in them. Energy packs that look suspiciously like they came from my Boy Scout bag.

Ava stumbles in.

"Check his pack."

"Your back," she protests.

"No, supply check first. Any medical supplies?"

I try to stand but when I see black spots instead of Ava and the cave, I drop back to my knees. Blood loss is making me dizzy.

I stagger over to the fire and flick the blade into the coals. Then I grab the gun and check it. No more bullets. Figures. I toss it aside again.

"There's a tinfoily blanket thing, a prescription bottle full of something. Pain pills?" She sounded hopeful.

"Water purifying tablets." She sighs in disappointment and I can't help agreeing with that sentiment. I could use an oxycodone or ten. "A flat plastic thingy. There's also about ten energy supplements."

No rope. No MREs. No lighters. Apparently he found the Boy Scout bag but some stuff had fallen out. The blanket, energy bars, and water purifying tablets were good, though. Very good.

"The plastic thing is a bladder to hold the water and the purification tablets. Are there still embers in the fire?"

"Yes."

I think I see her stab at it. "I want you to go out to the mouth of the cave. There's some kindling there. Throw it on the fire. Go over to Afonso's body. Don't look at his face but pull off his pants. Wipe down my wound and when it's clean you're going to put the hot knife to my skin."

She sucks in a horrified breath. "I'm not doing that."

I grab her hand. "You do that or I'll die."

# CHAPTER SIXTEEN

## AVA

Every time I turn around, it seems like things are migrating from bad to worse. A girl can't even take a pee without someone hijacking her cave. Now, Mendoza's been stabbed and I feel as if we've hit rock bottom on the shit-scale of "things that could go wrong."

Of course, I shouldn't say that. Another plane could always crash into the jungle, this time on top of us.

"Then again, that might be a lucky break," I mutter to myself. Then I shake the thought away. I don't want to die. I want to live, and it seems like every time we catch a break, something else screws us over.

"More . . . wood on the fire," Mendoza tells me, stopping my frantic train of thoughts. The wound looks as clean as I'm going to get it. "Make it good and hot."

"All right," I say faintly. I push the blade into the coals a little deeper, and add more wood and more leafy debris. I blow on the fire, and the flames leap up. "You tell me when it's hot enough, okay?"

"When it's red hot," he says, unwinding the belt from around his wrist. He bites down on it, and a shiver goes up my spine. Oh God, oh God, this is going to suck.

Moments pass, and Mendoza groans quietly. I know he's got to be in a lot of pain. I want to wring my hands, but my mangled pinky and swollen wrist make me settle for squeezing my index finger, over and over again.

"Good enough," Mendoza says. "Just hurry up . . . do it. Losing too much blood." His words are slurred through the belt, and there's a sleepy droop to his eyes that tells me he's going to pass out soon. I need to get my shit together.

I nod and grab the knife out of the fire. Immediately, I realize that's a mistake—the handle is red hot and I hiss back a yelp of pain and drop it back into the coals. I can feel my fingers immediately blistering up, but there's no time to think about that. *Dumb, Ava. Dumb.* Blinking back tears of pain, I wrap my hand in my shirt and grab the knife again.

"Here I come," I tell him, and then feel stupid again. "Not that anyone else would be coming after you with a hot knife. Then again, you seem to have as many enemies as I do, so hey." He doesn't chuckle, but talking makes me feel better, so I keep babbling as I pull his blood-soaked shirt away from his back. "I don't know how to break this to you, Mr. Mendoza, but I think Darwinism is trying to vote you out of the gene pool."

The cut looks awful. It's deep and bleeding a slow trickle of thick, dark blood. It doesn't look like it's anywhere vital, but I'm not a doctor. I'm a freaking hand model. Even as I gape at the wound, a fly buzzes nearby.

Right. Cauterizing time.

I suck in a deep breath and don't even bother with a count of three. I push the flat of the red-hot blade against his wound. The sizzle of skin, like a frying egg, hits the air, and then the smell of burning flesh. I gag, and press the blade harder, because I don't know how this shit works. I don't know how long I need to leave it, or if I even did this right.

Mendoza's gone limp. He didn't even scream, which is pretty badass of him. I pull the knife away and study the wound. There's a big, blistering mark where I pressed the knife, but the wound is ragged on one side and the knife I have is tiny.

"I think I'm going to have to cauterize it twice. I'm so sorry. It's the knife. It's so small."

He doesn't answer me.

Panic hammers my heart, and I shove the tiny knife back into the coals of the fire and then bend over Mendoza. "Rafe?"

He's still breathing. Passed out, then, either from blood loss or pain. Or both. Well, that makes this easier for him. I finish heating the knife and press it to his wound again, wincing only a little this time as it cauterizes his flesh. The skin is blistered and purpled, but it's sealed. With that, I take my shirt off, wet a clean corner, and bathe away the dirt and blood from the rest of his skin. Once his back is cleaned, I roll him onto his side and examine his eye, peeling back the bandages. It looks awful, worse than before, and that worries me. We don't have antibiotics, but we have water purifiers now, at least, so I can at least bathe it with clean water.

Over the next few hours, while Rafe sleeps, I keep myself busy around camp. It's either that or go crazy with worry. I keep the fire going, hauling in more wood every time I venture out. If the wood's wet, I create a pile on the other side of the fire, hoping that the heat will eventually dry it out more. I get more water, use the tablets, and wash Rafe's eye and rebandage it. I wash his other wounds, too, since he's covered in scrapes and scratches. I clean up the cave, get fresh leaves for a bed, and gather things that look useful. I find a sturdy vine hanging from a tree, and after I make sure it's not a snake, I bring it back with me. Since it's not long enough, I get more vines, and then spend a good hour or two braiding my finds together to make a makeshift rope.

I also find wood that will make a decent spear, and make a few more of those. You can never have too many weapons in the jungle, and I keep seeing wild animals. Night is coming on, and the fire won't keep a determined predator away.

Which means I need to get rid of the body.

That takes up a good chunk of the afternoon. I keep Afonso facedown so I don't have to see what happened. Rafe said it wasn't good, and I trust him. I tie the rope around his arm and loop it around my torso like a harness so I can drag him through the jungle, but he's heavy, so I don't make it as far as I want. I have to settle for letting the body slide off of a rocky precipice and into jungle vines below. Good enough. I give the body a salute. "Not gonna miss you, Afonso."

Rafe wakes up at sunset, when I've stoked up the fire and put another damp, hissing log onto the flames. He groans and cusses in Spanish.

I immediately go to his side, bringing the bottle of water with me. "How are you feeling?" I want to kiss him all over his banged-up face for rejoining the land of the living, because I don't know what I'd do if he went to sleep and just never woke up again.

"Like hell," he says, and tries to sit up.

"Stay off it if you can," I tell him, pushing a hand against his shoulder. "Give it time to heal. We're not going anywhere tonight."

He nods and lies back on his side again, then touches the bandages on his face. "Eye feels like hell, too."

"I cleaned it while you were out," I tell him. "Sorry if I made it worse."

"Is it bad?"

"Let's just say you're not going to win any beauty contests with that look."

He nods.

I pass him the water bottle.

He takes a small sip, then tries to pass it back to me.

"Drink the whole thing," I tell him. "You need to replace the blood you've lost and I've been drinking water all afternoon." River water, but hey. Today it didn't rain too much, and that means the wood was drier than usual, so I'll take it.

"I should get up and get rid of the body—"

"Taken care of," I tell him, and I feel a little bit of pride at the surprise on his face. "I'm not totally helpless you know."

"I think you're pretty great, actually. How's the wrist?"

I stupidly preen under those words and take the water bottle back from him when he finishes drinking, then offer him a fruit. "It actually doesn't hurt as much." He grunts in what I presume to be happiness. "I'm not sure if we should save the snake or eat it. How much longer do you think we'll be . . . out here?"

He props up on an elbow. "We should eat the meat before it

goes bad. And as for us, we'll go up the river tomorrow. See if we can find anyone else."

I nod and break the cooked snake in half and offer him part. We both choke it down, and then it gets quiet again. I'm guessing Mendoza's not in a talky mood, what with passing out and cauterized wounds and all, but I desperately need conversation after a day of being in my own head.

"So," I say brightly. "Do you want to play another round of our game?"

He scrubs a hand down his face, then crooks his elbow to act as a pillow. "I guess." He sounds tired.

"All right, I'll start." I stir the fire, contemplating what to talk about. Nothing sexual, because the last thing we need is more tension in camp. We're too exhausted and Mendoza's lost too much blood. I study my awful, awful-looking hands. They're upraised with welts from bugs. The blisters are puffy and dark on three of my fingertips, and one burst earlier, which means an ugly scab. There's scratches, my nails are ragged, and my one pinky is bloated and terrible. My hand modeling days are over, at least for the next year or two. Even the smallest imperfections can cost jobs. I once lost a job because they didn't like the way my nail beds looked.

Thinking about hand modeling makes me think about Rose. That's an easy subject, then. I curl my legs under me and move closer to the fire. "When I was in third grade, I moved to a new school," I tell Mendoza. "Back then, my hair wasn't this weird brown, but blond. I was very blond, and very pale. I moved to California, and I didn't know anyone. And kids are mean to people that are different, you know? Anyhow, back then, my eyes—the heterochromia—really stood out. The kids picked on me, called me names, you name it."

"Kids are shitty."

I dug my toes in the dirt of the cave. "Kids are kids. A week or two passed, and I started making up illnesses to avoid class. I'd spend half the day lying down in the nurse's office just to avoid people. And one day, while at the nurse's office, in walks the prettiest girl with blond hair and the same pink shirt I was wearing. Her name was Rose, and she had to go to the nurse's office daily to get her insulin pump monitored." I smile at the memory. "She sits next to me, and asks why my eyes are so weird. I tell her that I was born that way. Then she shows me her insulin pump, and says she was born different, too. She then declares that I'm going to be her new best friend. And after that, people weren't shitty to me, because they loved Rose. And if Rose liked someone, then she was okay." My eyes fill with tears. "Rose is the one that got me into hand modeling, you know. She told them they had to have some sort of work for me, and no one's ever able to tell Rose no. Turned out someone had a cancellation, and I filled in. The rest was history."

Rafe's silent.

I sniff and give a shaky laugh. "You pass out on me again?"

"No. Just thinking."

"About what you're going to tell me? What terrible secrets?" I tease. "You want to tell me about your childhood?"

"Not really," he says. "My mother hated me and the man she was married to wasn't my father."

Well, that's a mood killer. So much for my game. "How about you tell me a fun fact about you, instead?"

He yawns sleepily. "I'll try to think of something."

We're both quiet for the next while, and I put on a big log so it can burn all night. Then, I lie down by the fire. I figure Mendoza's asleep again, and my thoughts fill of Rose. Beautiful, headstrong

Rose who thinks she can always get her way with a smile and a flirty laugh. Rose with her insulin pump. Are they taking care of her? I wonder. Can we even be friends after this? Will I be able to look her in the eye and not resent what her choice in men has put me through? I don't have answers to this, so I close my eyes and try to sleep.

Just when I'm about to drift off, Mendoza speaks. His voice is soft with exhaustion. "I thought of something, Ava. A fun fact."

"What's that?"

"I have an island."

This strikes me as . . . absurd. "Uh-huh."

"I bought it," he says, voice dazed with exhaustion. "Had a place in a favela in Rio called Tears of God. Got too dangerous, so I bought an island. Moved a bunch of people there. To keep them safe."

"Go to sleep, Rafe," I tell him softly. I hope he's not hallucinating. I don't know what I'll do if he gets sick and dies. Ava of the Jungle has just about hit her limits.

# CHAPTER **SEVENTEEN**

### RAFAEL

The next morning I spend a long time watching Ava wake up. I imagine her on the island, in my bed. My room faces the east because I like to see the sunrise. I'm usually the first one up. It occurs to me that the other men that join me for a run along the beach are almost all single, which makes sense because if you have an Ava in bed with you, why in the hell would you be running at dawn when you could be spreading her legs and feasting on her juicy pussy?

I run my tongue across my lower lip. I haven't tasted her. Am afraid to, really. I'm the rabid dog at the end of a weak leash wearing a frayed collar. Tasting her will snap the last threads of my control.

Deliberately, one by one, I force my fingers to relax from their clenched position and reach over to wake Ava.

"Rise and shine." I shake the bladder of water. It'll be another couple of hours before we can drink it since that's how long it takes for the purification tablets to do their job, but it holds three liters of water, which will keep us plenty hydrated.

"It's too early, Rose," she mumbles.

It's pathetic that I'm happy that it's her friend's name she mutters in her sleep, not some asshole boyfriend's. I rub some nonexistent sleep out of my eye and shake her again.

"Rise and shine. Time to find civilization."

She stretches and the motion thrusts her breasts in the air, and the blanket slips down around her thighs. There's a tantalizing stretch of skin exposed between the waistband of her yoga pants and the bottom of her ragged shirt, which pulls up when her arms go over her head. My mouth waters at the sight. I take a swig of the water hoping the stale taste will wake me out of my lust-induced fugue, but then she shifts again and her shirt rides up even farther until the round curve of her breast is almost revealed. Not even the tightness and pain in my back when I move breaks my concentration as I try to will the fabric to go even higher.

I can't pull myself together until she sits up and rubs her eyes like a toddler. That forces me to shake myself awake.

She blinks and glances around. "What time is it?"

"Seven or so." The sun has been up for a couple of hours. I start packing our supplies into the nylon knapsack.

"Hey. Don't we need that?" she protests as I stamp out the fire. "Aren't we looking for more stuff from the plane today?"

"No." I don't look up from the ashes I'm creating. I can't spend another night in a cave with Ava and not take her. We're too isolated and the need in my body is overriding every other thought. "We need to get out of the jungle."

"Oh, because of your injuries?"

"Yeah," I lie. "Because of those."

I've had worse than a knife in my back and a gouge in my eye but then again, I haven't had to take care of a model at the same time. I shoulder the knapsack, ignoring the pain in my back. I lift the knife so I can take a look at my eye in the blade's reflection.

"Oh for God's sake," Ava says and stomps over to me. She knocks my hand away and lifts up the bandage. At the first touch of her hand on my temple, I freeze and all my good intentions fade, too. "Your eye looks good. No oozing puss or grossness. Should I smell it or something? I saw someone do that in a television show."

"Maybe check it again?" I ask not because I doubt her word but because I want her to stand there all day and look over every part of my body. I can actually see a little out of my bad eye, which means the swelling is starting to go down. I'll be fine. And the scar on my back is nothing. I have a scar on my chest from a wound I received nine years ago—the first time I was sent to do wet work. Guy knifed me before I could terminate him. She should check that out. Hell, I have scars all over my body including—I jerk away.

"Did I hurt you?" She sounds unhappy or worried.

"No." And then to soften the harshness of my response, I add gruffly, "Thanks for looking out for me."

"Well, you are my ticket home." She gives me a wan smile.

"Right. Let's get moving."

I heft the foot-long blade in my hand, the one Afonso tried to gore me with, and lead the way out of the cave. It would do me good to remember that her touches and concern all have to do with getting out of the jungle. Of course she's going to be nice to me. I'm the only one around who can save her pretty ass.

"Stay close and walk in my footsteps."

"Sure." She answers just as abruptly.

We make our way to the bank of the river where we mud up. The mosquito repellent that was in the Boy Scout bag must have fallen out along with other things. Once done, we start walking downstream.

There are no paths in this part of the jungle, not even overgrown ones, and that means there's no village nearby. We walk silently for a long time. I can feel her eyes burning through my back. She has questions she is dying to ask.

Around midmorning she breaks. "Do you know why I play the game?"

"The one-question game?" I want to make sure I understand her.

"Yes. I play it because then I can pretend we aren't in the jungle and that we're on stage two of getting to know each other."

"What was stage one?" I ask against my better judgment.

"Stage one was when you took me to the café and bought me food. Granted, now I know that you were doing that as part of your mission or whatever, but at the time, it was flattering."

"Seems to me you get to stage one plenty of times."

"Not me. Rose. Her other friends, maybe, but I haven't been to stage one for a while." Is that wistfulness I hear?

I stop and turn abruptly. "You have to be kidding me? How's a girl like you not getting chatted up nonstop? You must be having stage one dates all the fucking time."

She grins then a true, happy smile stretches across her face. It's a good thing my boots are planted shoulder-width apart, because that sort of beauty knocks a man on his ass if he's not prepared. "Have you seen Rose? She's a model. A real runway model. I've got pretty hands." She holds up her hands and we both look at them.

One is covered in mud and the other is still swollen and purple. Her hands are not pretty anymore. They are soft, but right now, the only modeling she'd be doing would be in a survivalist magazine. I see the moment that realization hits, because her grin fades away and the light in her eyes dies out. "Okay, maybe not right now, but I did have pretty hands."

Suddenly nothing seems more important to me than for Ava to know how fucking beautiful she is. I cup her neck and tilt her head back and for once when I look at her, I don't try to hide a thing. "I don't know who you've been hanging around but you're a knock-out. You've got the type of body that makes men want to fight for you. Your face is like a goddamn sun; it's so beautiful that you can't look directly at it. If you were any more fucking gorgeous, I'd probably die of a heart attack. In fact, I'm going to have to mud up some of your features so that when we do run into natives, they don't try to keep you as some goddess that they worship." I run a muddy, sweaty finger over her forehead and then down the bridge of her nose. Her eyes soften and her lids get heavy. Even with my shitty experience with women, I know what that means, and my body strains toward her.

I step back, drop my hand, and turn away. That's all I can give her now. Reaching down I shift the monster toward my inseam, hoping that the little extra fabric there can give me some breathing room.

I resume walking and she follows, but this time the dam's broken and the questions come relentlessly.

"Do you really own an island?"

"Yeah. It was owned by a former Columbian drug cartel owner. He terrorized the locals, cleared land for an airstrip, and built a compound. He was killed by a rival gang when he was in

Sanibel doing business. It was semi-abandoned. My men and I
pooled our resources and bought it. We moved everyone there who
wanted to move because the Brazilian government wasn't friendly
anymore."

"What's it called?"

"Tears of God."

"Where'd you get that from?"

I hack at the branches. Her hand slips into the back of my
pants, and whatever room I had left disappears. It's tight but I
decide that I don't want to lose her touch, which probably means
I'm losing my mind. Hopefully we'll find some natives soon and
they can just spear me to death and put me out of my misery.

"And God shall wipe away all tears from their eyes; and there
shall be no more death, neither sorrow, nor crying, neither shall
there be any more pain." I quote Revelation.

"And is there no death or sorrow or pain?"

I snort. "No. No matter how high the fence or how strong the
barricades, death illness, heartache—all find you."

"So why the island?"

"Because it was the safest place I could find for the people who
trust me to protect them." I pause. I probably shouldn't be sharing
this information with her, but she deserves to know why I was following her. "A friend of mine was taken by the U.S. government. He
helped me form the Tears of God. It might have even been his idea.
Hell if I know. We were captured by rebels in Tehran. They brought
us to Dasht-e Kavir and said if we could make it out of the desert
then we'd be free. We were meant to die but a few of the natives
found us and helped us. When we got to safety, they begged for us
to take them with us." I squint up at the canopy of leaves remember-
ing that hot day when Davidson and I were faced with abandoning

our saviors or taking them with us. There really wasn't any debate, though. We wouldn't have survived without their help. "We walked out of the desert, away from the army, and set up base in a small slum in Brazil. Seemed like a good place to hide from the world."

"How did the other people find you?"

"Word got around. A kid is sold for food or maybe a daughter is offered up for protection. We hadn't broken ties with everything back home to become slave traders or kid killers. But the slums are dangerous. It's a kill-or-be-killed mentality, so we fought back and we fought back hard. Touch us and you suffered—not just you, but your whole line."

I could feel her shiver behind me, but she never removed her hand. "Sounds biblical."

"That's my mom's influence. She read me the Bible when I should have been playing video games and watching porn. She lived a shitty life and the Bible was her refuge. She wanted me to be a missionary." *She wanted me to atone for the original sin of being born. As if life isn't enough of a curse.*

"And it sounds like you are."

"How so?" I look over my shoulder.

"You have an island where you send people you've saved." She shrugs as if it makes total sense to her. "Isn't that the definition of being a missionary? Saving people?"

"The Tears of God ain't heaven, Ava," I say more harshly than I intend.

"Maybe for some people it is."

# CHAPTER **EIGHTEEN**

## AVA

Just when I think I have the guy figured out, he surprises me again. There are so many layers to Rafe Mendoza that I don't know what to think. I think he's a thug, and he helps me escape the bad guys. He says I mean nothing to him, but he watches me with such hunger in his eyes that it makes me shiver. And he says he's just a mercenary, but then he tells me about an island he bought that he's turned into a refuge for people.

Most of all, he tells me he's a virgin by choice and then jerks his cock in front of me.

So yeah, there's no putting Rafe Mendoza into a nice, safe box.

I can't exactly put my feelings about him into an easily classifiable category, either. I hate that he wants to sell me out. I'm utterly confused about his decades-long celibacy—so long he probably is a virgin, particularly if his only experience with a girl was just getting the tip in. And I'm terribly, horribly, completely attracted to the man. Giant cock or no, there's more to Mendoza than what's in his pants.

All I know is that when he told me I was beautiful earlier and traced mud down my nose? It took everything I had not to drag him against me and kiss the hell out of him.

I think he guessed how I felt, too, because he immediately turned away, leaving me all confused. Didn't he just say he found me attractive? Didn't he want to get rid of his virginity?

I touch my hair self-consciously. God, I probably look like a fucking wreck. Maybe that's why he turned away so abruptly. My bug bites probably have bug bites. Not a sexy look by any means.

And really, the jungle isn't exactly conducive to hot, steamy sex anyhow. I think of the cave we've spent the last two days in and shudder. I think of how long it's been since I've showered. I sniff one armpit, and wince. Okay, yeah. Fragrant. I'm probably covered in head-to-toe jungle grunge.

It's quiet as we walk through the jungle, and Rafe doesn't seem to be in a chatty mood, so I mentally fantasize about how I'd take his virginity. We'd have to have a nice hotel room. Something special, with a big bed and a big tub. Order some wine, maybe some strawberries. I'd wear some lingerie that would cinch up my slightly-too-wide waist and play up on my breasts. And we'd need lots of lube. Lots and lots of lube. I visualize tearing Mendoza's shirt open and straddling his hips as he lay down on the bed. The look on his face as he realizes just what I intend to do with him, and then that wonderful hunger in his eyes.

I shiver a little despite the warm, humid air. If we get out of here alive, I'm definitely putting that plan into action.

We follow along the banks of the river for a while, my hand holding on to the back of his pants as he moves forward. I have a spear lightly gripped in my bad hand, but I mostly use it as a walking stick. Mendoza's got Afonso's machete and has been using it to hack through the jungle. There have been a few caimans and snakes, but mostly on the other side of the riverbank. I'm hoping we're making too much noise for anything to come investigate us. My gaze moves along the river as we walk. It's murky and congested with debris, the water a muddy, uninviting brown. Trees and brush overhang the edges of the river so we walk a short distance away but keep it in sight. We haven't seen anyone in this jungle mess, and I don't expect to.

Which is why I'm surprised when, about midday, I see something on the opposite bank, under a few overhanging trees. "Is that . . . a boat?"

Mendoza pauses and squints. "My sight's shit right now. Let's get a bit closer." I follow close behind him and we move farther down the river, into the brush at the bank. Sure enough, it looks like a small six-foot fiberglass boat with a motor on the back. Excitement flares through me and I wrap an arm around Mendoza's chest from behind and squeal. "Oh my God, it's a boat! It's a boat! We're going to get out of here!"

He adjusts himself automatically at my touch, and maybe it's weird, but I'm starting to get used to the idea of Rafe having a constant erection around me. He then shakes his head. "Let's not get too excited just yet. That boat might be there because that means the enemy is nearby."

I freeze in place. "You mean . . . Fouquet?"

"Or Fouquet's men. They're going to come looking for that purse or for you."

"Shit," I breathe. "What do we do, then? Go back deep into the jungle?" The thought makes me want to cry.

"Nah," Rafe says, and he turns to grin at me. "We're gonna steal their fucking boat."

An excited giggle escapes my throat. I don't think I could adore the guy more than if he had turned around and told me he had brownies. "I like the way you think."

He starts to strip off his pants.

"What are you doing?"

Rafe peers at me from under the bandages swathing one half of his face. "I'm going to get in the river and swim across to bring the boat."

I stare at him, aghast. "Are you frickin' high? You have a stab wound in your back—"

"Which you cauterized."

"And you have a bad eye that can get infected and is a whole lot less sexy to a girl."

He stares at me for a moment.

"I'm serious," I say, putting my good hand on my hip. "I'm all for nursemaiding and sponge baths, but the moment you start dripping green shit from your eye socket, I am out."

Rafe snorts and starts to unbutton his shirt again.

"Oh no you don't," I say, and start to pull my own shirt off. "I am so going in that river and you are not."

"Don't be ridiculous, Ava," he says to me. "It's dangerous."

"It's all dangerous."

"I can probably swim better than you."

"I'm a champion swimmer," I lie to him. "Won three medals in high school for the breast stroke." I pull my shirt off and since

I'm now in my bra, I give a little wiggle of my breasts to see if he's paying attention.

He is. Boy, is he. His gaze immediately swoops down to my tits. And I feel in control again. "Here's the thing, Rafe," I tell him. "You are no good to me if you're all infected and dead, okay? You staying alive and whole means I stay alive and whole. And I'm willing to make a deal with you."

"A deal, huh?" He pushes a hand against the front of his pants, but it's obvious that I've awakened the beast once more. He can't hide the fact that he gets an erection. Not in cargo pants. Not with that dick.

"Yup, a deal," I tell him. I wonder if my nipples are hard. Because the idea of my deal is making me turned on. "You let me get that boat and I promise that when we get back to civilization, I play nurse and give you a sponge bath."

"It sounds like I win both ways," he says, and his gaze flicks to my breasts again.

"You do." *And you aren't the only one.*

But his white knight side isn't letting me win so easily. Even as I slip off my pants, he glances across the muddy, nasty river. "Champion swimmer, huh?"

"Three medals in high school," I agree.

He sighs and looks back at me. "I don't like this."

"I don't care. I don't like the thought of you getting gangrene, either."

Now he just looks amused. "Pretty sure you can't get gangrene from a river."

"Pretty sure you're just stalling," I tell him, and hand him my pants, then my shoes. I'm a little freaked out over the thought of getting in that water, but it looks like bad news for Rafe and his many wounds. Mine are all under the skin—blisters, a broken pinky, etc. His are far more troubling and more likely to get infected.

"Sponge bath, huh?" He's trying to be nonchalant about it, but there's a husky note in his voice that tells me he's already thinking about it.

"Yup," I say cheerfully. "I'm swimming that river."

He frowns but takes something out of his pocket. "Take this at least." He hands me the small knife.

"Good idea," I say and clench it between my teeth. I give him a sassy wink, and before I can think about alligators or piranhas or snakes hiding in that murky brown water, I move to the river-bank and step in.

It's warm and silty. Ugh. I also can't see my feet. Double ugh. I move into the water slowly, wading out. Then I start to swim awkwardly, because my wrist hurts when I push it against the water.

"I thought you said you were a champion swimmer," Rafe calls as I more or less dog-paddle into the river.

"I lied," I call between knife-gritted teeth.

He curses.

And then I'm concentrating on swimming to the boat as fast as I can. I'm terrified, and fear makes me paddle faster, especially when something brushes against my foot. It could be an old branch fallen into the water. It could be a twenty-foot-long snake. It could be a fish. I don't stick around to find out. I just swim faster.

The water gets deeper toward the middle of the river and I can't touch the bottom, but it shallows out again on the other side and I make it to the side of the boat. There's a rope tying it to the shore, so I hide on the side of the boat and use my knife to cut it. When the boat is freed, it begins to drift, and I realize I have no idea how I'm supposed to get in the damn thing. My bad wrist aches something awful, and I don't know that I can use it to spring myself into the boat. Then again, it's too unwieldy to swim it back to the other side.

Something bumps against my leg in the water again, and I panic. Grabbing the side of the boat, I ignore the trembling weakness in my wrist and haul myself over the side. A blinding flash of pain shoots up my arm as I tip the boat to the side, but I manage to roll into the bottom. I lie with my legs propped up on one of the seats, and a small, choked sob escapes me. My wrist hurts worse every damn day, and right now it's white-hot agony. I don't have time to baby it, though. I force myself to sit up, holding my wrist against my chest. There's a paddle at the bottom of the boat, and I reach for it. I don't know how to work a motor, but I'm sure I can figure out how to paddle.

It's only when I reach for the paddle that I realize there's something else in the boat with me. With a mixture of horror and awe, I pull the heavy machine gun into my lap.

Oh, holy shit.

I've just stolen the boat of someone with a goddamn machine gun. Eyes wide, I stare across the river at Rafe. What the fuck do I do now?

He's not looking in this direction, though. He's gazing down the river, machete in hand. I'm tempted to pitch the gun into the bottom of the river, but we might need it. So I start paddling my way to the other side.

Hopefully I can get to Rafe before the owners of this gun come back.

# CHAPTER **NINETEEN**

## RAFAEL

*She swam across the river for me.*

I can't get that thought out of my head. The ground I'm standing on is shaking. There's a tectonic shift in the Earth's crust but apparently no one can feel it but me. When she took off her shirt and her barely covered breasts jiggled in front of me, my tongue stuck to the roof of my mouth. I couldn't muster up a single argument to prevent her from sliding into the river, because I had no brain activity. Her tits are *that* magnificent.

"Look what I found!" she cries and lifts what looks like an AK-47 triumphantly above her head. There's a long magazine dangling from the chamber of the machine gun. The gun isn't going to get us out of the jungle faster, but we're no longer low on the food chain. A couple of bullets from that baby and we'll be eating something better than snake.

I mentally punch myself so I can get my head in the game. Enough with the fucking mooning. So she swam across the river. She wants to get out of this humid land of suck as much as I do. I tell myself that repeatedly, but what my head wants the rest of me to believe isn't sticking.

My dick is as hard as ever and there's a tightness in my left breastbone that is making me feel like a goddamn schoolgirl— the kind that writes her crush's name in a notebook littered with flowers and hearts.

Shit.

I'm in love with this woman.

Not only do I want to bone her from here to Ecuador but I want to spirit her away to my island, put her on a throne and lie prostrate at her feet until she tells me to rise and suck her toes. And if I'm very good, I will be allowed to place my mouth between her legs and eat her pussy until she's too boneless to sit upright.

If my dear mother wasn't dead, I'd seek her out and have her take a switch to my back again. I need someone, anyone, to beat some sense into me. For both Ava's and my sake.

I clamber down the embankment and raise my hand to wave her over to my side of the river. She picks up the paddle and dips it into the water. The boat's prow heads downstream as she paddles on the left side.

"Switch sides," I holler and then make rowing motions on both sides of my body. She catches on immediately and flips the paddle to the right side. I see her laboring. It must be a bitch to hold the paddle when her pinky is swollen. As she closes in, I step into the water to help her drag the boat ashore.

"Get out of the water," she scolds me. "There's something awful in it. Something tried to eat me when I was swimming."

"Because you're a juicy piece." I grin as I drag the boat to the sand so I can climb inside. The danger's gone and her smile of joy is making me giddy.

"Juicy piece of what?" She smiles back and my heart goes into overdrive. I might just die of a heart attack on the banks of the Amazon.

There's a small, selfish part of me that wants to stay in the jungle, where I can keep Ava to myself. I'd tell her that we couldn't find our way out and we'd live in the cave, just the two of us. The jungle is full of food and water, and I could provide for her.

When I take her back to civilization, she'll go back to her fancy life with her model friends and the rich men that hang around them. I'll be reduced to stalking her, watching her from afar and jerking off in my hand.

My hand tightens on the prow of the boat for just a moment as I contemplate the jungle fantasy once more. Then I throw the nylon sack of supplies into the boat along with the damn purse of Ava's. "You're juicy everywhere."

The words come out more gruff than I intend, and I can see by the tightening of her lips that she's disappointed in me. And that's why I need to get her back. Because here in the jungle, I might be happy, but she would never be. She needs soft sheets, expensive clothes, and a man who knows how to pleasure her.

Because even if I didn't have a dick the size of a club, I had no experience and my ability to bring this woman to orgasm while fucking is probably slimmer than a piece of paper in that damn bag of Ava's. I give her a tight smile and start to swing into the boat, when I hear the unmistakable sound of a chamber being loaded.

Jesus *fuck*. Can't we catch even one break?

Ava gasps and raises the gun but then lowers it almost immediately.

"What?" I mouth and reach in to grab the machete I took from Afonso.

"They're kids," she whispers in horror.

I lift my hands, knife clenched in one, and turn around slowly.

And see a band of boys, tense and dirty. The tallest one is about ten inches shorter than me. He's not holding the semiautomatic, though. That would be his friend to the right, who is about Ava's height but has good muscle tone. From the look of his face and hair growth, though, this kid is just out of puberty. He might be thirteen, if that.

The rest of the kids range from ten to thirteen and they are armed to the hilt, looking like boy soldiers from Uganda. Their dark skin is decorated with homemade tattoos and belts of ammunition. Whatever happened to the good old days when natives were armed with homemade spears and wore leaves around their groins? Now they have more guns than a survivalist camp in Utah and wear cargo pants where they store a dozen more magazines for their toys.

Too bad he isn't holding a handgun on me. I'd flip that shit on his face so fast, he'd forget he even knew how to hold a gun. But a semi with a bullet in the chamber at this close range? I'd likely be shot in the other eye.

"Do you speak Spanish?" I ask with my hands still raised.

The leader turns to the tall boy next to him, who nods.

"Who are you?" Tall Boy asks.

He doesn't want to know my name. He wants to know if I present a danger to him. I do. I'm six feet five inches of muscle with seventeen years of killing to my name. Even if one of these children does get a shot off, I have the ability to take them all to hell with me. But I'm no kid killer. I never was.

I take a risk. When we were in Rio, the Tears of God favela was well known. People from all over sought refuge there. We became known for not only meting out vengeance but providing a safe haven for others, too. No matter what your past was, so long as you could prove to us you had changed or presented no danger to the community, you were welcome.

I lower my hands and then turn my right biceps toward the group. Once you are part of the Tears of God, you receive a tattoo. It's a large stylized eye with a knife spearing a teardrop beneath it. Everyone has one—every man, woman, and every child over the age of thirteen. Mine is crude because Davidson did it with a knife and ink for a fountain pen when we escaped the desert where we'd formulated our plans.

"I am from the Tears of God. You touch us and the entire world will become blanketed with death. You will die, your mother will die. Every person who is related to you will be dust and even heaven itself will forget you. Help me and I will do everything in my power to destroy your enemies and give you aid when you need it."

Tall Boy's eyes widen. He turns to his friend and starts speaking swiftly. I catch a word or two. They are speaking a variant of Spanish. Special Forces required you to pick up several languages depending on where the government thought you would do your best work. I didn't know enough to speak but I could understand.

"He . . . Tears of God . . . help us . . . enemies."

"What's going on?" Ava asks.

"I told him that I would hurt him if he hurt us and that I'd help him if he helped us."

"That's good," she says with approval. "But you really aren't going to hurt them, right?"

"I don't want to." But in a battle between keeping Ava safe and hurting these boys? Yes, I'd do that. I just don't want it to come to that. Right now they're distracted and I could disarm one and down the others, but a stray bullet could hit Ava.

The two boys finish their conversation and the tall one turns back. He jerks his handgun downstream. "You come help us clean our village and we will let you go."

"What'd he say?"

"He wants us to come to their village and clean."

"Like do their laundry? Clean their bathrooms?" She sounds confused.

"I suspect cleaning the village means something other than sweeping the floors of their homes. Duval has to be monitoring the flight. The purse must have a tracking signal. When the plane didn't land, he probably fired up a GPS tracker and sent out scout troops to retrieve the case. These boys' village must be the closest form of civilization to the crash site. Given that we haven't heard them in the jungle, they must have just landed and started occupying the village."

"Oh shit. That's bad, right?"

"Maybe. My men are following Duval, which means if Duval's mercenaries are there, Garcia should be hot on their trail." I turn to the boys. "How many men came to your home?"

The tall boy holds up eight fingers. "Only eight, but too many guns. They kill chief and two others and then everyone surrenders."

He raises both arms and then lowers them. "We were gone hunting and returned to see home under attack."

"My woman needs to be kept safe. Can you do that while I come with you and clean your home?"

The tall boy translates and the leader nods.

Eight men. I have the AK Ava found in the boat, this kid's semiautomatic, five children and my woman to protect. I scrub a hand down my face and turn to deliver the news to Ava.

# CHAPTER TWENTY

## AVA

"You *what*?"

The look on Rafe's face is grim. "I told them I'd go into their village, help them get rid of the mercenaries, and when it's safe, we'll call for you." He hefts the gun we got from the boat. "Should be a lot easier with this baby."

I just stare at him like he's crazy. "Rafe, you're falling apart. You're in no condition to go raiding a village." Wasn't it just yesterday that I cauterized a stab wound and rebandaged his eye for him? The eye he can't see out of?

"We don't have a lot of choices," Rafe tells me. He tilts his head, gesturing at the armed boys behind us. "They're our best option. And if we can get into that village, we can get a real place to sleep for the night, and safety. And we can make it back to civilization in the morning."

All of those things sound wonderful. More than wonderful. But the fact of the matter is that I'm scared. Rafe's not in peak condition at the moment. Hell, I'm not, either. I'm so tired and icky feeling that I could fall over and go to sleep for an entire day. Maybe two. I can't imagine what he feels like.

And he wants to go raid a village?

"I should be the one going," I tell him.

He stares at me, incredulous. "I'm the mercenary."

"You're also the one with the stab wound in your back."

His mouth twitches as if he's trying to hide amusement. "I'm also dressed."

I cross my arms, refusing to feel weird about being in my bra and panties. "I was swimming a river, thank you very much. And you didn't mind how I looked five minutes ago. I saw you checking me out."

"Five minutes ago, I didn't feel weird about having an erection. In front of child mercenaries I do."

Good point. "I still don't think you should go in."

Rafe holds the gun out to me. "Do you know how to use this?"

"You just pull the trigger, right?"

His eyebrows go up. "And if it jams? Or you need to reload?"

He's got a point. About the only thing I'd be good with, weapon-wise, is the paddle in the boat. "Okay, fine. If you have to go in, you have to go in. But I'm going with you."

"No, you're staying here."

"Rafe, goddamn it, I am not—"

"Ava, if I have to worry about your safety, I'm not going to be able to do what needs to be done."

"How do you think I feel?" I exclaim. "I'm going to be worried sick over you!"

His expression softens and I catch him gazing at my mouth. "Are you?"

That husky note that returns to his voice makes my nipples prick with awareness. They're all, *Oh, hello Ava, not so tired now are we?* I cross my arms over my chest to hide them. "So I'm supposed to just sit out here in the jungle with my thumb up my ass?"

"No, you're going to sit out here and wait for the all clear. And if it doesn't come, you get the hell outta Dodge. You understand?"

"Can I just point out how much I hate this plan?"

"You can, but it doesn't mean we have a better one."

Hell.

Ten minutes later, Rafe leaves despite my protests, and I'm left with two boys on this side of the river. They have guns and speak a form of Spanish, and spend a lot of time staring at my breasts, even after I get dressed again. Boys. Typical.

They offer me some fruit to eat, though, and I scarf it down while they talk quietly among themselves and laugh at my manners. One comments on my hand, gesturing at my awkward-looking pinky.

"What, are you a medic?" I ask him. I doubt it, but I show him anyhow.

He says something and gestures at my wrist, then at my pinky. I shrug in answer. I don't know what he's saying. "It's just swollen."

He taps his cheek and points at my eyes. "Ow?" he asks.

Oh. He thinks I've hurt my eye, like Rafe. I shake my head. I know my eyes look strange to most people. I have one green one and one very dark brown one, and it's unsettling to a lot of people that see me at first glance, because when my pupils are dilated, my brown eye can look very dark indeed. "Not hurt," I say with a shake of my head. "They're just like that."

He starts to say something else, but we're interrupted by the distant sound of gunfire. Our friendly smiles fade.

We've just been reminded that across the river, Rafe and the other kids are risking their lives.

I can't relax after that. The fruit in my belly churns sickly. I think of Rafe, wounded. Is he safe? Is he misjudging things with one eye covered, and one of the bad guys is getting the drop on him? Is he going to die a virgin with that hungry look in his eyes?

Am I never going to get to experience that hunger for myself?

There's more gunfire in the distance, and the kids look worried. Rafe can take care of himself, I mentally chide my worried mind. He's done this sort of thing before.

It doesn't matter. I've made a deal with myself. If he comes back safe, I'm going to fuck the hell out of that guy when we get back to civilization. If we weren't in this crazy situation, I'd say I'm falling for him.

But I can't, because I have to save Rose.

Time passes slowly, and it gets later and later. I hear the sounds of the jungle, and the buzz of bugs. They bite the hell out of me, but the kids at my side aren't affected nearly as much. They must like my pasty skin better. We don't have a fire, and I don't ask for one. I'm guessing things are touch and go, because the kids keep their guns at hand and they constantly watch the edges of our encampment.

It's late and despite the worry gnawing on me even more than the bugs, I'm drowsy and tired. I'm half asleep when someone starts crashing through the brush. Both boys jump to their feet, alert, and I grab my paddle, ready to swat anyone that comes near.

A voice calls out in the darkness, and the boys run forward, guns clutched.

"What?" I cry. "What is it?" Did we lose? Oh fuck. What do I do if Rafe is gone?

Oh fuck. If Rafe is gone . . . the thought fills me with despair, and not just about my situation. If Rafe is gone, he'll never smile at me again. Never give me one of those hungry looks. Never touch me tenderly. Never grab Godzilla when he thinks I'm not looking.

I don't know what I'm going to do if Rafe is gone. The thought is staggering to me. How is it that he's become so much to me so quickly? Rose is the one that gives her heart away—I'm the practical, jaded one.

But not, it seems, when it comes to Rafe.

As if my thoughts have conjured him from the jungle, a figure appears in the night shadows. He's tall and muscular, but I see the dirty fabric of the eye patch before anything else, and I choke back a sob of relief.

"Rafe!" I launch myself forward and fling my arms around his neck. "Oh my God! Are you hurt? Is everything all right?"

"Everything's fine," he says, and his voice is weary. His arm goes protectively around my waist, though. "We took care of the village," he tells me. "There were some casualties. A few boys got too eager." There's sadness in his voice. "Eight of the enemy dead."

"You got all eight of them?" I'm elated at first, and then I picture it. Eight men with guns, and Mendoza went in with a few schoolboys and one rifle? I smack his arm. "Goddamn you, that's so fucking dangerous!"

"It had to be done."

It did, and I know he did it for these boys, so they wouldn't have to live under the thumb of asshole warlords with guns. He did it because he's a good guy that wants the good guys to win. And he did it for me. I know that as surely as I know he'd do it all over again.

It's who he is. And I love that about him.

It's why I put my hands on the sides of his face and kiss his mouth, hard. I mash my lips against his, tasting sweat, and dirt, but also . . . Rafe.

He stiffens under me, and I don't know if it's from surprise or if it's because I'm being completely inappropriate. I don't care. All I know is that I desperately need him to kiss me back, right fucking now. So I part my lips and slide my tongue along the seam of his, coaxing him to open up underneath me. To give me a chance.

Rafe groans and his arms tighten around me. The gun drops to the ground and then his hands are moving all over my back, as if he needs to touch me everywhere he can. My tongue glides into his mouth, and I'm met by his hungry one. Everything about Rafe is hungry and wild with need, and it makes me crazy with lust, too. I kiss him roughly, my tongue flicking against his, encouraging him to fuck my mouth with his tongue, to show me his intent.

His hand tangles in my hair and holds me in place, and then he takes me in the deepest, wettest, sultriest kiss I've ever had. I feel like his tongue is going places no tongue has ever gone, and it makes me weak in the knees. By the time we break apart, I feel like I'm the one that just conquered a village—I'm exhausted but utterly triumphant.

We're both breathing hard.

"What was that for?" Rafe asks.

"For coming back safe for me," I tell him, and cling to his chest for a little bit longer, just because I can. "Do me a favor and don't leave me behind again, okay?"

# CHAPTER **TWENTY-ONE**

## RAFAEL

"I promise not to leave you behind with boy soldiers in the jungle again."

She rolls her eyes at my specific promise but doesn't move. I lean down and capture her mouth again. We are sweaty, smelly, mud-covered creatures but I've never tasted anything better than her mouth. She kisses me back, her mouth opening wider under mine. Her tongue is bold and hot. I can't stop from growling, which apparently is a good thing, because she presses closer to me, so close that my painfully aroused dick is carving a divot in her stomach. I try to move away but she drags me closer.

"No, I want it. I want *you*," she moans against my lips.

And that breaks me. I haul her roughly against me, my hands on her ass lifting her so that the juncture of her legs rubs my granite-hard cock. She responds by wrapping her legs around my waist and then grinding against me.

I hold her tightly to me. Not even a leaf could fit in between the two of us. My hand digs into her hair to grip her scalp while my other arm is an iron band around her waist. I spread my legs for balance and allow her to ride me.

Her heels dig into the small of my back and it's that tiny pain that keeps me from coming in my pants.

A distant shout pierces the fogged lust of my brain and I'm reminded that we are still in the middle of the Amazon jungle, covered in mud and not yet out of harm's way. With a herculean effort, I break away from her hot mouth.

She stares down at me, her hands clutched around my neck. "Why'd you stop?"

"Because we're in the middle of the jungle, baby."

Her legs tighten around my waist at my use of an endearment.

"I want you," she repeats.

"I don't want to hurt you." I'd kill myself before I'd harm even a hair on her head.

"You won't," she assures me. "It's going to be good. I'll be gentle." An impish grin settles on her face.

I tug on her hair lightly, reminding her I've got several inches and at least a hundred pounds on her. "It's not you I'm worried about."

She places a finger on my lips. "You are not going to hurt me. Do you trust me?"

I nod because my tongue's down my throat. "Before . . . before we get Godzilla out, I want to eat your pussy. I need to feel you come all over me, just once." Before I ruin it.

She shivers. "It's going to be awesome."

"We'll be in a hotel by sundown," I swear. "And I'm going to save Rose for you."

"You will? How?" Her eyes widen and her fuck-me lips fall open. I resist the temptation to kiss her again. I have a feeling the shout came from Garcia and that he'll be on us in a minute.

I let her drop slowly to the ground. There's a barely formulated plan in the back of my head, but I can't stop now that she's staring at me like I've hung the moon.

"Duval has been using her to keep you in check, so he's got to be keeping her close, and there's no way this buy goes down without him being directly involved. The buyers wouldn't stand for it."

"You really think she's here?"

"I bet my good eye she's in Pucallpa right now with Duval and they're waiting for this to be returned." I kick the bag at my feet.

"You'd trade the information for Rose? What about your friend?"

"We'll get him out, too."

"How?" Suspicion dots her words but so does hope. I'm banking on the hope. Banking everything I've got.

"We're going to steal it back after we get Rose."

"And if you don't?"

"Then we'll offer the government something that they want more than the information."

"What's that?"

I give her a wry smile. "Can't reveal all my secrets."

"What do you want from me?"

I lick my lips. "You know what I want."

A smile spreads across her face. "I do, don't I?"

I have to stop staring into the sun. It's hurting my good eye and burning a path straight to my heart. Turning around, I squint at the large figure moving toward us. As I suspected, Garcia was close behind the mercs.

The boy who speaks Spanish, Carlos, rises from his spot under a large palm, where he must have sat while Ava and I mauled each other. He points the tip of his AK toward Garcia.

"Friend," I tell him. He lowers the gun as we watch Garcia hack his way to us.

"You look like shit," he says in greeting.

"Better than you on your best day." I pull him in for a rough hug and then grunt when he slaps me too hard on my wounds. "Looks worse than it is. Ava, this is Garcia. Garcia, you know Ms. Samson. And this is Carlos. His village is that way." I point toward the west.

"The gunfire?" Garcia asks, wondering if the bullets he heard being exchanged were from us or some other encounter.

"That was us. I'll tell you about it in the boat. *Vamos*, Carlos?" I ask.

He nods and leads us down to the embankment. Ava and Carlos step into the rickety metal rowboat with its lightweight motor on the back, while Garcia and I push it away from the sand.

"You going to go blind?"

I finger my makeshift bandage. I'm already seeing light in the periphery, so I suspect my eye will be just fine. "Not from the wound," I joke.

Garcia looks sharply at Ava but doesn't say another word as we both lift ourselves over the side of the boat. Once all of our limbs are inside, I give Carlos another nod and we're off.

"Where are we?" I ask, pulling Garcia's attention back toward me.

"The Padre Abad Province. The plane crashed about fifty kilometers northwest of the flight path."

"When did you hear?"

"Duval must have the bag chipped, because he knew that there was something wrong before the Peruvian government did. He and about twenty men flew from Lima to Pucallpa a day ago. It took them another day to get kitted out for a trip into the jungle. There was some infighting. Not everyone wants to make the trek into the Amazon."

"That must be why the crew was so light. Only eight," I told him.

He snorts. "Shit. Must have been like playing on the easy mode."

We'd faced a lot tougher odds in the past, which is why I was angry that we'd lost any of the villagers. The leader of the boys was back with his people, burying his dead.

"There were some fatalities," I reply flatly.

Garcia winces.

I have him relate what's been going on since Ava and I've been downed.

"I wasn't able to find a guide right away, so they had a head start on me. I heard the sound of the AK about four clicks south, but by the time I got there it was over." He shrugged.

The firefight lasted all of about five minutes after I'd garroted three of the guards. The youngest of the boys had gotten trigger-happy and the five mercs left rushed toward the sound, spraying gunfire into the brush. An older male villager broke away from the crude imprisonment and was shot dead. His woman ran to the fallen body and one of the assholes shot her, too, before I got to him.

There were a couple of bullet wounds, including to the boy shooter, but that was it. The father of the leader came over and told us to leave—that we'd brought bad fortune to their village. Couldn't argue with that.

We are lucky to have the boat ride to Campoverde.

Carlos lets us off and I leave the AK with him, although I have to wrestle it from Ava. She's become attached to it.

"I'll get you a gun," I swear.

"Promise?" She doesn't want to be afraid anymore.

"Promise."

Reluctantly she lets it go and the boy takes off. He's eager to get back to his home.

"What now?"

"Now we buy a vehicle and find a place to stay. Tomorrow we'll head to Pucallpa." I grab Ava's good hand, ignoring Garcia's glare. She takes a deep breath as she stares up the reddish-brown clay road. There are buildings made of brick, corrugated sheet metal, and concrete. It's sparsely populated but after a few days in the jungle and the worry she might die, I can tell she's thrilled to see signs of semi-modern civilization.

"Will I get to shower?" she asks hopefully.

"Yeah. After we get some wheels, we'll find showers, food, beds. Clothes." I can't help but stare at her soiled T-shirt and remember the amazing sight of her bra-clad tits as she rose out of the water. The fabric clung to every honeyed inch of her and had it not been for the boy soldiers, I probably would have thrown her down on the embankment and sucked all the Amazon water off of her.

She notices me noticing but only smiles in return. She apparently does not care if I stare at her tits or her ass. She also doesn't seem to care if I touch her. In fact, I think she likes it. She's even shown curiosity instead of fear toward Godzilla. Wet, clean Ava sounds like a personal piece of heaven.

"Let's go," Garcia says sourly.

Ava makes a funny face and I bark out a short laugh, which serves to make Garcia's frown deeper. The walk from the riverside to the center of the small province is short. Campoverde consists of one central paved road serving a number of small clay offshoots and a smattering of businesses including a small grocery, a supply store, and what looks like might be a motel. There are more bicycle rickshaws in the center of town than people.

The locals look at us like we're apparitions—pale-skinned Ava in particular. Although their stares could be chalked up to the fact that we are wearing more dirt than is on the ground.

"You have money." It's not really a question. Garcia wouldn't come out here without being fully equipped.

He nods and pulls out a wad of pink-colored Nuevo Sol. "How much do you think one of these will cost?"

I spot an old VW Golf. "Maybe fifty bills?"

"That's it?" Ava asks.

"It's a couple of grand in U.S. dollars," I explain.

Garcia locates the owner and engages in some rapid-fire negotiations in Spanish. From the car seller, we rent a small residence. One bedroom, one bathroom and a kitchen area. It's modest but has running water, which is key. The family will stay with neighbors in exchange for our money, and the two families will share the payment when we leave.

"In you go, baby," I say as I open the door to the small bathroom. She leans against me, as if all her energy has disappeared now that she's out of the jungle. It's the post-adrenaline crash.

"Baby?" Garcia says with raised eyebrows.

I close the door and listen to the water start up. I'm heading toward my own crash.

"Give me the rundown on the situation in Pucallpa."

"I have Bennito and Rodrigo with eyes and ears on Duval. He's rented a bungalow at the Manish Hotel Ecológico. His brother, Fouquet, is with him, and he has three bodyguards. Two of whom are in the bungalow with him, and the other is in the main building. I saw them bring a woman. Her face was covered, so I wasn't able to get an ID."

*Rose.* I don't tell my plans to Garcia just yet. He's on edge and I want to get a lay of the land before I propose a new course of action.

"Cozy. How are we situated?"

"We have the bungalows on either side," Garcia says smugly.

"Good. Ava and I will take one and you three can be in the other."

"When are we ditching *her*?" He jerks his head toward the bathroom.

"We aren't."

Garcia's hands tighten around a wooden chair back. "She's a liability. A dead-weight distraction."

"You missed 'demon.' Isn't that why Fouquet didn't fuck her? Because her eyes are mismatched?" Maybe she is a succubus. Don't know if I really care at this point. I'm willing to give up my soul for her.

"If saying she's the devil's child keeps her out of your bed, then yes, she's a demon."

"Get used to sleeping with Lady Lucifer then, because she's coming to the island."

"The fuck you say," he blurts out.

"The fuck I say." I close my eyes.

He sputters and drones on about how he can't believe I lost

my balls to some chick in the jungle and how I must have been bitten by a mosquito and am now suffering from malaria-induced hallucinations. Ava and I have a deal. I'm going to save Rose and she's . . . she's going to save me.

"Is he going to be okay?" Ava asks when she comes out of the shower looking pink and white and glorious.

"Yes, I'll be fine," I answer for Garcia. He's working on cleaning out the wounds on my back and doesn't want to talk to her, probably for fear he'd fall under her spell. And yeah, then I'd have to kill him because Ava's mine now. She's coming to my island. I don't know how we're going to have sex. It's possible we won't. But I'm going to learn how to give the best oral in the world and along with a few toys, I'll keep her satisfied.

But I can't see living without her. No. The truth is that I do know what living without her is like. That's what I've been doing for the last thirty-five years. Existing.

Her presence lights up the dark night and makes a jungle trek seem like a too-short resort vacation. She's brave—foolishly so— and smart. And I want her more than a starving man craves sustenance. More than a cursed man cares about his consequences.

Hell, her smiles are all I need to power through. As Garcia digs into my wounds, I don't flinch, because I barely feel the pain. What's pain when Ava's here holding my hand, spreading her multicolored sunshine all over me.

"You done?" I ask Garcia, impatient to be alone with Ava.

She smells good. Our bellies were full of bush meat, beans, and fruit. Ava ate a roadside Popsicle made of fruit and sugar and cream so enthusiastically, I thought I'd come in my pants just watching her. Even Garcia had a glazed look in his eyes.

"Patience, *hermano*." He is working slow, and I don't think it's because the wounds are dirty but because he is trying to delay the inevitable—Ava and I alone.

But he needs to leave.

She's not holding my hand anymore. She's stroking it. Her one hand is cradling mine and with her other hand, the one with the swollen pinky, she traces the veins on the back of my hand and rubs a fingertip across each knuckle. I didn't know a touch like that could feel so erotic. It's a good thing I'm lying on my stomach, because my dick is driving a hole into the mattress.

"I need more bandages. They're in the sack in the outer room." Garcia points to the open doorway.

Ava squeezes my hand and hops up to do his bidding. I watch her curvy ass swing out the door and sigh like a schoolboy. Garcia doesn't waste time.

"She needs to go," he repeats. "The buy is going to take place any day now and we can't have you distracted."

I don't take my eyes off the vacated doorway, because soon Ava will return and I'll get to watch her as she approaches. She's showered and her skin looks edible. I want to lick it and see if it tastes like cream or honey. Maybe it's both. Her heavy tits sway under a borrowed T-shirt. Mine of course. I nearly wrestled Garcia to the ground when he threw one of his at her face, which is why he's now trying to convince me to leave. He'll stay here and guard the *girl*.

"Not happening," I say. No one is sleeping near Ava except for me. No one is guarding her but me. I trust Garcia and the others, but tonight, it's me and Ava.

# CHAPTER **TWENTY-TWO**

## AVA

God, I'm so clean it's orgasmic.

There are so many things now that we're back in relative civilization that I'm never going to take for granted again. Things like soap and fresh water. Being outside and not having a hundred bugs land on you. Food that didn't walk past you three minutes ago.

Actually, just food, full stop. I can't seem to quit eating. Even now, I'm so full of camp food that I could barf, but when I dig through the sack for bandages, I see a few chocolate-flavored PowerBars and have to resist the urge to cram them in my mouth.

But Rafe's friend hates me enough already.

I've seen him shooting unhappy looks in my direction all day. It doesn't matter that I'm ragged and covered in bug bites on every inch of my skin. You'd think I'm the devil incarnate here to cause problems. I can guess why. Rafe's changing his plans for me. Instead of "ditch Ava" it's now "work with Ava."

And while that wasn't my original plan, I'm gleefully stoked that it's the plan now. Dare I get the hot guy and save my best friend? Can this shitstorm turn into a best-case scenario?

One can only hope.

Even my swollen hand feels better. The pinky looks bad but I can bend it without too much pain, and the swelling is going down around my wrist, too. I grab the bandages and return to the bedroom area, where Rafe's lying flat across the bed and his buddy Garcia works on him. They both look up as I enter, and I feel a bit self-conscious at my clothing. I'm wearing a T-shirt that's a few sizes too big for me and a pair of cotton boxers, since that was all that they had to give me that was clean. My bra and panties are soaking in a sink full of soap, and someone's promised to go get me "real" clothing in the morning.

Garcia frowns at me and shakes his head, moving over Rafe's wounds again, but Rafe extends a hand for me, that intense look in his eyes that he saves only for me. I hand Garcia the bandages and sit back down in my chair next to the bed and take Rafe's hand again.

I'll be the first to admit I'm a little touchy-feely with my guy. He's my anchor and the only thing that's keeping me from panicking about the situation. He's keeping my worry over Rose at bay. He's keeping me distracted from the fact that his friend hates me and we're still in a strange country with dangerous information and not a lot of friends. Because when his hand touches mine? Everything's all right. I know Rafe's got me.

I sit down in my chair again and cross my legs. They're clean and freshly shaven, but welts, cuts, and bruises still cover them. It's not a sexy look, but Rafe reaches out and drags his hand down one calf, a thoughtful, almost reverent look on his face as he touches me.

I shiver, desire sliding through me, just like that. My thighs press together and I shoot another look at Garcia. His lips are pressed together unhappily at the sight of Rafe touching me.

"You done?" he asks Garcia again, but his gaze is still on me. Always on me.

"Almost," Garcia says, and his tone is more than a little irritated. "You can sit up now."

Rafe gives my leg one last caress and then he sits up. His cock is tenting the front of his pants, and I wet my lips at the sight of it. He's giving me another hungry look that promises what his kiss wanted to deliver on the riverbank.

"Can you see yourself out?" Rafe asks, raising an arm and rolling his shoulder to flex his muscles. The sight of that makes my mouth dry.

Garcia's brows go down. "We need to talk first."

I gesture at the door to the bedroom. "Why don't I just go get myself a drink?"

Rafe nods, but his gaze is devouring my face, my breasts, my legs. He brushes a hand over his mouth, and I know he's not thinking about anything Garcia is going to say. He's thinking about me. Me under him. Me on top of him. Me with my mouth on him. Him with his mouth on me.

Aaaaaand now I'm thinking about it, too. I force myself to get up and walk out of the room, closing the door behind me. Immediately, I hear Garcia start talking, his voice low, and then Rafe begins to argue with him. Part of me wants to stay and snoop, but I have bigger, better ideas on my mind.

I head for the bathroom of the small bungalow and dig through drawers and cabinets, looking for two very particular things: condoms and lube. If I'm taking Rafe's virginity tonight—and oh, I *am*—we need both.

The bathroom doesn't have anything good except travel-sized shampoo and conditioner. There's a washcloth and an ice bucket and it gives me ideas, but I'm more interested in finding condoms. I head back to the living room and dig through Garcia's bag. Success. One condom. One. I eye the package but it doesn't read as "extra large." Well, damn. We'll figure something out. I set it down on the counter for later.

I return to the bathroom and grab the ice bucket and washcloth, and run the tap until the water's nice and warm. I add a little soap, and then fill the bucket.

Tonight is going to be the first night we're going to be clean, well fed, and not afraid that a bug is going to bite something unmentionable. I plan on enjoying every moment of this, and I plan on touching Rafe all over.

And we're going to start with the sponge bath I promised.

The arguing escalates, and I shut off the water, listening. A moment later, I hear a muttered "fuck it" and then the door to the home slams shut.

I peek out, and Rafe's standing in the living room, shirt off. He rubs his mouth and stares at the door, then shakes his head.

"Did your friend leave?" I ask Rafe, opening the door to the bathroom wider.

He nods.

"He's not a big fan of mine," I point out.

Rafe glances over at me. "He thinks you're distracting me when I need it least."

Ah. Well, he might not be wrong about that. But I'm not

changing my plans. Regardless of how I feel about Rafe, I need his help to save Rose. It's just an added bonus (so much bonus) that I happen to be nuts over the guy, too. I tuck the bucket under my bandaged hand and drop the washcloth into it. "If he thinks you're distracted now, he hasn't seen anything yet."

That gets Rafe's attention. So does the swing of my hips as I move forward. Around this man? I feel pretty, no matter the bug bites and the bruises.

"What's with the bucket?" Rafe asks me. He's getting the hungry look in his eyes again, which makes me excited.

I bite my lip, reach into the soapy water, and lift the towel up and give it a squeeze. "Time for your sponge bath, just like I promised."

His brows go up. "You going to play nurse for me, Ava?" He moves toward me, and I can tell that he's excited about the thought. Everything in Rafe changes when he's thinking about me. Even the way he moves is more predatory, more hungry.

And God, I fucking love it.

"That's right," I say, keeping my voice light. "I want to check your wounds over for myself, and make sure you're squeaky clean before bedtime. So back onto the bed with you."

His eyes flare with need, and he moves toward me to give me a kiss.

I neatly sidestep, because I'm in playful mode now. If we're going to have sex, we're going to have lots of foreplay first. "Naughty, naughty," I tease. "If you want your bath, you'd better get in that bed pronto."

The promise of a rubdown makes him climb into bed again, wincing at his wounds. He sits up on the edge of the bed and stares at me, impatient and hungry for touch.

But I'm a girl, and we are expert teases. I set the bucket of soapy water down on the nightstand and pick up a pillow instead. "Here. Let me help you get comfortable. Come lean back against the headboard and I'll get you fixed up." Rafe does as I ask, and then I direct him once more. "Lean forward and I'll give you a pillow."

He leans forward obediently, which lets me slide a pillow in behind his back. My objective is twofold, of course. I'm acutely aware of the abrasions and recent wounds on his back, no matter how patched. A pillow will help.

Also, it gives me a chance to stick my breasts in his face.

I do just that, making sure to rub them against his chest, and then his jaw as I pretend to fluff the pillow. My breasts are loose under the shirt, and he groans and reaches up to grab a handful.

I gasp, because it sends a bolt of heat rocketing through my body the moment he touches me, and his thumb grazes my nipple. He buries his face between my breasts and groans deep again. "Ava. Goddamn, sweet Ava."

"You're a very naughty patient," I chide him and pull away, even though I want to cram my breasts back into his face and see if he'll tongue my nipples. Flustered, I straighten my shirt and turn to my water bucket. My breasts feel aching and tight under the shirt, and I want to rip it off and climb all over him. *Patience, Ava.*

"You're a torturer," he rasps.

I wink at him. "Torture's half the fun, baby." With my good hand, I squeeze the towel and then lean forward. "Can I soap you now?" The V-neck of the T-shirt is probably giving him a good look at my cleavage, and when his gaze goes there, I know I've found yet another way to drive him insane.

"If you touch me," he warns, "I might bust in my pants."

"Then I'll clean you up." I sit on the edge of the bed and delicately trace the washcloth over his collarbones. Fact is, he's a virgin. Sticking the tip in does not count—at least not in this scenario. I'm not expecting him to be more than a one-pump chump. At least, not the first time. There's no expectations of screaming from the rafters from orgasm after orgasm. For me, this is about him, because I'm getting off on making him wild.

Sex doesn't have to be about someone dicking you until you can't stand. It can be about soft, sexy touches and playful words, and I want to show Rafe that. I want to show him that I don't care about his scars, or the fact that he's got an absurdly large (and kinda painful-looking) penis. Sex can just be about enjoying each other and enjoying what the other person offers.

*Then* it can be about him dicking me until I can't stand up.

He closes his eyes as I drag the cloth over his chest. Rivulets of water move down that tanned skin, and my plan is suddenly working against me. Now I want to put my mouth on that skin, taste those warm muscles for myself. Bite his hard pectorals. Do all kinds of naughty, wicked things to the man. I sigh as I dip my cloth again and trace it down his belly. "You sure are a good-looking man, Rafe Mendoza."

He cracks an eye open at me. "I'm scarred everywhere."

"Chicks dig scars."

He snorts.

"I'm serious. If I saw you at a party, I'd probably have to pick up my jaw." I slide a wet finger over his belly button. "Those dark eyes, that thick hair, your gorgeous tan. Mmm." He's quiet, and when I look over at him again, the intense, aching need is back in his eyes. I know just how he feels. My pulse seems to be centered between his legs, and my nipples are aching for his mouth. I feel achy with need everywhere. All of this from a half-assed sponge bath and a promise of pleasure later.

No reason I can't up the ante, though. "Why don't you take those pants off so I can finish wiping you down?"

He hesitates, and my heart aches a little. I know he's worried about Godzilla and his size. He's worried about whatever happened in the past. Time to distract him again. This time, when I lift the towel from the bucket, I let it stay sloppy wet and drag it across my breasts, so the fabric of the shirt sticks to me. "Oops. Look what I did. How clumsy."

# CHAPTER **TWENTY-THREE**

## RAFAEL

"Fuck, Ava, you are so beautiful." I drag a hand over my suddenly parched mouth. I know what I want to wet it with, though.

"You're a fan of post-jungle couture?" She waves a hand over her frame and I guess I'm supposed to see some flaws, but all I notice are her generous curves, the shiny glow of freshly washed skin, and the open, welcoming look on her face. "I clean up pretty good."

"If you were any more beautiful, my heart would stop." I tug on her hand so that she's no longer kneeling between my legs. I'm afraid that just staring down at her in that position is going to have me coming all over her face. Plus I have plans for her. I run my hands down her thighs to the backs of her knees. Her calves are slightly muscled and she has a delicate ankle. There's a hollow behind her ankle bone that is begging to be kissed. Actually, there isn't one part of her body that isn't made for my lips.

Her hands find their way to my shoulders. The touch is light.

"You won't hurt me," I tell her. I need her to be certain of tonight, not because I expect her to have sex with me but because I don't want her in my bed out of some misplaced idea of gratitude. I want that touch to be *sure*.

"You sure?" Her hands sweep lightly over my back muscles and down the jagged sides of the knife cuts.

"Nothing you could do would ever hurt me," I tell her. Even if she ran away from me. Even if she decides that she doesn't want to have anything to do with me—none of that would be her fault. She didn't hurt me. The situation would kill me. The idea that she couldn't love me back would hurt me. But those are all my feelings and I'll own them.

I'd take any number of knife cuts to my body for this one night with her. To be able to place my lips against her skin. To suckle on her tits. To hear her cry my name as I tongue her to an orgasm. Anything that I will ever endure or suffer after this will be worth it. *Worth. It.*

I slide my hands up those silky legs to the back of her thighs, pulling down the boxers, and tug her forward. Her scent is rich, not just soap and water, but . . . arousal. A musky, earthy scent that suddenly has my mouth pooling with saliva. No bakery in France ever smelled so enticing or fragrant.

Then I lift her T-shirt up and find nothing but bare skin. She's shaved everywhere. The smooth skin between her pale thighs is the most erotic vision I've been privileged to view.

"Beautiful," I repeat reverently. I press my nose against her and inhale the scent of her need. She shudders at the touch and her fingers dig into the muscles of my shoulder. I want nail marks. I want her so wild that she flays me with her nails and teeth. I'm going to wrench hair-pulling, throating-scratching orgasms from her tonight. "That's right. Show me how much you want this."

"I do," she says. Her own breath is choppy. My breath is coming in short, uneven pants, too. I've never been so excited, so fraught with anticipation. Every part of me is reaching toward her. She's the magnet and I'm a mass of tiny metal filings finding home for the first time in my pathetic life.

I tuck my hand between her legs, and holy fuck is she wet. My plans, the ones that involved a long, drawn-out finger-fucking, go out the window.

"Hands on the bed, sweetheart," I tell her as I scoot off the side of the mattress to sit between her thighs. She leans forward, her breasts dangling in front of me. The T-shirt that barely disguised any of her charms pisses me off, because I want to see those lush tits swaying in front of my face. I take the bottom of the T-shirt in my teeth and with my two hands rip the whole thing right up the front.

She yelps in surprise and slaps her hand against her chest. "Holy shit, did you just bite and rip the T-shirt off?" She laughs, a sound that is cut off when I suck one of her juicy tits into my mouth.

"You're fucking right I did."

With my rough palm, I abrade her other nipple until it is taut and ready for my mouth. Her legs start shaking and I have to abandon her tits to hold her upright, and the motion brings her sopping pussy right to my mouth.

I groan at the sight and scent of her. The liquid of her pussy is dripping down her thighs. There's a trail of juice that doesn't end until it's halfway down her leg. I lap it up. I lap that wet, succulent path all the way up to its source. There, in the hot, sodden cavern between her legs are so many things I want to suck and bite at one time. It's a wonderland and I barely know where to start. Do I tongue her cunt until she creams on my tongue? Do I suck on her lips? Do I lash her clit until she can't stand straight? *Don't fuck it up, Rafael.*

"Shit, sweetheart. I can kill a man a dozen ways. I can last for two weeks in the tit-frozen north. I can lead you out of the jungle, but I don't know what I'm doing here and I don't want to fuck it up. I'm so hungry for you. If I don't get my mouth on you . . ." I trail off and lick her from asshole to clit and back again.

"That's good. Whatever you're doing now is good," she pants out.

"I want you to keep talking to me. Keep telling me what you like. What you don't like." I want inside that pussy. I may never get my dick in her, but I will tongue her better than any motherfucker who ever existed. I will get so proficient at making Ava come with my tongue, my fingers, my words that she will never want for anything. She will always be satisfied. Always.

I place a thumb on either side of her red, engorged pussy lips and arrow my tongue inside her.

"Oh God, yes, Rafe. Do that. Again."

Her cunt is soft and tight and so very wet. If we were in the desert, I could live just drinking her juice. I stab at her, thrusting inside and memorizing everything. When my jaw rubs against thighs, she trembles. When my tongue rubs against her lips, she moans. I catalog every moan, shudder, and movement.

My cock is leaking inside my cargo pants, and I know I'm going to come just from licking her. Fuck, I could come just from her smell alone, and with my nose buried in her soft skin and my tongue so far up her cunt, I know I won't last.

"Use your fingers," she gasps out, a scratchy sound that tells me she's having trouble breathing and that she's hoarse from holding in her cries. It makes me want to reapply myself so she loses any semblance of control. "Suck my clit."

Her shaking hand covers her clit and massages it. Her fingers flick against my nose, and I watch her touch avidly for a few moments so I can see exactly what rhythm she likes. The touch is gentle and then harder until she's mashing down her clit and bearing down on my face. Her legs give way and I lift her so that she straddles my shoulders, and I steady her ass with one hand so that her weight is off her toes. With my other hand, I plunge two fingers inside her.

"Yes, oh yes, Rafe. Just like that."

Her cunt walls close down around my fingers.

"Harder, baby. Fuck me harder."

I shove another finger in. Shit, she is so tight.

I'm harder than I've ever been. A million liters of blood are coursing through at a breakneck pace. My heartbeat is pounding in my ears so loudly I can barely hear Ava's pleas for more.

*I'll give you more. I'll give you everything.*

There may not be tomorrow with her. I might not get another chance with her, but if I never get between her legs again, her joy and pleasure in this moment has to be so memorable that she won't be able to touch herself without thinking of my tongue and my fingers and how I made her body light up. I'm glad I'm sitting on my ass and that she's bent over above me. I don't know if I could take it if I saw her passion-drunk face or her heavy tits flushed with desire.

I barely have any control left. The urge to pick her up and plunge between her legs has a fierce grip on me. I can see it now. Her legs are spread wide with my hands hooked under her knees. Her nails would be digging into my forearms and her head would be thrown back in delirious ecstasy.

But my gaze would be fixated between us and the vision of my cock shuttling in and out of her sweet cunt.

Clenching my jaw, I remind myself that scenario is never going to happen. Instead, I have a goddamn amazing alternative. I'm palm deep in Ava's pussy. She's showing me how to bring her off. I've got her lube all over my face, my palm, and inside my mouth. I'm going to give her an orgasm so hard she will feel it in the soles of her feet.

Nudging her hand away with my chin, I lick her clit slowly, trying to map out her reactions. I run my finger up the underside and tickle the tip with teasing lashes. She squirms, which is great for teasing, but I want to make her explode.

Inside her channel, I scissor my fingers, stroking every nerve ending I can find. Her hips buck forward when I find a small, spongy patch of skin. She gasps, a singular noise that sends a tremor down my spine. I drag my fingertips slowly against the front, making sure I hit that spot again.

Everything tightens. Her toes point and the muscles in her thighs harden.

I clamp down on her tiny nub with my mouth, sucking it hard into my mouth. She screams and I don't let up. Applying as much pressure as I can, pumping my fingers into her cunt, sucking her clit so hard my cheeks are hollowing out.

She grinds down on my tongue, fucking my face. I use everything I've got—tongue, jaw, teeth, fingers—until she comes, one shuddering, clenching motion after another, and I keep swallowing.

It's miraculous. Fuck solar power, wind renewal sources; her orgasm could power the world. I think she made people pregnant three countries over. If Garcia tells me later that there was an earthquake in the ocean, I wouldn't doubt it.

She cries out my name. "God, Rafe. God. Don't stop."

Never. I won't ever stop. I keep thrusting and sucking until she comes again.

With every breath, I fill my lungs with her musk. Her cream is flooding my mouth, and I'm surrounded by her. My balls tighten and the orgasm shoots down my spine and rockets up and out of my cock. I spill into my pants.

As she collapses against the bed, her legs heavy on my shoulders, I'm thrilled that she's the first—and only—woman I've ever tasted. That her voice is the only one that's ever screamed my name.

I can feel a smile split my face and stretch from ear to ear, because I fucking made her come so hard she couldn't stand on her own power and she screamed my name so loud the boys in the village probably heard the echo.

But I'm not done. I've only kissed one part of her body. I've got so much more to explore.

I lift her easily and throw her onto the bed. She lands on her back with her legs spread, and her big breasts jiggle. I could easily slide my dick between those two lush pillows with the valley wet from her juice and my come.

Her body is slick with sweat.

"Come inside me, Rafe. I want your hard cock inside me." One of her hands rises to grip her tits while the other hovers over her swollen pussy.

"No." I shake my head. "I've got other plans for you."

I'm not ruining this night with any pain.

She wants me despite the size of my dick, which has made prostitutes run away screaming. Not to mention the scars. I don't understand how she wants me, but I'm done questioning it.

I crawl up her body, kissing the small rise of her belly up to the underside of her breast. Her tits are amazing. Full and ripe with nipples red like berries. I run my tongue along the curve and into the valley between them. Between us I thread my fingers through the folds of her sex that are wet with my saliva and her come until I can slip inside her again. She welcomes me with a tight squeeze.

"I can make you come again," I tell her, leaning up to rub my nose against her neck. "I'm learning you. I know you like this." She writhes under my hand as I find that hot spot in her cunt. "After I'm done sucking and licking every inch of your body, I'm going to fuck you with my tongue and fingers until I've sucked every ounce of come from your pussy."

"I want this." She grabs my cock in her hand—that hand that is softer than a lamb but surprisingly strong. Or maybe I'm just weak putty at her touch.

"No, Ava, we can't." But my body betrays me. It lunges against her touch and she laughs, a low, sultry noise that reeks of sex.

"Oh, Rafe, we can. I'm so wet right now."

She tugs at my wrist and I reluctantly withdraw. With determination, she guides my soaked hand to my shaft. She wants dick inside her. Fuck.

Could I bring in Garcia? His eyes flared with interest he tried to hide. I'd do anything for this woman. It would kill me to see another man between her legs, but if this was the only way to hold her, could I do it?

"I can bring someone else . . ." She cants her hips toward me, my wet dick rubs against her inflamed pussy lips, and I strangle on the words. "Fuck, sweetheart. You are killing me."

Her hands cup my face, and her beautifully mismatched eyes burn into me. "I don't want anyone but you, Rafe. Only you. I know I can take you. Let me try."

She wraps her legs around my waist and thrusts upward so that she's riding the ridge of my cock. I grip the base of my cock tightly. Coming hasn't made me less hard. None of this makes me less hard. I'm only growing larger, thicker, and longer. Every gasp in my ear and every brush of her skin against mine makes me crazier.

I lunge to my feet and pull her body to the edge of the bed. "I'll make you come again."

Using the head of my shaft, I rub it through her swollen lips up to her clit and back again. Her hole is so tight and small there's no way I'm getting inside her, but I can put in just the tip.

"You safe, Ava? You on the pill or got the shot or whatever the shit women do these days? Do we have condoms?"

She taps her stomach. "No condom necessary, I think. I have an IUD. But I haven't been tested in a year."

"Don't care." I'm not ever going to have sex with anyone. My dick and I will only ever want Ava.

I hold my dick at the entrance of her small opening, waiting for her permission. She sucks in her bottom lip. "I haven't had sex in a year, which is why I haven't been tested."

"Good enough for me."

We both know I'm safe. I'm a virgin. A thirty-five-year-old virgin who has killed more people than Ava has ever slept with.

I ease the broad tip inside her, drawing out her lube and spreading it all over her lips and cunt. I repeat the action again and again, dipping in just a tiny bit and then retreating. My dick is screaming for more action, for deeper penetration, and I have to squeeze my cock to the point of pain.

My balls are drawn tight against my body as the urge to paint her with my come rides me hard. But I'm not coming until I hear her sweet sounds of release.

I circle her clit with my cockhead and then slap the pert flesh with my shaft.

"Hold your tits up for me, sweetheart. I need to suck on them."

Eyes glazed, she does as I command. She places her hands underneath those ripe mounds and pushes them together. Without breaking my steady pattern of dip, circle, and press, I lean forward using all my core muscles to keep my body hovering over hers. I draw one nipple into my mouth and then the other, working back and forth between the two.

Her head thrashes on the mattress.

She needs more pressure. She needs it *harder.*

Her hand curls behind my neck, and I hear her whisper hoarsely in my ear, "I want you to fuck me."

"I am, sweetheart," I say behind gritted teeth. "The best way I can."

"I need you inside me."

I grab her ass and pull her against me. Her come, my come, I don't know where the slickness all comes from, but it's wet between us. She digs her heels into my back and rides the hard, rigid length.

I work her roughly against me using all my power to give her the *harder* that she so desperately wants.

"I want you to come for me, Ava. Now," I order, taking a break from mouthing her nipples.

She does. Her legs clench me tight against her body as it arches off the bed. I feel her come soak my cock and I almost lose control. My hips jerk and the huge head of my erection slips inside her wet, hot hole and that small contact is enough to set me off.

With a roar, I rear back and grab my cock. With a few rough jerks, I pull the orgasm from the base of my spine. It barrels out, spurting long, milky jets onto her bare mound, over her belly, and onto the curves of her breasts.

She lies beneath me, panting and wide-eyed.

I stare at the mess I've made and I find I'm not sorry at all. No. There's only one thought in my head, only one concept that runs in a tight circle inside my brain. I bring my hand down on her belly into the viscous fluid and smear it everywhere. I even drag two fingers of it down over her pubis and into her hot cunt, shoving my sperm up inside that tight channel.

My entire world has narrowed down to four letters. *Mine.*

# CHAPTER **TWENTY-FOUR**

## AVA

Well.

I pant, trying to get air back into my lungs. I've just come so hard my brain feels it should be leaking out of my ears. Between my slick thighs, Rafe slides his fingers inside me, pumping over and over again. It's sending aftershocks skittering through my body with every movement of his fingers, but I don't tell him to stop.

I feel good. Actually, I feel amazing. But I still feel hollow deep inside, and it's something that even his pumping, thrusting fingers can't satisfy. In the crudest terms, it's the hollow ache that can only be satisfied by a good, deep dicking.

And we haven't even come close to that.

"Rafe," I murmur when I can breathe again. My hands trail over his shoulders. "How are you . . ."

I pause, because it feels weird to ask. *Are you hanging in there? Are you getting all weirded out?* Does he think I'm not going to notice that he flinched away from sticking that baseball bat inside me? Rafe is many things, and so is Godzilla. "Ignorable" is nowhere on that list.

"I'm the happiest goddamn man alive." His voice is raspy, and he pushes his fingers into me again, fascinated by the slick glide. "And you're so goddamn beautiful it hurts."

"That's a lot of goddamns," I say lightly. I feel a bit silly. Really good, pretty boneless, but silly. "Save a little for later."

"Later?" He looks up at me, finally, after intensely scrutinizing his fingers working in and out of my pussy. "You need to come again, baby?"

Me? I bite back the laugh that threatens to erupt and flex my hips instead, rocking on his fingers so they slide into me even harder. They make a wet noise inside me, and his fascinated gaze goes back to my pussy. "You still haven't come, Rafe."

"Oh, I did," he breathes, pushing those fingers in me again as I rock down. "I came all over you."

"But not inside me," I tease, and squeeze my inner muscles around his fingers.

He hisses and I know he can feel me working him. He shakes his head. "Nah. I'm good."

"You're not." I continue to work his fingers, and he pumps inside me even harder, and I bite my lip, because I'm getting all aroused all over again. "You mean to tell me if I reach down and grip your cock, it's going to be all soft and limp in my hands?"

Rafe groans and presses his face against my thigh.

"That's what I thought," I say in a soft, teasing voice. "We're not leaving this bed until you're deep inside me, and you come so hard I feel it in my throat."

Instead of telling me that it's arousing to hear me talk like that, or that I'm sexy, he shakes his head and presses a kiss to my thigh. "I can't. Jesus, I want to so badly, Ava, but I can't. I'll hurt you."

"You won't," I exclaim.

"You're too tight." His fingers push inside me again, as if to prove his point.

"Then loosen me up." I spread my legs wider, gripping my knees and presenting him with my open flesh.

His gaze goes there, then he shakes his head again. "I've had hookers turn me down at the sight of my cock, Ava."

*Yes, but they weren't in love with you*, I want to say. I bite back the words. It's probably just jungle fever. Stockholm syndrome, something along those lines. I've grown attached to Rafe Mendoza over the last week, and right about now, I'd do anything for him. Maybe I'm not in my right mind to be declaring love right at this moment, so I won't.

It's clear my virgin needs to be eased into things. "How many fingers do you have inside me right now, baby?" I ask him.

"Two," he says, voice gruff. "And you're so fucking tight."

"Put a third one in me."

He doesn't pause, and that makes me happy. He wants this, even if he says he doesn't. In the next moment, he pushes into me harder, and I wiggle around the feel of those three fingers. Definitely bigger, but not out of the realm of what I can handle. I'm so slick from his come and my own juices that I feel I could handle anything right about now. He pumps them into me cautiously, watching my face.

Time to get a little theatrical. It feels good, but to win over Rafe's reservations, I need to act like it's the greatest goddamn thing I've ever felt in my life. "Oooh, yeah," I moan, and squeeze my pussy around him again.

"You like that, baby?" He thrusts into me again.

"God, yes." I bite my lip and groan, pressing my arms against my sides so my tits thrust up a little higher, a little more noticeable with each grind of his hand into my pussy. Thing is, I had a boyfriend once who was the nicest guy and lousy as hell in bed. I'm a champion at faking how good something feels. And I bet I can get Rafe over his hesitation. "Spread your fingers inside me, Rafe. Push me to my limits."

He does, and I bear down on them even as he thrusts again. My pussy's making wet, sloppy noises against his fingers, and the sound fascinates him as much as it embarrasses me. But the wetness is a good thing, because we're not stopping at fingers.

"Feel good?" he asks, voice husky and so full of want that it makes me ache.

I nod. "I still want more, Rafe. I want you."

"Can you take four fingers?"

*Yeah, I'm gonna have to*, I think, but I nod. If he needs this before we move to the next round, I'll give it to him. "Do it."

He pulls back, and when he pushes deep into me again, everything feels tight and tense despite our efforts to loosen me up. "That's good," I tell him, bucking against his hand. "Keep doing that."

"You're fucking swallowing my fingers in that gorgeous cunt of yours, aren't you?" He pushes into me again, then out, then begins a slow, wicked rhythm that makes me forget that I'm supposed to be working *him*. I feel my nipples tighten in response, and the low, delightful pressure begins to build in my belly again.

"You feel so good, Rafe." I raise my hips, trying to chase the orgasm that's building. "I need that big fat cock of yours, baby. I want you inside me when I come."

A hiss escapes him and he grunts. His hand slides free of my pussy, and I feel weirdly bereft. I look down to see him working his cock with his hand. It's gleaming with my juices and his come, and as I watch, another jet of semen fountains from the purple head of his huge dick.

"You came without me." I sit up on my elbows, a pout on my lips.

"Not done," he grits out, working his cock. His intense eyes gaze up at me. "Never done with you."

"Mmm." I reach between my legs and trace a finger over my clit. It's slick from our mingled juices, and I suck in a breath as I feel my orgasm start to build again. "You're not going to make me finish myself again, are you?"

"No." He pants, still working his hand over his cock. "Just . . . need a moment."

"Take your time," I say sweetly and continue to touch myself. Not much, just enough to keep my body feeling pumped and the orgasm close by. Minutes pass, marked only by Rafe's rasping breath and my occasional gasp as one touch takes me a little too close to the edge.

Then, quicker than he should be ready again, he leans in and begins to kiss my thigh, his mouth hungry and full of need. "I want you again, Ava."

"You want to touch me?"

"Fuck yes." His mouth moves to my pussy, where I'm touching myself.

I shield my flesh with my hand. "Then I want your cock inside me."

He shakes his head. "Lemme just eat your pussy, babe. You taste so goddamn good."

"I'm making the rules now," I tell him, scooting back on the bed and sitting up. "Didn't you get four fingers inside me?"

"Yes," he says, and his hand goes to his cock. It's like he can't stop touching himself at the sight of me, can't pace himself.

"Don't you think your cock is about four fingers?"

"Bigger," he grits.

"Well, I can take bigger," I tell him. I wait until his gaze catches mine and then I deliberately slide my fingers to my pussy, where I'm still wet and needy. "Don't you want in here?"

Rafe groans again, a sound like pain. There's sweat on his brow. "I don't want to hurt you, Ava."

"You won't," I tell him. "Why don't you let me be on top? We'll go as slow as we need to that way."

He hesitates again, but I know I've won. Most men love the mental picture of a woman on top. I slide a hand to my breasts and begin to tease my nipples as he gives it some thought, and that decides him. With a muffled curse, he turns and flings himself onto his back on the bed.

And Godzilla sticks straight up in the air.

I'm not gonna lie, it's a damn intimidating dick. I've bluffed and told Rafe that his size doesn't bother me, but I need to conquer Everest if we're going to move ahead. The sight of him thrusting upright has my thighs clenching with a firm feeling of *NOPE*, but I ignore it and try to judge his girth for myself. I put a hand at the base of his cock; my fingers don't go all the way around it. Jesus. Again, my thighs go *NOPE*. But Rafe's watching me with such tension on his face that I want to ease him. I want to make him feel better about himself. That he's not a freak with a monster penis and no woman will touch him.

Because I love touching him. And I want to make him feel good.

So I sling a leg over his thighs and straddle him. "I'm going to go nice and slow, all right?"

His eyes are tense slits, but he nods at me.

I move forward, trapping his cock against my pussy and I crawl up him, positioning myself. I lean forward so my breasts can brush against his chest, and his gaze goes there, utterly fascinated. That riveted gaze makes me feel bold, so I rock my hips against his cock, sliding back and forth over his length. I'm rewetting him, because I'm still slick as hell, and I'm gearing myself up to take him.

Rafe groans, and his hands move to palm my breasts. "I love your tits, Ava."

I bite back my own gasp, because his fingers feel incredible plucking and teasing at my nipples. "They kinda love you back, you know. That feels so good. Keep touching me." He does, and I continue to slide over his cock, getting used to the size of him, the sheer girth, lubricating him with my juices even as Rafe teases my nipples until they're peaked, tight, and aching.

I lift my hips and reach down between us. His cock is slippery, but still so gosh-darn big. I fit the head of him against my opening, determined not to be afraid. People have sex with big dicks all the time, right? Look at porn. Except I suspect Rafe would make porn stars jealous.

"I'm going to move down on you," I tell him.

"Ava, we don't have to do this," he tells me. His hand moves to my breast and he squeezes it again. "I can lick your cunt all night long."

"Hush." I settle the head of him against me, and then let gravity do its work. Except gravity doesn't seem to want to work. I'm wet, but I'm not loose enough to take him. I push down against him, determined to make us fit.

A sharp little pain drags through me as I push down on him, and I suck in a breath.

Rafe freezes under me. "Ava, no—"

I ignore him and rock my hips, bracing my hands on his chest, determined. He groans and his head goes back against the mattress as I work the head of his cock into me. It's a tight, uncomfortable fit, but I feel a surge of triumph that we're making progress.

"Fuck," Rafe growls. "You feel so fucking tight and just . . . ah, fuck."

"I've got you, baby," I tell him. "You feel good. So big." Half of it's the truth anyhow. I feel like I'm being stretched over something far too large for my body, but the fact of the matter is that between gravity, my slickness, and my small movements, we're making progress. He's slowly sliding into me.

I bite my lip and rock down on him again, and then we're at the halfway point. "We're just going slow this time," I tell him. "Next time, once we're used to each other, it won't be quite so . . . torturous."

The look on his face is stricken and he tenses under me. "Torturous? Ava, am I hurting you?"

Oh, damn it. *Bad choice of words, Ava.* I shake my head and give him my best seductive smile. "If I was hurting, would I do this?" I flex my hips and bear down on him, and he sinks farther into me.

And, okay, that sent unpleasant twinges all through my innards. But underneath me, Rafe hisses and his eyes close. "Oh, fuuuuck."

And that's worth every moment.

I continue to wiggle and move over him in small, rocking motions, until my hips are meeting his and, incredibly, I've taken his entire outrageous length inside me. "There we go," I say softly, and rake my nails lightly down his abdomen. "How do you feel?"

"I need to move, baby," he groans, and the cords in his neck are so tight. It's as if his entire body is straining under me.

"Then move," I tell him, and rock my hips a little.

I'm surprised at the intensity of his thrust. He pushes, and I feel like my entire body jumps a foot. A startled gasp breaks from me, because I'm stuffed so full of him that I can feel everything, every throb of his cock, every drag of his skin against mine, even the press of my IUD deep inside. And I definitely, definitely feel him rub against my G-spot.

There's a huge plus to having a guy so big he can rearrange your organs, I realize. I've never had a guy hit my G-spot just through penetration before. But with the size of Rafe in me? There's no way he can't.

He stills at my gasp, his hand sliding down my side. "Ava?"

"Do that again," I breathe, and hold on to him. I know I'm on top and I know I'm supposed to be in charge, but fuck it. "Pump into me again, Rafe. Now."

He does, and all my nerve endings flare with excitement. I moan, and my legs clamp against his sides. "Oh fuck," I breathe. "That's amazing."

"Yeah?" He sounds shocked.

"God, yeah. Do it again."

He thrusts again, and my toes curl with delight. Oh wow. *Wow.* "Rafe," I moan. "Oh Jesus, that feels so good—"

"Ava," he groans, and there's urgency in his tone. "I don't know if I can last—"

"It's okay," I tell him. "Do what you need to." *I'll just sit over here on your big cock and like, revel in how fucking glorious it is.*

A feral sound rips from his throat, and two seconds later, we're rolling and he flips me onto my back. His hands grip my shoulders and he presses a kiss to my mouth, then begins to thrust into me. Deep, hard, incredibly powerful thrusts that shake my entire body with the intensity of it. And oh, sweet Jesus, it's amazing. It's the deep dicking I've been craving, but times a hundred. "Rafe," I moan, clinging to him. "Oh God, yes. Fuck me harder."

"Ava," he snarls. "Fuck!"

"Yes," I shriek when he bucks into me again. "God, yes!"

But he groans and I feel the heat of him wash over my insides a moment later. His body shudders against mine. He's come, and I'm . . . almost there.

"No," he groans. "Ah, fuck. I'm so sorry—"

"Give me your hand," I tell him, still wriggling under him. He adjusts, leaning heavily on one elbow, and I take his hand and put it on my clit. He's still stuffed inside me, so deep I feel changed, and when his fingers start to play my clit, it takes me mere moments until I'm over the edge with him, my nails dragging up his back and his name shrieked at the top of my lungs.

As his fingers slide away from my clit, I give a soft sigh of contentment, wrapping my arms around his sweaty shoulders. There isn't an inch of us that isn't covered in either sweat or semen or my juices.

I've never felt better, either.

# CHAPTER TWENTY-FIVE

**RAFAEL**

It takes more willpower than I expect to extricate myself from Ava's warm embrace. She's fallen asleep on top of me, and moving out from under her soft body isn't high on my list, but a knock at the door tells me time is up.

I've made Garcia wait too long as it is. I swipe my pants off the floor and shrug into a cotton camp shirt. I stink of Ava and sweat, but Garcia will have to suck it up.

"You done?" he snaps with irritation when I step out into the small space outside the bedroom.

I'm too satisfied to be able to summon any irritation at his tone. "For now." I pour myself a cup of water. The post-fucking glow is going to hang around for a while. By U.S. standards it's primitive in Campoverde, but compared to the jungle, the dusty water tastes like sweet tea. "What have you got?"

While Ava was punching my V card, Garcia had been busy. There is a new pack in the corner, which suggests he's loaded up on supplies. Outside the window, I see the VW Golf we bought, and on the table, he's fieldstripped the handbag.

"I didn't find anything else in the pockets or lining except for the GPS chip." The leather shell is on a chair, and I run my fingers around the inside. It's smooth except where glue adhered the felt.

"No memory card? Those fuckers are tiny these days." I'm grasping at straws. If Garcia says that there's nothing here, there's nothing here.

He shakes his head. "All we have are the folders, which are just teasers for the buyers. Information that is harmless but intimate enough to lead the buyer to believe it's genuine."

"You think it's a head fake? That Duval is selling false information?"

"No. That would be too dangerous. The North Korean crew would disembowel him and send pieces of his body to all his relatives. And the Libyan group would take his family and crucify them in front of him."

Pulling a chair out, I flip open the folders. The first one contains email exchanges discussing gifts for a newlywed royal couple. One contains a bawdy, off-color joke that would create a seven-day news cycle of defensiveness followed by an apology that would be pushed aside for the next drama. It's not worth enough to pay eight figures for and it's not worth enough to kidnap a U.S. citizen and then threaten to kill him if the information isn't intercepted. The next one is a transcribed phone call between another politician and his lover. That one is more damaging but nothing that would require this kind of payoff. There are sticky notes stuck to the papers, but they don't seem to flag anything in particular.

Duval has more, but exactly what it is and where we can find it, we are still in the dark.

"They never told you what it was we are supposed to steal?" Garcia asks.

We came too late in the game to find out how the offers went out. By the time the government had blackmailed me into cooperating, the buy was being set up. We had only a couple of weeks to mobilize, locate Ava, and then get our asses down to Peru.

"No. You were there when I got the message that they wanted me in Virginia ASAP. I get there and learn that Davidson is being held in some remote prison and that he doesn't get out until we bring the goods."

He sighs. "Yeah, I know. I was hoping we'd missed something."

"Do you think it's a red herring? Got there by accident?" I point to the table full of folders. "We've got a GPS-chipped purse with five folders. The folders contain printouts of phone calls and emails that have somewhat scandalous information, but nothing that is worth this kind of elaborate buying scheme. The folders themselves are plain cardstock."

He rubs his head because obviously he's thought about this a lot while I was getting my pipes cleaned. "I've got nothing. If they didn't have Davidson and there weren't fifty mercenaries running around Pucallpa ready to fire at anything that looks at them crosswise, I'd think we were being trolled for some elaborate hoax. But Duval's got something that makes people believe it's worth a lot of money and effort."

"What about Ava? What's the angle there?"

"She's just a Kleenex."

"A what?"

We both turn to find Ava standing in the doorway. She has a sheet wrapped around her body, which does almost nothing to hide her curves. Garcia's eyes linger too long on the upper part of her chest until I growl in annoyance.

He swipes a hand down his cheek and across his mouth before turning back to the contents of the table. "Disposable, like a Kleenex. You use it and you don't care if you trash it because there are plenty more where that came from."

"Ouch," she says and hitches up the sheet. There's a lot of hurt in that one word, and like the besotted fool I am, I need to soothe that pain away immediately. I kick Garcia under the table in a not-so-subtle gesture for him to clarify and take the hurt away.

"Garcia's not saying he thinks you're Kleenex, and I sure as shit don't."

"Before you got roped into being a mule, they were using another girl. College student who'd been fucking one of Duval's underlings. She got her throat slit in an alleyway by the Chinese contingent. I don't know the reason why. Could be because she got mouthy. Could be they didn't like the perfume she was wearing. But they needed another disposable mule, and you were it. They could keep you in line because of your friend Rose, and if you died, oh well." He shrugs and spreads his hands palms up.

Ava blanches at Garcia's recitation. Even a few days in the jungle and being a mule hasn't really prepared her for this chat.

"Are you saying Rose isn't safe?"

Garcia and I exchange a look. Rose wasn't safe the day she allowed Duval to stick his dick in her, but that's not what Ava wants to hear.

"She's in Pucallpa and she looks healthy," Garcia says.

"Oh, thank God," she breathes, and then wobbles over to the table to collapse in my lap. "You're going to get her out, right?"

Her mismatched eyes are full of hope, and when her ass wiggles against my hardening dick, I can't help but wonder if she fucked me because she thought that is the only way I'm going to help her. I make the mistake of looking at Garcia, whose narrowed eyes are accusing her of the exact same thing. But then do I really care about her motivations? If saving Rose is the price of having Ava by my side, it's a small price to pay and one I'd offer a thousand times over.

I press her face into my neck. "You got that right, baby."

Over her head, I glare at Garcia, who rolls his eyes.

"You're pussy-whipped," he mouths.

Don't care if I am, I decide. It's time to get moving. The longer we stay here, the more likely it is that Rose gets her throat cut and Ava decides to leave me. "Why don't you get dressed?" I tell Ava, reluctantly pushing her upright and off my lap. "We need to get on the road."

She sucks the edge of her lower lip between her teeth and throws a sidelong glance toward Garcia, who is busy packing everything but the GPS locator. "I don't have a shirt," she whispers.

I can't stop a stupid, delirious grin from stretching across my face, because her shirt is the one I tore off. "I got you covered."

Standing up requires a not-so-minute adjustment of the woody in my pants. Garcia pretends not to notice but Ava smirks. Over by the wall, I pull another camp shirt out from the pack and toss it at her. "You best get dressed on your own," I tell her when she hesitates. "If I come in there and I see your naked tits, we're not making it out of the room for another thirty minutes, and that'll make hard-ass here even grumpier."

She turns a beet red color but disappears, clutching the sheet tight against her body.

"I'm a grumpy hard-ass?" Garcia asks as he rises from his chair.

"Also the best gun this town has ever seen," I say and swipe the locator up and jerk my head toward the exterior door. "We'll be back, Ava. Garcia and I are going to piss and then get rid of this GPS tracker."

A muffled *okay* from the bedroom follows us out the door.

"Worried about you, man," Garcia says as soon as we're far enough away from the hut that Ava can't hear us. "You seem awfully attached to this chick. Promising to save her stupid-ass friend? How're we going to do that?"

"I'm thinking we make a trade. Give Duval all this shit in exchange for Rose, and then we steal it back before the buy just like we originally planned."

"We're making things extra hard on ourselves because you want to get laid," he grumbles.

I stop because I need to address this shit before it gets out of hand. I lay both of my hands on his shoulders. "We don't even know if we've got anything. Maybe it's one part of the puzzle, maybe it's the whole damn thing. But you and I and the rest of the guys are the best damn team ever assembled. It's why the government came to us and not someone else. Duval's got no chance against us in the end. He's a two-bit criminal with a taste for high drama that's going to bring him down in the end. We got this. Plus, aren't we all about trying to help those who don't have it in them to help themselves? Isn't that the whole fucking point of the island and the home we're building there? I want to save Davidson as much as you do. We just have a couple more strays to take care of."

He drops his head to his chest and takes a few breaths. I wait as it sinks in, as his fear for me subsides and his sense of justice kicks in. It doesn't take long. He chuckles, a rueful, rough sound. "Sorry. Got sidetracked there."

"No worries, man." I let him go. We let a comfortable silence settle in until we reach the river. Then we drop down the embankment and plant the locator in the mud and cover it with a few rocks.

Afterward, he says, "It's been a long time for you, hasn't it?"

"You have no idea, Garcia. No idea." I slap him on the back.

Ava is ready for us, dressed in a camp shirt that has never looked so sexy, and a pair of loose-fitting pants that she's holding around her waist. Garcia crouches next to the bag and pulls out a rope, which he holds out to Ava.

She stares at it like it's a snake.

To Garcia's credit, he doesn't get mad. "It's for your pants. To hold them up," he explains.

"Oh, gotcha. Thanks." She takes the rope and winds the length around her twice. I help her make a knot and then we pile into the sedan.

As Garcia guns the engine, I pop open the glove compartment and pull out the handgun.

"Nice. How much more we got?"

"There's the AK you took off the villagers and two other long guns. There should be another magazine in there, too." He pats the dash.

"Good to know." I chamber a round and hold it loosely in my lap.

"Is the drive dangerous?" Ava tries not to sound worried, but fails.

"Just being extra cautious," I reassure her. The road between Campoverde and Pucallpa is paved but completely dark at night. Only the headlights from the car illuminate the long stretch ahead. "Why don't you try sleeping," I suggest.

She nods and stretches out on the seat.

Garcia and I keep a watchful eye for oncoming traffic. The mercenaries have likely missed their check-in time with Duval, and if I was him, I'd have sent out a scout hours ago. But Duval's not a mercenary. He's a criminal with a lot of money and a thirst for more.

The road whips by, black against black blocking any meaningful scenery. We keep the music off so we can listen for oncoming traffic. In the backseat, soft whiffles signal Ava's asleep.

"Do you think those emails and shit have a code in them? And the buyer knows?" Garcia asks, his fingers tapping the wheel.

"Could be. Never thought of that." I hate these fucking spy games. We're mercenaries—soldiers for hire. We protect our people by killing others. We're physical creatures, not thinkers. Have a target to take out? Have a body that is in need of protection? Have something you want destroyed or taken? We can do that. But we don't decipher codes and we don't think up elaborate schemes involving multiple buyers and red herrings.

I'm too straightforward. Maybe if Bennito were in charge it'd be different, but he's not. He's a twenty-five-year-old computer whiz we saved from a life of imprisonment because he hacked into a major website and played an ode to the current girl he was boning at the time. The relationship died a quick death after the police showed up at her house to question her.

If we don't know what to steal, our plans—no matter what they are—aren't worth shit.

We let the silence fall again as we contemplate how to deal with Duval's information.

Or at least I was contemplating that. When Garcia opens his mouth, I realize something else is bothering him.

"What you plan to do with her?"

"I don't know." I hadn't given it much thought.

"You can't really think she's going to want to come to the island. The only women there are those who've already been used up by life. They're hiding. She's the opposite of those women. She's a model, for Christ's sake." He's not saying anything that I haven't tossed around in my own head. Doesn't make it any more fun to hear them trotted out in front of me. "She's not going to be happy picking fruit from the trees, planting crops, and weaving baskets."

"Someone weaves baskets on the island?"

Garcia growls. "It's just a fucking example."

The darkness stretches endlessly in front of us. I set aside the levity for a little truth. Garcia deserves that. "I don't know if she'll come back with me. I don't know if this is the only time I'll have with her. But even if it is, it'll be enough."

"Bullshit," he spits out, hands tightening around the wheel. One time when we were very drunk, Garcia admitted that he had loved a woman once. A girl, really. Her brothers hadn't been keen on a wetback—their words—soiling their sister. They told him that he wasn't good enough for her and he must have believed it, because Garcia hasn't had a woman in his life for as long as I've known him. Bachelorhood was just one of the many things we had in common.

"You're saying that if you could, you'd go back and erase all those times that you had with your girl—the one from back home?"

He's quiet for so long I wonder if he plans to ignore the question.

"No," he says finally.

"What happened to her?" We don't talk about this shit often—only when our defenses are low and there's nothing to keep our mouths from rambling. I'm going to blame it on the fact that Ava fucked all the good sense out of me.

"She got killed in a drunk driving accident while in the car with her new boyfriend. He was handpicked by her brothers—one of their friends or something. He'd had a few too many to drink, got in and drove his convertible through a four-way stop, and crashed into a fire hydrant at about sixty miles per hour. Broke her goddamn neck."

I let loose a long, low whistle. "What'd you do to him?" There was no way that Garcia didn't fuck that boy up.

"I beat him into a coma. Because I was a juvenile, I was given the option of going into the army or going to prison. I chose the army. Or rather they chose me. I guess they like the fact that I didn't mind hurting people."

"Sounds like Uncle Sam. Come over here and have this gun. You want to kill people, here's a fucking list. Go do it and don't ask questions."

Garcia gives a half grunt, half laugh. "That sounds about right."

"You ever find anyone that means half as much?"

"Never wanted to. For some folks, there's only one, and she was it for me."

"Then why'd you leave her? Why didn't you just run off?"

"I wasn't it for her."

Meaning he asked her to run away and she refused. I shift in my seat to look back at Ava. Her hands are tucked underneath her cheek and she looks like an angel kissed by the moonlight.

I'm probably not it for Ava, either, but I'm going to enjoy the hell out of the time she gives me.

It's because I'm turned around that I don't notice how fast the oncoming traffic is approaching. I see only the lights and then hear Garcia curse. There's a ping and then the car begins to skid sideways.

Garcia struggles for control as the back wheels dig into the ditch. I reach over the seat and push Ava's falling body back onto the seat.

"What's happening?" she cries as she tries to sit up. The skidding motion of the car drives her into one side.

"Put your seat belt on, Ava," I shout and then brace my hand against the dash.

The car spins around, once and then twice. The nearly bald tires have no traction. We skid into the middle of the road. Lights flash in our lane.

Fuck, in *our* lane.

A horn sounds.

The lights bear down on us. Behind me I hear a muffled scream of fear and in the reflection, I see Ava with her hand over her mouth.

"The gas, Garcia. The gas," I yell.

Just before impact, Garcia guns the engine and we go flying across the road and into the ditch. The little sedan is rocked slightly by the wind as the truck speeds past, whaling on the horn in angry fear.

"What happened?" Ava gasps.

"Tire shot out." Beside me Garcia is dumbstruck. He hasn't moved. "Where's your gun, man?"

"Seat." His breathing is labored. "Under the seat."

I don't have time to dwell on why his voice sounds strange. Whoever shot out our tires is out there. And that kind of shot? It had to be done with night-vision goggles, which means they have a serious advantage on us. We need to mud up. The cool mud layer will reduce our heat signal and level the playing field.

"How far do you think we are from the river?" I ask Garcia while feeling around on the floor for his gun. I locate it wedged between the seat and the console. I place it on Garcia's lap and twist around. "Ava, pull down the center compartment and reach through to the back."

"What about you two?" she asks.

"Don't worry about us." I take the butt of my gun and smash out the interior lights.

Garcia's hand is on his door. At my nod, we both roll out of the car, making as small of a target as we can. I duckwalk to the rear and open the car door to grab the pack where we stuck the folders. After sticking my arms through the straps, I army crawl on my stomach over to Garcia, who's already flat on the ground with his gun up.

Pucallpa can't be more than a few hundred clicks away. If we have to abandon this car, we'll find another one that will carry us the rest of the way.

No gunshots greet us. Whoever shot at us must be some distance away. That's to our advantage. We'll hear them . . . I hope.

"How many?" I mouth quietly.

"No more than one," Garcia guesses. "Maybe two? But only one is a decent shot."

"Only takes one bullet to kill us."

He grunts quietly.

I tap the ground. "You stay here with Ava. I'll go forward and see if I can spot the shooter. Snipers don't like to get close. If I circle around, I might be able to see him."

"I have a better idea. Be ready."

Before I can ask him what the hell he means, he jumps up. A slight flare appears as the gunpowder is engaged thirty degrees to the left. Garcia's body jerks once and then twice. I shut out what I know has happened and run hard toward the pinpoint of light that has already died out. I hear footsteps approaching fast, and drop immediately to the ground. The bullet whizzes over my head. The shooter is twenty-five feet in front of me, standing like a dumbass. I shoot his leg.

The muzzle of his gun swings toward me, and I surge forward and blow the top of his fucking head off. In the gauzy moonlight I see the figure jerk backward and then collapse. I'm on top of his corpse in less than twenty seconds. The sniper rifle lies to his right. I grab it and then sprint back to Garcia.

Ava's on her knees outside the car and Garcia's in her lap. She's using her shirt to sop the blood gurgling out of his mouth. Even in the darkness I can see the stain on her hands, which are clenched over his chest.

"Rafe," she cries out. "He's been shot."

"You dumb fuck." I crash to my knees beside them. Ava gasps in shock but I ignore her to repeat it. "You dumb, stupid fuck."

Garcia closes his eyes and makes an impatient huffing noise. "He'd have picked us both off if I hadn't drawn his fire. Stupid night-vision goggles."

I throw the pack off and paw through it for the first aid kit. His hand, warm and slick from his blood, stops me. "No," he says. "It's not just my lung. I'm gut shot."

His hand drags mine to his side. When I peel away the fabric, the entry wound pulses as if it's alive.

"Fuck." I swipe my hand across my mouth and taste the metallic flavor of Garcia's life. "No, we're going to save you." I wrench open the kit and grab the gauze. "We'll glue you up and drive into Pucallpa and get the bullet out of you."

"No," he repeats. "I'm not going to make it. We both know it. Take her and get out."

"No man left behind, brother. Not happening." I twist out of his grasp and press the gauze to his wound. It's soaked and ruined immediately. The fountain of blood keeps coming.

Ava's crying but she tries to help, our hands fumbling to pack the wound tight and stop the blood.

"I'm going now. See my girl." Garcia smiles. "Here, I'm it for her. I can see her."

He clasps my arm and pulls me close, death giving him strength. "You're right," he gasps into my ear, his breath cold when it should be warm. I press harder against the wound even though I know it's useless. My throat tightens.

"What about?"

"Everything. Her. You. What we fight for. The moment. Savor it." Each word is labored. I clench my teeth from striking out, from weeping, from running back and putting a dozen more bullets into the shooter's face.

"I got him," I say, knowing that's one thing Garcia would have wanted.

"Never doubted you, Brother."

And then that's it. His fingers tighten momentarily against my arm and then he's gone. No breath, just a dead, lifeless weight.

I shove the med kit back in the bag and then pick him up.

"Get the door, Ava," I order. She scurries to obey, my voice harsher than she's probably ever heard before. I slide Garcia into the backseat and then strip the car of all of its supplies. Garcia had gotten us a lot of shit. Guns, extra ammunition, clothes, water, cash.

In a fair world, Garcia would have died on the island with a beer at his side and his fishing pole between his legs. But we don't live in a fair world—haven't since we were born, and not even then.

"Can you carry a few things?" I ask.

She nods, still sniffling and looking a hundred times lost, hurt, and confused. I'd like to take her in my arms, but that's the last thing I *should* do.

My mother told me I was a killer, that I killed from the moment I was conceived, and I haven't stopped. I want to laugh off the curse, but the dead body of my friend reveals the truth. Even if Ava truly wanted me, not the man who can save her friend but *me*, I would still need to walk away. For her own safety.

Garcia's a dark reminder of my own cursed existence. I can't forget again.

I give her two of the AKs and another pack. It's lightweight and we won't be walking for long. I'll steal a car soon.

I take the rest of the stuff and then lead Ava away, back toward the dead sniper's body. I'm taking his night-vision gear.

"Stay here," I say, pointing to a small patch of dirt.

"I think I should go with you." She shivers but it's not from the cold. She rubs her hands up and down her arms, trying to remember what it feels like to be alive.

"No." I don't give her any chance to argue, just turn on my heel until I reach the dead sniper. I pull off his headgear that's splattered with brain matter and blood and slip it over my eyes. I can barely see the car from here—only the engine and Garcia's body make faint heat signals, and both are fading fast. I release two shots into the rear of the car and the second one hits. The gas tank explodes. Ava screams. I wipe moisture away from my face and return to Ava's side.

My *madre* said I was cursed. That I should keep the devil's wand to myself lest I hurt any other innocents. I'd kept to myself for most of my life because I hadn't wanted to hurt those who didn't deserve it.

Garcia was right in one sense. Ava didn't belong with me, because men like Garcia and I are just one bullet away from death.

# CHAPTER TWENTY-SIX

**AVA**

Rafe's being distant. I can't blame the guy. His best friend just died in our arms a few hours ago. Since then, we've stolen another car from a pair of boys, driven into Pucallpa, abandoned the vehicle, and now we're heading to a hotel to meet up with someone else. Of course, I assume we're heading to a hotel, because Rafe won't talk to me.

He's shut down entirely.

And part of me wants to remind him that I'm here and I'm scared, too, and I want to comfort him. If he was visibly upset, I could handle that. If he was angry, I could get angry, too. But stone-cold silence? I don't know what to do with that. He's been so cheerfully competent this entire time, even when I'm ready to fall apart.

Now, I feel like he's falling apart and I've got no idea what to do.

"Come on," Rafe says at one point, startling me out of my woe-is-me attitude. I perk up, but he only takes my elbow and steers me toward a building.

It's a seedy-looking hotel with a boxy storefront. Lovely. I wrinkle my nose as we head inside and the smell of sour air-conditioning meets my nose. Rafe doesn't stop at the front desk, but heads for the stairs, dragging me along. We pass grubby doors with dirt halos around the doorknobs. Rafe seems to know what room we're looking for and pauses in front of a door. He knocks twice, pauses, knocks three times, pauses, and then knocks once. A moment later, I hear chains coming off the door, and we're greeted by a young man about my age, with a head of dark, curly hair, wearing a baseball cap turned backward. He gives me a curious look, then turns to Rafe.

"Where's Garcia?"

"Dead," Rafe says flatly. "We got ambushed. Snipers. Night vision."

The man's face falls, and he looks devastated. He flicks a glance at me, then moves to Rafe. "What? But—"

"I don't want to talk about it," Rafe says. He slings a pack on the bed. "Shut the door and lock it. You know which hotel the exchange is going to be at?" He is cold and terse with the new guy.

"Yeah. Chatter says it's still at Manish Hotel Ecológico. One of the bungalows." He turns and looks at me, his mouth crooking up, only to wobble. "Hey, Ava."

I'm a little startled he knows my name, but then I remember that Rafe and his boys have been watching me since this mule thing started. "Hey," I say softly.

"I'm Bennito." He swallows hard, then his jaw clenches, and he looks at Rafe.

I do, too. He's busy rifling through the things we've brought—guns, ammo, cash. It's like he's deliberately trying to ignore us.

Both of us. And that hurts.

My stomach growls and Rafe picks up a gun, unsnaps the cartridge to check the bullets, and then snaps it back in again. "She needs to eat."

"Room service?" Bennito asks, gesturing at the phone. "I got you the adjoining room. Wasn't sure . . ." His throat works. "Garcia's shit is in there, but . . ."

"It'll come in handy," Rafe says in that emotionless voice. "And not room service. I don't want anyone knowing we're here. Take her to the corner, get her something to eat."

Now both Bennito and I look concerned. "Is it safe? Will they recognize me?" I ask.

"Here," Rafe says coldly and takes the baseball cap off of Bennito's head. "Now you have a disguise. Just go around the corner. Bennito can call if there's trouble."

"'Kay, boss," Bennito says. He stuffs a gun in his waistband and tugs his shirt over it, then looks at me. "Shall we go?"

My mouth works silently. This all feels wrong. Stupid and wrong. He's letting me leave to go to the goddamned corner store? After a week of practically peeing together in the jungle because it wasn't safe to be alone? I feel oddly betrayed and hurt.

*His friend died, you selfish idiot. Maybe he needs a moment.*

Right. Maybe I'm too busy thinking about me right now. "We'll be back," I say softly. "You want anything?"

He shakes his head.

Okay then.

It feels so bizarre to go down the street with Bennito. Like I haven't just been pawned off to a stranger. Like we're not in danger out here. But no one on the streets notices us. If anything, I suppose we blend in, because we look scruffy as all hell.

We get to a run-down corner store and my stomach rumbles again. "Get whatever you want," Bennito says, and runs a hand over his mouth. "I think I'm gonna buy some cigarettes."

I nod and absently head down an aisle. I'm starving, so everything looks good. I grab some beef jerky, some chips, and a stack of chocolate bars. God, I definitely need chocolate. It's good depression food. I pick up some junk for Mendoza, too, because I know he's got to be hungry.

I pass a toiletries aisle and grab a toothbrush, toothpaste, a razor, a comb for my ragged hair, and some lip balm, because my face is a mess. I grab a bottle of lotion, too, even though the thought of trying to repair my hands feels like going after the sea with a spoon. They look awful. Like I've been trying to catch bees with my hands or something.

I spot condoms, and pick through the selection. I don't suppose condoms matter, since Rafe was a virgin. He'd probably be too large for anything they made anyhow. I hesitate, and then spot a bottle of lube and grab it.

My arms are full of crap when I return to Bennito's side, but he doesn't comment, just gestures to the counter. I throw it all down and give Bennito a challenging look when he spots the lube. Again, no comment.

Jesus, I wish *someone* would talk to me.

We exit the store a few minutes later, and Bennito buys me something to eat from a street vendor. I don't know what the food is, but it's hot and warm and I gobble it down quickly, because I want to get back to the hotel room and to Rafe. We buy Rafe some street food, too, and I cradle it in my good hand as we skirt around mototaxis and walk back to the hotel. There are chickens in the streets, and the entire area strikes me as a bit run-down, despite it being a city.

When we get back to the hotel room, though, Rafe's in the shower in his room. I stand awkwardly in Bennito's room for a moment, holding Rafe's rapidly cooling food. Should I go in after Rafe? Take him in my arms and hug him despite his prickliness? Or is he the kind that will hate that? I wish I knew.

Bennito clears his throat. "So you still have the contents of the bag?"

I'm thankful for the distraction. "Yeah, but it's just junk. Some colored folders with papers in them."

He cocks his head, clearly curious. "Can I see them? There has to be something there for them to keep tracking you. Otherwise, there'd be no point."

I shrug and set Rafe's food down on one of the tables, then dig through his bag until I find the folders.

Bennito takes them with a *hmmm* in his throat, and immediately starts flipping through the printouts. "These are web page printouts."

"So?" I'm not following.

"So maybe there's something embedded on these websites that corresponds. Maybe it's a code." He rubs a finger across one of the sticky notes, thinking. "Give me some time and I'll figure it out."

I nod and look over at Rafe's room. "I . . . guess I'll go see how he's doing."

"Did you, ah . . ." Bennito clears his throat. "Did you need to stay in this room? There's two beds. The other only has one."

It's sweet of him to offer. Maybe he thinks my relationship with Rafe is a lot less consensual than it looks. "I like sleeping with Rafe," I tell him, even though we haven't done it much. I don't plan on letting Rafe escape my clutches all night. He needs to talk to someone, damn it. It's not natural to get so quiet. Not after what happened. I'm still in shock myself and I barely knew the guy.

I give Bennito back his hat, take my bag of junk food and toiletries, and sit down on one side of Rafe's bed, shutting the door between the rooms. With my comb, I detangle my hair slowly as Rafe showers. My curls are a rat's nest but with some careful work of the comb, I'm able to get my hair to something decent. It's a riot of natural sleep-waves, but at least it's not snarled and matted.

Rafe's still in the damn shower, so I lean back against the ugly headboard of the bed and pull out a chocolate bar. I'm starting to feel . . . I don't know. It's a mixture of depression and shock and loss and despair, and pity. Pity for Rafe, who has to be torn apart, and pity for myself, who could use a hug, and the person I want one from most has shut me out.

I think of Rose. My best friend, the only person in the world that I'm truly close to. My parents have always been distant workaholics, happy to pawn me off on daycare or a nanny or a babysitter so they could do their own thing. We've never been close, but Rose and I? We're close.

Like Garcia and Rafe were close. My throat closes up and hot tears start to flood my eyes. What if I can't save Rose? What am I going to do? A day or so ago, I felt in control. Like I could get the guy and save my best friend. Now I feel like all that control has disappeared. Rafe's pushed me away, and all of my hopes for saving Rose hinge on him.

I think of Rafe, and how he must be feeling at the moment. Does he feel like Garcia's death is my fault? Like I'm to blame? Unhappy, I shove a piece of chocolate in my mouth. Rose and I would always split a chocolate bar, because she couldn't afford the calories, but she had a major sweet tooth. Whenever she was sad, she'd want chocolate. I guess it's a habit I'm picking up. Unfortunately, the taste of chocolate reminds me of my missing bestie, and I put the rest of it aside.

I allow myself a bit of surreptitious weeping, but by the time the shower turns off, I'm done. I'm composed, too, and I want to be there for Rafe. However he needs me, in whatever capacity he needs me, I want to be there for him.

When Rafe comes out, though, he's dressed. No sexy towel slung around his hips. No damp skin. He looks at me, and his eyes are a bit red-rimmed, and my heart aches for him. Then, he looks away and gestures at the door. "You should go hang with Bennito. Help him with the project."

I sit up in bed, extending my legs because I know he likes to look at them. "I want to stay with you, Rafe. Please, talk to me." I pat my side of the bed, indicating he should sit.

He grabs the TV remote and shakes his head. "I'm not in the mood, Ava." He sits at a nearby table, flicks the TV on, and focuses his grim gaze on it.

Loud Spanish jabber from a TV show fills the room. I watch Rafe, but he seems determined to focus on the TV instead of me. I sit up and crawl forward on the bed. "Rafe, come on."

"No, Ava." His voice becomes hard and he finally looks at me again. His jaw flexes, and his entire expression is one of anger. "I don't have time for a pity fuck right now, all right? You'll still get Rose back, okay? No need to bargain with your body anymore."

Each word slams into me like a fist. I gasp and recoil back on the bed, hurt making tears spring to my eyes again. "Fine," I choke out. I gather my plastic bag full of things and contemplate where I can go. In the other room with Bennito, a stranger, so he can give me pitying looks, knowing I've been kicked out? I change my mind and head for the bathroom instead. If Rafe can hide in the shower, I can, too.

"Ava," Rafe says, voice weary, but I slam the door behind me and lock it. I immediately turn the water on to drown out my tears, and wipe my eyes. Fuck him. Fuck all of this. I strip my clothing off and get in the shower. It's ice cold and I don't care. I still wash up, because being clean is a luxury. I shave everything— arms, legs, and even run the razor over my pussy, shaving everywhere. Fuck it.

By the time I turn the water off, I'm calm. Funny how an ice-cold shower can restore clarity to a hot temper. As I towel off, I realize what Rafe's doing.

He's pushing me away. He's hurting, and he's trying to push me out. And I've been too wrapped up in the fact that he's lashing out at me to realize that this isn't like him. This isn't the man that's so carefully thoughtful of me. The man who'd rather swim a crocodile-infested river with a knife wound in his back than put me out. The man who'd rather eat my pussy all night than dream of inflicting a bit of pain on me.

The man who went thirty-five years without touching a woman because he was afraid of hurting them.

I think of his scars on his groin and his chest. I think of the hints he's dropped about his awful mother, and the girl that died when he tried to fuck her. I think of the boys that came after him and punished him.

Everyone he's cared for has hurt him or died on him. No wonder he's all fucked up at the moment.

That won't be me, I decide. I dig through my bag and find the lubricant. It's a cheap off brand I've never seen, but lube is lube. I pull the tiny tube out of the package and leave the bathroom behind.

I'm not letting him push me out.

## CHAPTER TWENTY-SEVEN

### AVA

I saunter out of the bathroom, completely naked, and prop my arms against the doorframe. The tiny bottle of lube is in my hand, hidden. And I wait for Rafe to notice me. My pose makes my breasts thrust into the air, and I bend one knee so my hips are canted slightly in a sexy angle. Rafe might be a freshly deflowered virgin, but I'm skilled at this sort of thing, and he does not know what he's up against.

It doesn't take long for Rafe's attention to swing to me. Once it does, I see him blink, see his gaze move over my naked body, from my jutting breasts to the freshly smooth mound of my pussy. That gets his attention. I watch the lust flare in his eyes, and then his jaw clenches again and he forces himself to look away.

But there's one thing about Rafe that's super obvious, and I can see his cock springing to life in his pants even if he's trying to deny me. Encouraged, I saunter forward. "I know how your mind works, Rafe," I say in a sultry voice, moving to his side of the bed. "I know you're trying to shut me out, because you're hurting, and maybe you're scared of losing more people. But here's the thing with me. I don't like being shut out. I need you. I need you in more ways than just this stupid transaction. I need you to hold me, too. I need you to touch me and love me, and distract me. To remind me of the good things in life even when the bad things happen."

I stand there, next to his side of the bed, and wait.

He stares at me a little longer (mostly at my pussy) and then rubs a hand over his mouth. "We're not doing this."

All right. I'm not a woman without a plan, and if he's going to play hardball, I am, too.

He closes his eyes and leans back against the headboard. "It isn't safe for you to be here with me, Ava. Trust me."

"Oh, I trust you." And since his eyes are still closed, it's time for me to put my plan into action. I open the bottle of lube and squirt a fair bit onto my hands, then rub them together to warm it. His face turns toward me, but he's still keeping his eyes closed.

He thinks he can win this game, does he? He has no idea who he's up against. I slide my oily hands over my breasts, greasing them up, and tug at my nipples. "Mmmm," I breathe, making the sound as sexy as I can. Truth is, I'm getting pretty turned on at performing for Rafe. I want to see his eyes light up at what I do. I want to distract him from his misery. I want him to *connect* with me again. And if it means being dirty, raunchy, cock-needy Ava? That's what I'll do.

His gaze goes to my breasts, now slippery and bouncing against my hands. I see the moment his mouth goes dry, his eyes darken with hunger. His hand slides down to his cock and he presses against it as if adjusting himself. "What are you doing, Ava?"

"Convincing you that you want to touch me." I stroke my fingers over my nipples, hardening the tips, and then slide my hands down to my pussy. I know I'm leaving a wet, shiny streak of lube all over my body. Don't care. The fascination in his eyes is enough for me. "It's not a pity fuck," I tell him. "It's not me fucking you for Rose. It's me fucking you because I like fucking you. And because you turn me on. And I need you."

My fingers slide between my folds. I'm a little wet, but the lube helps things. I move to the table and squirt a bit more into my hand, and I know Rafe's watching my every move now.

And because I'm feeling daring, I turn around and bend over, spread my legs, and present him with my ass. My fingers slide between my legs and I push them into my pussy, knowing he's getting a face full of the sight. It's a total porn-star move, but it's also turning me on like mad, because I'm picturing how much I'm blowing his mind. My fingers slick in and out of my sex, and I moan at the wet sounds they make.

"Fuck, Ava," Rafe groans. I feel his hands grab my hips, and it's the first move he's made to touch me since Garcia's awful death. "Tell me not to touch you, baby. Tell me that you're better without me."

"I need you, Rafe." I work my fingers in my pussy faster. I need him, and I need the orgasm he can give me. After taking Rafe's monster cock? My fingers feel like the saddest substitute.

"Tell me I can fuck you," he growls, and I feel his teeth rake over my buttock, sending a shiver of need through me.

Oh God, *yes please.* "I want you to fuck me with that big Godzilla dick of yours."

He groans and tugs my hand out of my pussy, and my fingers leave with a wet, needy sound. "Get on the bed," he commands.

Okay, that's hot. He's in control, and it makes my nipples tighten and my body ache with more need. I get on the bed on all fours, not caring that I'm probably getting cheap lube all over the hotel blankets. Fuck the blankets. I hunch down on my elbows and stick my ass in the air for him, spreading my legs wide.

I hear Rafe fumbling with his pants, hear the zipper go down and the rustle of fabric. I don't want him to second-guess anything. I want him mindless and inside me, so I slide a hand back to my pussy again and push my cheek against the bedsheets. "You want inside this pussy? Rafe? It needs your cock so bad. It's aching for you." God, I hope Bennito can't hear our dirty talk in the next room.

Actually, I don't care. Let Bennito know that Rafe's nailing me. I'll share it with the world if I need to. He's sexy as hell, my mercenary.

Rafe makes an agonized sound, and I feel the thick, enormous head of his cock press against the entrance to my sex. "Tell me to fuck you, Ava."

"Fuck me."

He pushes, and I tense a little, expecting a taut sort of pain like before. But there's nothing. I'm stretched wide for him, and I'm needy and lubed up, and I cry out because he feels so freaking amazing I can't stand it.

Over me, Rafe freezes. "Ava?"

"Good," I moan. "Oh so fucking good. Fuck me hard, Rafe.

I need you to pound into me." I wiggle back against him to show that I mean it.

He makes another agonized sound that's not quite a groan, and not quite my name. He slams into me with Godzilla, and it's shocking and so incredibly good that I cry out again. Now I'm positive Bennito can hear us fucking.

Still not caring.

Again, Rafe thrusts into me. "You're so fucking tight—"

"Tight for you," I pant. "My pussy's just for you, baby."

"Fuck," he growls. "Fuck, you feel so good."

"You feel better," I tell him. "So big and thick, I can feel you all through me. I love your big, fat cock, baby. Love how good it makes me feel. Love—"

"*Fuck*," he says again, and I've forgotten all about the fact that Rafe's not too experienced with sex, because he shudders over me, coming. His hands clasp my hips tightly, and he grinds his cock into me as he orgasms.

And really, it's still okay that he's come after a few quick thrusts. I know how to get mine. "Keep moving," I tell him, and reach between my spread thighs to touch my clit.

"Goddamn, Ava," he says, but his entire body shakes as he gives me another halfhearted thrust. Even Rafe's limp dick is still better than most dicks, and I rub my clit faster, moving in tiny, fast circles helped along by the lube that's all over my hands. He grinds into me again, and I suck in a breath, because now I'm coming, too. My toes curl and I whimper loudly as he pants over me.

Even a messy fuck with Rafe's still amazing. It takes me a few minutes to come down from the orgasm, and he's still slowly pumping into me with his half chub. I can feel the slippery wetness of his come all over where we're joined, and I moan, because he's sending happy aftershocks through my body with every slide of his cock inside me.

"Can I hold you?" he asks, voice hoarse.

"I'd be pissed if you didn't," I tell him, and he moves down on the bed next to me, and pulls me against him. I'm the smaller spoon, and his cock is pressing against my backside, slick and hot, and still stirring. Rafe can keep a hard-on longer than any guy I've ever known. Maybe it's because of his size.

He reaches around and holds me against him, his hands going to my breasts. I feel his breath on my neck, and he kisses it softly. "I'm sorry."

I squeeze his hand, and in the process, squeeze my own boob. "What are you sorry for?"

"That I said those things—"

"Shh," I tell him. "I know you didn't mean it. I know you love me," I tease, trying to keep him smiling.

"God," he says softly, and kisses my neck again. "You're incredible."

"You are, too. I don't understand why you don't think so."

He's silent for a long moment. Then, he strokes his fingers over my shoulder reverently. His voice is low as he begins to speak. "My mother was raped when she was sixteen but her family is devoutly religious. They would not allow her to get an abortion. She hated me. I don't blame her. I was the evidence of everything that had gone wrong in her life. She poured herself into the church and told me to avoid the opposite sex. My dick was monstrous, she'd said, and that it was a sign that I'd been born evil. Cursed."

"That's not true." I hug his arms against me tightly.

"Really?" He's miserable. "Because the one time I did try to have sex, I killed a girl."

"You say that but there's no possible way. Did you see her die in front of you?"

He shakes his head. "Two days later. Her brothers came for me and said she didn't wake up. That the doctors told them she'd hemorrhaged internally for two days and died as a result."

"You couldn't have done that damage, not how you described it. Unless you lied to me." I know he didn't but he needs to hear it.

"No, never," he says hoarsely. "I barely touched her . . . but there was the blood and then . . ." He trails off.

"You didn't kill her. I don't believe it and you need to stop beating yourself up with it. Here's the thing," I say, tracing a finger over the thick veins in his hands. I've got such a thing for hands and I love his big, rough ones. "When you're hurting, I want you to come to me. I want you to trust me. We've got each other in this, you know?"

"Garcia," he says, voice quiet and full of pain.

"I know, baby," I tell him softly. "I know. Whatever happens, we can't shut each other out, okay? I feel like I've lost Rose." I choke up a little, and swallow it down. Now's not the time. "I don't want to lose you, too."

I feel him nod against my neck, and he holds me tighter. "You're it, Ava."

"Hmm?" I don't understand.

"Nothing," he says. "Just something Garcia was saying."

I stroke his hand with my slippery one. I ignore the lube all over us, just like I ignore the sweat that's making our skin stick together. He holds me close—no, he's clutching me against him as if I'm a lifeline. He's breaking my heart, my big, strong guy. From what I know of Rafe, he doesn't love easily, and I don't know how he's going to handle the loss of his best friend.

I'd do anything to make it better for him. Anything.

But for now? All I can do is love him and remind him that life's worth living.

# CHAPTER **TWENTY-EIGHT**

## RAFAEL

I towel off as Ava finishes up in the shower. She is asking impossible things of me. And worse, I want to give them to her. My mother had said that I needed to spend the rest of my days atoning for the people I had killed. My unborn baby sister. The high school girl. When I came home on leave, my mother would cross herself as I passed over the doorway and sprinkle holy water outside the door to cast out the demons I had carried home with me.

The souls of those who'd died at my hand clung to me, she claimed. I believed her then and believe her now, because Garcia's death hangs around my neck like an anvil.

Ava's sweet face is so hopeful when she speaks of Rose and even if she won't admit to it, not saving Rose will change things. I know this and deep down, I believe that Ava knows it, too.

But there is no point in dwelling on this. Tomorrow will happen, no matter what I do today. What shape it is, who I have with me? I can change that. In the next room, Bennito is bent over the table, drawn away from his computer.

"Dude, you sounded like you were killing her in there." He holds up his hand to high-five me. Glad that Ava isn't here, I grunt a nonresponse and take the chair opposite.

He leans over the table. "We always joke about who's got the bigger gun, but it's always been you, hasn't it?"

"Yes." And suddenly I get all the jokes. The pie jokes. The baseball jokes. The boning jokes. I heard them before, but now they have context and meaning. *Heft.*

"Cool." He sits back and looks at me more admiringly than ever before. Because I have a big gun and know how to use it. There's something wrong with that thinking. Something I'm going to have to talk to Bennito about so when he finds his Ava, he doesn't screw it up with his machismo. But for now, we share a moment for a few seconds before I flick my fingers at the items he has laid out on the table.

"What have you found?"

His attention is easily diverted. "Shit, this is some cool stuff. You remember how each of the folders had small sticky flags?" I nod. On each page, there are two or three translucent flags with colored tabs that matched the folder. "Well they aren't fucking notes. You stick them together, like so." He holds up a small stack. "They form a fucking USB chip. Wild, huh?"

Spy shit. It's the weirdest shit in the world.

"How do you stick it into a USB port if it's that thin?" I pick up the tab. Now that Bennito has pointed it out, it did have more rigidity than an ordinary Post-it flag, but it still looked paper thin. I couldn't see any circuitry, either.

"You don't. It works through a receiver. The receiver works in tandem with the USB stack. It's pretty genius whoever designed this. I know that USBs were getting smaller but I swear that this was only a concept design. The flag is made of grapheme, which is a single layer of carbon atoms packed into a honeycomb pattern. The conductive layer is at the end."

I scrub a hand over my face. "Duval sends out his mule with the sales information but his buyers can't access the information without the receiver."

"Exactly." Bennito nods. "But if he's going to sell the information, then the receiver must not be encrypted."

"Is there any way to copy the data from the USB to our computer?"

"Not really. The information can only be read through the corresponding receiver."

"We need Duval, then."

"Or the receiver."

"And how many bodyguards does he have with him?"

"Twelve, and then there are the multiple goons surrounding his buyers. The Manish Hotel Ecológico is overrun with black-suited, earpiece-wearing foreigners. Looks like a hit-man convention."

"Why here in Pucallpa?"

"Dunno. I'm your computer and electronics guy." He wheels back to the computer and taps a few buttons. A video screen pops up, and I see two men standing on guard outside a bungalow.

"That Duval's place?"

"Yup. He's got that supermodel with him. She spends most of her time in a cabana flipping through magazines. He's usually talking on the phone or arguing with his brother."

I watch the screen. "What are they arguing about?"

Bennito laughs and rips open a potato chip bag. He shakes it toward me. "No thanks." I wave my hand.

"What don't they argue about? If Duval says the sky is blue, Fouquet says its green. If Duval wants to order fish for lunch, Fouquet wants meat. If Duval is taking Rose off to fuck, Fouquet wants to join."

My eyebrow raises on its own. "And does he?"

"Nope. That's about the biggest argument that they get into. 'Why does Duval get all the pussy?' Fouquet shouts. 'Go buy your own whore,' Duval snarls back. Rose just sits on the lounge chair until Duval snaps his fingers."

"Nice." I wonder how much Ava knows about this. "Is she there against her will?"

"Who can say? I mean, if I was in her situation and it was either fuck Duval or be killed, I'd probably fuck Duval until someone could ride to my rescue."

I nod absently. If she's willingly with Duval, it will be harder to extract her, but does it matter? Everyone in Duval's circle, with the exception of his brother, is disposable, including—or maybe especially—the women.

"What's the chatter? Has Duval said anything about the USB drives? Or does he assume they are lost in the jungle?"

"So far nothing."

"We have to assume that Duval has the original information on some computer device. We should steal that. Have you run an infrared scan and thermal imaging to locate all the electronics?"

"Yeah." Bennito flicks open another file. He has already labeled the items. "Our main targets are the two laptops. One is Duval's. Not sure whose the other one is. Rose has a tablet and so does

Fouquet." He taps his pen against an object shaped like a lamp. "But I think the receiver is here. The base of this lamp is hotter than all the other ones in his bungalow. I compared it to the heat signatures from all the other ten bungalows." With a few keystrokes, he places an overlay of transparent maps on top of Duval's.

"Is the lamp in Duval's bedroom?"

"Yeah," he drawls.

"Maid go in there?"

"Oh yeah." Bennito and I are on the same wavelength. In another country, maybe we could sneak a man inside, but in Pucallpa, there's no way that cleaning is done by a male. We need Ava for that. "Is she going to be up for that?"

"It's not her you should worry about." I rise and stalk over to the window. The safest plan for all of us, the one that would result in the least amount of injury and with the highest likelihood of success, is sending Ava in as a maid. She cleans, steals the base of the lamp, drops it out the window to a waiting Bennito who in the span of time it takes her to make the bed would have the receiver switched out and returned. I turn the plan over in my head. I don't like leaving Ava alone here. Too many shitheads with no morals running around. But I don't like her being so close to Duval, either. "We steal a uniform. Ava goes in, snatches the receiver, and then leaves. You and Rodrigo need to swap out the contents, and then we'll send her back in with the replacement. At the same time, we offer the USB shit to Duval outside in exchange for Rose. When we get Rose, we get on the first plane to Lima and then to Virginia."

"Sounds like a good plan to me."

"The only problem is that both Duval and Fouquet know what Ava looks like. Even if we were to disguise her somehow, she has the mismatched eyes. Think Pucallpa has a place that sells colored contacts?"

We exchange dubious looks. Pucallpa is at the mouth of the Amazon jungle. It sells jungle-related shit. Not cosmetic enhancements like colored contacts. You'd have to get that shit in Lima, but maybe we could buy a wig somewhere . . . I stare at Bennito.

"Stand up."

"No way, man. Do I look like a chick to you?"

"Stand up," I repeat. Bennito sighs and throws his chip bag on the desk. He gets to his feet, brushing his hands on his pants, leaving orange dust behind. Bennito stands a little under six feet and is shaped like a square. He's not going to pass for a woman, not with all the makeup in the world. Bridge troll, possibly. Woman, no.

"Fuck," I curse and wave my hand at him. "Sit down."

"Thank Christ," he breathes.

"Call Rodrigo and tell him that he needs to get a maid's uniform. Size 10 or so. Maybe 12." Bennito nods and I leave him to take care of the details while I go tell Ava that she's going to have to enter the hornet's nest to save her friend.

# CHAPTER TWENTY-NINE

## AVA

I really freaking hate this new plan. Me, going in and making the switch while in disguise? They sure do have a lot of faith in me. Considering that I'm the world's unluckiest woman to date, we should probably pay someone else to do this.

But we can't trust anyone else, and so I guess it's got to be me.

Hours later, we're sitting in the rented bungalow next to Duval's. I'm on the edge of the bed dressed in a frumpy, pale blue maid's uniform. My breasts have been bound down so I'm more boxy, and I'm wearing a wig. I've penciled my brows heavier and darker to disguise my face a bit more.

They even got me reading glasses to disguise my eyes, an ugly green pair that look like they belong to an ancient, unstylish librarian. They even have a dangly golden chain. And I've got orthopedic shoes to boot.

It's the world's unsexiest getup. Or at least, it should be, except Rafe keeps kissing me on the mouth and watching me with those intense eyes of his.

"I hate this," I tell him one last time. "I'm scared. They're going to look at me and figure me out."

"Baby, you're tearing me up," he murmurs. Rafe rubs my arms up and down. "You know I'm going to be right next door. They're not going to look at you. They don't know we're here. No one pays attention to staff. I promise. All you have to do is sneak in and switch it out." When I hesitate, he leans in and kisses me on my nose. "If I thought you were in danger, I wouldn't let you go."

I snort. "That's a lie."

His mouth quirks up in a half smile. "Okay. It is a lie, but it's the only option we've got. And I know you're brave. You went swimming with piranhas, remember?"

I nod and suck in a breath. Really, walking into a bungalow filled with a few shitheads isn't the worst thing that's happened to me in the last few days. The Amazon jungle had been a nightmare full of snakes and jaguars, and bugs the size of my hand. This was just a hotel bungalow.

I walk in, pretend a little, walk back out.

I can do this.

"You should wear these." Rafe lays a pair of plastic yellow gloves in my lap.

He's right. My bad wrist is purple and yellow on the underside and still hurts like a bitch. On the good side, the swelling is almost completely gone and I'm nearly fully functional again. It remains to be seen whether there will be any permanent damage. Even Rafe's eye patch is gone. We're better, so . . .

All this should be okay. It should go perfectly.

But I'm not lucky, and I worry something will go wrong. It always seems to. So I nod and lean in for one last kiss before I go. His hand grips the back of my neck, cradling my head as he leans in and possesses my mouth. His tongue slicks against mine, until we're gasping and clinging to each other, mouths mating wildly. For a man that's eschewed sex for thirty-five years, he's a damn good kisser. Either that, or a fast learner. If this is him rusty and out of practice, he's going to make me melt into a puddle when he's skilled.

And oh God, I really want to be around to see that.

I cling to him and reluctantly break the kiss. "Hey, Rafe?"

"Mmm?" He leans in and nips at my lower lip, sucking it into his mouth.

I fight a moan. God, he's all handsy now. God, I love that. "After this, what about you and me? What happens to us?"

That stops the playful kissing. He pulls back and looks at me. He's got that intense, possessive look in his eyes, but he pushes me away. "We'll worry about that afterward, okay? Let's just get through today."

"Geez. You need to work on your pillow talk, babe." There's a shine to his mouth that I can't resist rubbing off with my thumb. And then I taste it, just to see his eyes flare.

Because I'm a flirt like that.

I turn around and Bennito leans in the doorway, eating a bag of some of the chips I bought for Rafe. "You two gonna suck face all afternoon or we gonna get this show on the road?"

I draw in a breath and manage a smile for both of them. "I guess we might as well do this." I wish I sounded more confident. Hell, I wish I was more confident. The gloves are loose fitting, thank goodness, and don't hurt at all.

"I'll be right outside, Ava," Rafe says in a low, urgent voice when I head for the door. "If you get into trouble, just shout my name."

I nod and slip out the back door of the bungalow. I take the long route around, back to the main lodge, and from there, I go to the cleaning supplies room that we bribed someone to show us. I have the key (more bribery) and get one of the carts and push it down the walkway toward the bungalows. My breath feels short and raspy, and I'm about ten seconds away from a panic attack. I should be thinking about what to say when they answer the door, but all I can think about is Rafe's mouth. Rafe's kisses.

Rafe saying, *Let's just get through today.*

Because I know that's a total bullshit answer. That's a *don't ask me for commitment right now, baby* statement, and it's freaking me out. I feel like yesterday, the answer would have been different, and it hurts. I know he's aching over Garcia's death, but how can he blow me off right now? Was what I asked for—hope for the future between us—such a bad thing?

Am I such a bad person that I'm good for a fuck and nothing else?

Even though I'm worrying and turning over Rafe's words in my mind, the moment I pull in front of Duval's little bungalow, I see Rose in the window, wearing a bikini. And I remember why I'm here. Why I crashed through the Amazon and have fought so damn hard to survive despite everything against me.

I'm going to save my best friend.

So I put on my old lady reading glasses and roll my cart forward and knock on the door.

"*¿Quién es?*" Someone calls through the door. *Who's there?*

Oh fuck. My mind goes blank and I scramble through a bunch of high school Spanish, looking for the right word for "housekeeping." I eventually settle upon "¿*Limpieza?*" and I have no idea if it's right or not.

My tremulous question must have seemed innocent enough, because the door opens, and there's Duval with a phone at his ear. He nods at me to come in, and then stalks away. Over his shoulder, he calls something at me in Spanish and I catch the word *cocina*. Kitchen. Right. I nod and wheel my cart toward the small kitchen at the back of the bungalow. My heart's hammering a mile a minute, but I get out sponges and towels like this is no big deal.

As I walk into the kitchen, Fouquet saunters away with a sandwich, dripping crumbs on the floor. He doesn't even look in my direction. I'm truly invisible, which is almost hilarious. Too bad my heart's beating way too fast for me to appreciate this.

The kitchen's an absolute fucking disaster. I should have guessed, since Rose is my roomie back home and she's a major slob. There's a blender on the counter and it's coated with the remnants of mixed drinks. Dishes are piled high in the sink, and there's spilled crap all over the counters, along with empty tumblers, napkins, and bottles and bottles of liquor. It's like they've been partying.

The sight of it fills me with helpless rage. While Rafe and I were trying to survive, they were sitting in this cozy bungalow, eating tons of food and mixed drinks and plotting how to take us out? Dicks. I worry about Rose. Is she going along with things because that will keep them from hurting her? It's possible, but I eye the blender, an inch of what looks like strawberry daiquiri at the bottom. That's her favorite mixed drink.

Surely she's not partying with these assholes. Not while I'm being forced to mule to save her life? Not while I've been shot at, had my wrist sprained, been downed in a plane, harassed, slapped around, and kidnapped by the other team?

No, she had to be playing it cool. My friend wouldn't do that to me. She wouldn't.

So I set to work cleaning the kitchen. I'm going to be in here longer than I anticipated, and I know Rafe and Bennito are waiting outside, but what can I do? Duval and Fouquet asked me to clean up the kitchen, and they'll be suspicious if I don't. So I clean. I wipe down the counters, throw away trash, clean out the blender, and fill the dishwasher. The floor's a mess but I give it a cursory swipe with my sponge, hoping they won't notice that I'm doing a shitty job. Actually, nobody's noticing me at all. Rose is sitting out on the porch, Fouquet is in the other room, and I can hear Duval in the front, talking on his phone. I slowly take a knife out of the silverware drawer and tuck it under a few towels. I feel better with it there, even if I know that if it comes to a knife fight, I'm fucked.

I finish with the kitchen and head to one of the bathrooms. It's equally gross in here, but I clean it up quickly, and then move farther down the hall. It's the bedroom. My heart speeds up again. Fouquet's in there. Sucking in a breath, I knock on the door and repeat, "*¿Limpieza?*"

The door opens a moment later and Fouquet comes out with a magazine. "*Gracias,*" he mumbles, and then heads out onto the sunporch with Rose. I wheel my cart into the room and begin to "clean." I want to head for the lamp first, but I feel like that will be too obvious, so I pick up dirty clothes off the floor and fold towels and try to be casual. When I head to the bed, I tuck in corners, moving ever so slowly to the lamp.

Then, I glance around. No one's looking my way. No one's even at this end of the house. Carefully, I unplug the lamp and then pick it up. The base unscrews easily and something weighty drops into my hand. I reattach the base and move to the window with the hard drive, then drop it carefully into the grass. Then, I resume making the bed.

I've just about finished when Rose walks in, a sarong around her hips. "Hey, we need more towels," she says, and then pauses when I jerk up. Her eyes widen and her voice lowers. "Ava?"

Shit. Count on her to recognize me despite my disguise. I put a finger to my lips and point at the door.

She shuts it, and rushes over to me. Her arms wrap around me tightly. "Oh my God, Ava, I thought you were dead. You're alive!"

The tears that wet the shoulder of my uniform are genuine, and I hug her back, so relieved to see her. Rose looks beautiful, as always, lean and golden and so pretty it makes me ache to look at her. "Shhh," I tell her softly. "We have to keep it quiet. They can't know I'm here."

She pulls away, her eyes stunningly blue and wet. "What? Why?"

"Long story," I say. "The plane went down but we somehow survived. I think we landed in a tree." I hold up my gloved wrist. "I hurt this."

She gasps as if the world has ended. "Your modeling jobs. Oh no!"

Like modeling has even been on my mind lately. I shake my head and grip her hand in my good one. "Enough about me, Rose. What's going on? Are you okay? Are they hurting you?"

If they've hurt Rose at all, I want Mendoza to shoot their nads off before he kills them. My hands squeezes hers tightly.

Her brows draw together and she looks prettily confused. "Hurt me? Why? Louis took me on vacation since I was stressed." She tilts her head at me. "Ava, what's going on? Why are you cleaning our room?" She frowns at my appearance. "Your face looks like hell. What did you do to your eyebrows? And—"

I shake my head. Rose, bless her heart, is the sweetest soul, but she's about as deep as a mud puddle. "I don't care about my appearance right now. Look, we have to get you out of here."

"Get me out? Why?" She blinks at me. "I'm on vacation, Ava. Why would I leave? Louis says when he finishes with his business we're going to spend more time on the beach."

Has my friend lost her senses? "Rose. You're not on vacation. They're holding you hostage."

She frowns, her brows drawing together, and then her face smooths out. "Don't. You'll make me wrinkle and my career will be over."

"I'm serious, Rose. You think I'm working for them because I want to? They told me if I don't, they'll kill you."

Her full lips part. "But . . ." Her jaw trembles, and I see it's finally sinking in that something about this is not right. "Louis told me he was paying you to do this for him."

"Paying me?" I hiss the words out. "Are you serious? Rose, he told me if I didn't, he was going to kill you. Why else would I do something so illegal?"

"I don't know." She stomps her sandal-clad foot. Tears threaten her eyes again. "I don't know anything! No one tells me what's going on! Why would Louis say he's going to kill me? He says he loves me."

"They're trying to shake down criminal organizations, Rose," I tell her softly. God, why is she so blind when it comes to men? Louis isn't the first loser she's dated, but he's definitely the worst. "And people are coming after them. The government, too. The men that saved me? They're mercenaries. Hit men. And they want the information that Duval has." I grip her arms. "Please, Rosie. Listen to me when I say that things are really bad, okay?"

She nods, her big blue eyes trusting and awash with tears. That's the problem with Rose. She's so damn trusting. It's like she's terrified of thinking for herself. Even at home, I'm the leader.

I rub her arm, trying to encourage her. "It's going to be okay." I look around, back at the window that I just tossed the drive out of. We can sneak out that way. "We're going to get out of here, and Rafe is going to take care of us, okay?"

"O-okay." She sniffs bravely.

"It's going to be fine, I promise." I look around the room, then nod at a chair against the wall. "Let's prop that against the door to keep them out." It could buy us a few seconds at least.

But Rose has been gone too long, and I've been in here too long to not draw suspicion. The moment I turn toward the chair, the door opens.

It's Duval, and he's got a gun in his hand. "Neither of you are going anywhere."

Fuck. Immediately, I step in front of Rose, spreading my arms to shield her.

"Louis," she weeps. "Is all this true?" She clings to the back of my dress, and her sniffles are turning into full-fledged sobs.

"Come away from her, Rose," he says in a low voice.

I tense, because I don't know what my friend is going to do. We've been friends since grade school, but . . . Rose is stupid when it comes to men.

She cringes behind me and bawls a bit louder. "N-no. I thought you loved me."

His lip curls. He doesn't even bother to answer, just flicks his gun at me. "Move aside."

I don't move. I can call for Rafe, but then what happens to me and Rose? The moment I scream, he's going to shoot. I can see it on his face. "Let Rose go and I'll stay with you," I bargain.

"You're both too much trouble," he says, and gestures at me with the gun again. "Step away from each other."

I watch his gaze go to the lamp. I move closer to it, because if he figures out that the information is missing, things are going to get ugly.

His eyes narrow even as I do. "How did you know?"

"How did I know what?" I bluff.

"Where the information is hidden?" He flicks the safety off. "You have one chance to answer me."

"I don't know anything about the information," I answer honestly. "I'm the only one that could fit in the maid costume." Staring down the barrel of the gun is making me rather nervous, and Rose keeps cringing behind me and sobbing. It's distracting the crap out of me. I know she can't stop, but I also can't think. "I'm just fucking the guy that sent me in. I don't want your information. I just want my friend back."

"Fine. Give me the information right now and I'll give her to you." Duval waves the gun at me again. "You can both leave if you hand over the information."

I pause. "Just like that?"

"Just like that," he echoes. "I'm guessing you stole it from this room."

Well, he'd have guessed right. I force myself not to look over at the window, to give away where it's gone. "I . . . don't have it any longer."

"That's what I thought," Duval says and raises the gun.

Rose screams, stumbling into Duval. It all happens so fast

that I don't feel it at first. It's just the quiet *pffffft* of the gun with the silencer, the hiss of air, and then my entire shoulder burns with a flare of pain.

The motherfucker shot me.

I slide to the ground in shock, and Rose sobs even louder.

"Shut the fuck up," Duval says, pushing her to the ground. "You spoiled my shot."

"You killed my friend," Rose weeps over me. At his words, I realize she saved me or he would have shot me in the heart or the head, but she rammed into him and his bullet missed his target. Her hands flick over my hair, my chest, and I realize they're wet with sticky blood. My blood. Oh shit. My entire shoulder hurts, my chest hurts, and it hurts to breathe.

And . . . I'm pretty sure I'm going to pass out.

Or I'm dying. God, I hope I'm not dying.

My hands go to my shoulder. Everything hurts and I gasp for breath, each lungful sending stabbing pain through me.

"Ava," Rose cries. In my fading vision, she looks up at Duval and snarls, "You're a monster. I hate you."

"And I don't need you any longer," he says. "It's clear we've been holding the wrong girl to bargain with."

And he holds the gun up and shoots her. Right in the head. Rose's body recoils and then she slumps over me, utterly silent.

And I can't even scream, because the world has gone black.

# CHAPTER THIRTY

## RAFAEL

The unmistakable sound of a discharged gun grabs me by the balls and shakes me. I push Bennito aside and race to the patio of the bungalow. The four guards turn to me with raised guns. So much for stealth.

I grab the first one and slit his throat and drive forward, using the guard's body as a shield. I double tap my Walther PPK into the foreheads of the two others. The fourth ducks and my bullet whizzes over his head.

I push the dead weight of the guard aside and kick the table over and duck behind it. The bullet from the fourth guard strikes the top, and shards of the glass rain down on me.

But I don't stop. I leap over the table, shooting toward his gun and then his head. His body jerks back when I land on top of him.

Digging my knees into his shoulders to hold him steady, I wrench his head to the left and snap his spinal cord.

I grab his gun and spin on my foot to shoot a hole in the French doors. The bullet cracks between the frame, and I waste no time throwing a chair through the fracturing glass. I dive through the jagged opening, uncaring that sharp edges gouge my arms and back. Inside are three more guards. My side is singed by a passing bullet, but I manage to roll out of the way behind a large wooden cabinet before my body takes any more damage.

The three guards fire on the cabinet, and wood slivers blow by my face. The cabinet, however, must be made of inch-thick wood, because I can't move the damn thing but the bullets aren't hitting me, either. My cover won't hold long.

I lean around the side, shooting twice for cover, to take stock of my situation. There is a dining room table, six chairs, and this giant wooden monolith. Beyond the dining room is the living area with a sofa and two side chairs flanking a television. Two of the men must be hunkered down behind the sofa. The third has crept into the dining room. His bad luck, because I pick him off.

A crunch on the glass outside has me spinning around but it's just Norse. I hold up two fingers and jerk my head toward the sofa.

He motions that he'll cover me and I surge forward. The two men rise when they hear me but either I or Norse pick them both off.

The outer rooms are completely empty.

None of the bodies are Fouquet or Duval.

I turn toward Norse and gesture my gun toward the closed bedroom door. There's no sound in there at all. The silence is ominous. Norse positions himself on the left side as I kick the door open.

Duval is shoving things into a bag set on the side of the bed. He raises his gun toward us but Norse has a bullet in his shoulder before Duval can even pull the trigger. Duval gets two shots off. I dive for the floor, sliding across the slick surface. I rise on a knee and shoot twice more in the gut. The gun falls from Duval's hand and he slides down the wall, leaving a slick trail of blood behind. His dead eyes stare at me.

At the foot of the bed lies a thin blond-haired woman slumped over another body—Ava!

Fuck.

There is so much blood. It's a river, staining the bamboo flooring and flowing away from the two bodies.

I scramble forward and lift Rose off and place her on the bed. Norse comes over.

"Dead," he says but I barely hear him. Ava's eyes are closed but fluttering and there's a slight rise and fall to her chest. *She's* alive. Relief makes me dizzy and I clutch her tighter to me. She whimpers in an obvious sound of pain.

"Ava. What has he done to you?" The urge to kill Duval again nearly has me on my feet, but Ava needs me now. The blood is soaked into her uniform, turning the blue dress nearly black. I don't know what is from her and what is from Rose. When I roll her to her back, she cries out in pain and I see that she is clutching her shoulder.

"Is that the only place she's shot?" Norse asks, on his knees beside me. I shake my head. He has a pillow from the bed and presses it against the wound. Ava screams at the pressure. With shaking hands, I run them over her body but see no other entry or exit wounds.

"I think that's it," I say, nudging the big blond aside. "See if there's a first aid kit in the bathroom."

"Stop hurting me," Ava cries.

"I'm sorry, baby. We have to stop the bleeding. You've lost a lot of blood." Footsteps behind me have me whirling around, but it's just Norse. He drops the first aid kit in my hands. "Not much there for her."

He's right. There are a few bandages, tape, and a bottle of topical antibacterial ointment, but Ava's going to need more care, particularly if she wants to use her arm in the future.

"Has the jet been chartered?"

"Yeah, there's one at the airport."

"Then let's get the hell out of here. Round every one up. Find us some cars and let's go."

Norse rushes off. With the kit, I have just enough to clean off the wound and bandage it. I babble nonsensical words as she twitches, moans, and weeps under my ministrations. I need a fucking morphine shot for her.

"I'm sorry, baby. This is going to stop hurting. I promise. We're going to get you somewhere safe and take good care of you."

Her breath becomes increasingly shallow and her skin begins to take on an ugly blue cast. Too much blood loss, my panicked mind tells me. This is the result of the curse. I kill those that I love. No matter how many people I try to save, I'm still the bringer of death, the killer of lives. Dread drives me into my mother's native tongue. I plead with her to stay with me. I castigate her for trying to leave me. *You are my life*, I tell her, *my one true love. If you die then I die. Do not die.*

"Yeah don't die," Bennito snarks behind me. "We really need the old man around."

I don't even glare at him for his audacity because I am too busy holding her from the embrace of death.

She moans again, agitated and in pain.

"Do you have a morphine shot?" I ask, trying not to be impatient. Ava's in pain and they need to fucking hurry it up, though.

Bennito shuffles toward me. "Yeah, we've got five needles in Garcia's Boy Scout pack."

Hearing his name is like a dart to my heart. I've lost him but I can't lose Ava.

I bite off the plastic protective cap and jab it into the inside of her arm. She screams at the sudden pain. Bennito winces and I bite my tongue to keep my own cries inside.

From past experience, the morphine shot will give her a couple of hours of relief at the most.

"Are there more supplies on the plane?"

"I think so. Garcia arranged for it."

Of course he did. How I will function with him gone, I don't know. I gather Ava in my arms.

"Let's go. We can be in Miami in under eight hours. What's the status of the other buyers?"

Before Bennito can answer, Norse reappears with Rodrigo behind him. They both have packs on their backs. "We need to evac ASAP," Norse informs me. "The gunfire has attracted attention. If they think Duval is dead, they'll take the information by force."

I table my anguish and worry over Ava's condition. Neither will help her now. I lay her on the dining table and slice off her housekeeping uniform. Norse hands me a sundress. With Bennito's help, we get Ava dressed.

"If we carry her through the lobby, it will garner too much attention. On the other side of the cemetery is a main road. I'll carry Ava through the cemetery. We'll meet you at the end. The airport is only a few blocks from there."

"What will you say if people ask questions?" Bennito says.

"Sunstroke. Go put this gun in Duval's hand. If the resort wants to cover it up, they can call it a murder-suicide."

Ava whimpers as I lift her in my arms. The sound tears in my gut. Steeling myself, I nod to let the men know I'm ready.

"Did you get everything, Bennito?"

"Yeah, the real receiver was under the window, and I put a dummy receiver back into the lamp. That might stall the buyers."

"Good."

I set off on a light jog trying to hold her against my chest as steadily as I can, but each step brings her pain. Her moans and tears that track down her face are worse than any knife wound or bullet that I've ever endured. I whisper encouragement to her. "After this you will be able to survive anything—earthquakes, tornadoes, you name it. You've been thrown in the fire and you've been polished into the sharpest, strongest steel."

She doesn't respond coherently and halfway there she finally passes out. With a prayer upward, I give thanks because I couldn't withstand another step of her painful sounds.

I've lost people that I care about, and Garcia's death would leave an opening in my heart that would never heal. But Ava is different. Her loss would be the end of me.

There was one older couple that came to the Tears of God favela years ago. He was old and his wife was dying. He wanted to ease her suffering. He knew, and so did she, that there was no hope of recovery, and they sought only palliative medication so that her death was easy.

He was in perfect health but the night that she died, he lay beside her, holding her hand, and his heart went with her. We found them both the following morning, clutched together, passing into the next life in the only way that they would have wanted.

I suspect that is what mine would do should she die. My heart would go with hers. But she is not going to die. A gunshot wound to her shoulder that passed through from front to back will not kill her. An infection and complications from the wounds would kill her but not the gunshot itself. We have a small hospital on the island. People who are involved in dangerous things need to know how to repair their bodies without alerting authorities. We will fly to Miami, refuel, and then to the island—we should be there in ten hours. I can keep her alive for ten hours.

We run past small concrete altars and granite headstones. Some areas are well tended and others are worn and covered in weeds and dirt. Her head lolls against my shoulder as I move swiftly through the graveyard.

Death's not taking us today.

A blur of motion on my left has me dropping to my knees. *Fouquet.* I release my precious bundle and crouch in front of her. I haven't come this far to die at this man's hands.

I charge him before he can shoot. His first bullet hits the ground and the next one pings off a granite headstone. No wonder he uses his fists. He's a god-awful shot. I plow into him, taking him to the ground. He manages to hang on to the gun, which he pounds ineffectually into my back. I grind a knee into his shoulder and slam one meaty fist into his face. And then another and another until he's comatose underneath me. I pick up the gun that has fallen out of his hands and shoot him in the head and the heart. I'm not leaving anyone behind that can come after us.

Running back to Ava, I gather her up again.

"The Jeep is ahead of us. We're going to make it," I tell her. My arms ache and my legs feel like jelly, but I push us forward. Norse drives the Jeep off the road and meets us halfway.

"What happened to you?" he asks, helping me into the back-seat. Bennito slides over to make room.

"Fouquet." I lift Ava up and Bennito reaches over to help me settle her.

"Do I need to go back?"

"No, he's dead." I shut the door and point forward. "Let's go."

We make it to the Captain David Abenzur Rengifo International Airport in short time. Guards patrol the exterior with their semiautomatic weapons slung over their backs. We're not dripping with blood, but we don't look exactly reputable. I'm beat up. Ava's shoulder is bandaged and she's slipping in and out of consciousness.

"I have a shot of adrenaline," Bennito offers.

"It's too dangerous. She'll have to try to walk." I prop Ava up. "Baby, I need you to walk through the terminal. It's a very short trip. I'll be on one side and Bennito on the other. All you need to do is to move your feet."

"I can't do it," she whimpers. "The pain is too much."

Even Bennito flinches at the anguished sound.

"I know, baby, I know. But we need to get you out of here. We're almost home where it's safe. You just need to stay upright for a hundred yards. I know you can do that. I know it."

She rolls her head to the side and looks out the window. I have no idea whether she is seeing the squat glass and metal building or whether it's just a haze of pain.

"I can try," she says finally.

"That's my girl." At those words, everyone is out of the Jeep and we head toward the entrance. A guard looks our way. I can see the men hesitate but pausing means guilt. "Go," I order harshly, and everyone begins to move again. The guard takes another step and then another.

We keep moving.

He takes one more step and I see Norse reach inside his loose nylon jacket.

"*El compañero*," another guard calls out. The man hesitates but we keep walking forward. When his friend calls for him again, he gives us one last look and then turns away.

We breathe a sigh of relief and no one stops us.

"Am I going to die?" she whimpers, her hand going to press against her wound as if by touching it, she could will the pain away.

"Of course not." I draw her hand away and clutch it in mine. I don't want her to hurt more, not even from her own touch. "No one is going to hurt you again."

"Where are you taking me? I don't have anywhere to go. Rose is gone." Her voice is hoarse from choking the tears back but she doesn't let them spill, doesn't let them draw undue attention to us.

"My island. Remember I told you about that."

She nods. "Where there's no tears or pain?"

"That's right. I've got people there who will fix you up."

"What about Rose? Did you bury her? She shouldn't be left here all alone."

"She's not alone," I tell her. "You were with her when she died. Her best friend. That means something."

"She didn't know what she was getting into," Ava says, and her eyes beg for understanding.

"Of course she didn't."

Ava gasps for breath and sweat is breaking out along her pale forehead. I tighten my grip around her waist. "Why does it hurt so much when I breathe? Are you sure I'm not dying? You wouldn't lie about that, would you?"

"Never. You are shot in the shoulder close to your lung. When you breathe, it pulls on the muscles, tendons, and nerves near your heart."

The explanation seems to calm her. "I'm being a huge baby, aren't I? You got stabbed and you didn't say a thing."

"It's different," I tell her.

She nods drowsily. "I got into modeling because of Rose. I wasn't good enough to be on the cover of any magazine or walk the runway."

"Then those people don't know what they are doing, because you are more beautiful than anyone I've seen on a magazine cover."

She gives me a weak smile. "Models are a different beautiful. They have to have angles and planes that look good under lights and makeup. They are unusual and striking. Like Rose. It's a different sort of beautiful." Her breath comes in short, agitated pants. "Rose got me the modeling jobs," she repeats.

Over her head, Bennito gives me a worried look. Ava is beginning to sound a bit delirious. She's lost in her past. Maybe it is the pain, maybe it is grief, but her legs are moving and we are almost there. I can see the private lounge ahead of us.

"Stay strong for Rose," I tell her. "The mind can fuel you in miraculous ways."

It's why I'm still alive. I have refused to die no matter how many times the reaper has been at my feet, waving his scythe. He might be here now. Ava might be seeing him but I won't let him take her.

Ava's beautiful face is contorted with pain.

"You're going to make it. Tell me more about Rose," I order.

Ava bites her lips but nods. So strong. So brave. "Rose wanted to be a model and I had no one at home so when she moved to New York City, I went with her. She took me to the modeling agency but I wasn't the right look. Too . . . big." She looks down at her magnificent rack. Stupid modeling agency. "But Rose kept bringing me along until one day I went to the bathroom while Rose was at a job and as I was washing my hands, a woman next to me couldn't stop looking at them. When I went to place them under the dryer she stopped me and pulled out a handkerchief and began to dry my hands off. It was the strangest thing. I thought she might have a fetish and want me to give her a hand job in the bathroom but she told me I had the most lovely hands and wondered if I had done modeling in the past.

"Of course I hadn't. I signed with the agency and with Rose's help, I ended up doing jobs all over the world using my hands." She lifts them up and we all look at them. They are elegant. She is long fingered and her palms are slender. Where most people have wrinkly knuckles, hers are smooth and perfect but her once-unmarred hands have scratches on their backs. There are several scabs from open wounds, and her nail beds are torn. Her right hand is purple and green.

"What will I do now?" she asks, and this time her pain is from longing and despair instead of from her shoulder. "I'm all alone."

"No," I answer more harshly than I intend. "You aren't alone, and you will never be alone again."

Each step toward the lounge is more painful and as she begins to sob, I know I can't make her walk another inch. I sweep her into my arms and stride into the lounge.

"Sir, is there a problem?"

"No, my friend is deathly afraid of flying. She had a little too much to drink in order to survive the flight. We just need to get up in the air and get going."

"Very well." He looks at us questioningly but does not stop us. Norse signs in and then moves off to alert the pilot.

We are not dressed like anyone else in the lounge. There are at least five groups—three of which are businessmen and two who appear to be travelers. The businessmen look at us suspiciously, and I wonder if any of these men are buyers for Duval.

I tuck Ava into a corner chair and Bennito runs off to get Ava some water. Rodrigo stands and appears to stare out the window, but I know he's watching the occupants in the reflection.

Before any trouble starts, Norse appears. "We're ready."

I can tell by Ava's pale face that the prospect of rising from her seat and walking across the tarmac is daunting. I scoop her up into my arms and walk out, uncaring what the other occupants might think. Our plane is leaving no matter what. We exit the lounge and walk into the humid afternoon air and then up the stairs into the plane.

"So rich you have your own plane," she jokes as I settle her into a seat. Fuck the federal regulations regarding air traffic. I reach beside her and press the buttons that recline the seat to a flat bed, and then cover her up with as many blankets as we can find.

"Nah, just rent it." I turn to Norse. "Any IVs?"

"Got it right here." He strings two up and hangs them next to the seat. "One's a morphine drip and the other's an antibiotic."

Within a couple of minutes we have the IVs pumping liquids into her and leads attached to her heart and a finger to monitor her vital signs.

"We spent all our cash to buy an island. Now we have to go out and make some more," I tell her.

"Is that what this is all about?"

"In part. They have one of ours. Kind of like they held Rose for you."

"Do you know if he's still alive?"

"Yeah, the people we're working for wouldn't kill him. He's too valuable an asset. They spent a lot of money to make him into what he is today." Her eyes droop as the morphine takes hold. "Get some sleep. Your body needs it. We'll talk when you're feeling better."

She barely nods. Beneath me, I can feel the rumble of the engines as the plane starts to move. "Norse, you monitor the feeds and, Bennito, I want you to start cracking the USB stack. We need to know what's on there."

I settle into my seat across from Ava and place my hand on her arm. I need the contact even if she doesn't.

"What are we going to do with her after she's better?" Norse asks.

"I'll cross that bridge when I come to it." A girl who lives the high-flying life of a model, even that of a hand model, wouldn't be interested in hiding herself away in my small island, no matter how idyllic it is. And we don't have the money to rent the plane to fly into Miami every time she has the yen for some social life. But there's a lot of time to think about the future. For now, I need to sleep. Forcing myself to rest, I don't even realize we are in Miami until the plane touches down.

Ava is still asleep when I sit up, shaking the cobwebs out of my head.

"I need you to come and look at this," Bennito says as soon as he notices I'm awake. The tone in his voice has me worried, and I'm not sure whether it's the harsh glare of the interior of the airplane or whether he has really lost all color in his face, but he looks like shit.

"Bad news, is it?"

"Pretty much the worst."

He slides the screen around so I can look at it. Norse and Rodrigo crowd behind me.

The emails and phone conversations that have been recorded and transcribed are no ordinary ones. The information on Bennito's screen is a collection of names and heads of state. Not just from the U.S. but from everywhere. The information reveals for the last ten years the payments governments have made to various insurgent groups to kill off political rivals, spies, and what I presume to be inconvenient lovers by the female names on the list. It's a hit list. A dirty, worldwide hit list.

"I kind of wish you weren't as good at encryption as you are," I tell Bennito.

"Shit, I know. But this was child's play. A fifth-grade coder could have cracked this." Bennito jabs the screen with his finger.

"Duval must've thought that he was invincible. But why?" Norse muses.

"Stupid is as stupid does. He's French and they always have a flair for the dramatic."

Bennito lifts the receiver. "Do we want to keep a copy of it?"

"No. If it's known that we have a copy, we will become targets. The only way we stay safe is by making sure that people fear us. But we can't have them always knocking down our door trying to kill us because we know too much." I take the receiver and place it in a small nylon bag that holds the USB sticks.

Everyone looks relieved that I'm taking responsibility. It's a ticking time bomb, and I think if I had opened an escape hatch and dropped the information out of the plane, they would've been just as happy. I hate spy games. It's one thing to kill a man. Lots of men need killing. I certainly don't mind protecting them in trying to keep people alive, either. But with secrets like these? There's always someone who's willing to kill to obtain them and to make sure they never see the light of day. Information like that can only harm you. *But it can also keep you safe*, a voice whispers at the back of my head.

When the pilot comes back to tell us that the refueling is done, we all breathe a sigh of relief.

"Break out the cards, boys, we're almost home," I say and then turn back to the still-resting Ava. Even though she is asleep, I begin to tell her about everything that she can expect. The palm trees, the fresh fruit we've planted, the windmill that we've set up to harness clean energy. I tell her that the island is thick with lonely men and that if she had lots of model girlfriends, we could set up a love connection. Norse snorts at this but doesn't voice any objections.

A small smile touches her lips as if she can sense, even in her unconscious state, that the mood is lightening.

# CHAPTER **THIRTY-ONE**

## AVA

I'm having all kinds of messed-up dreams. I know they're dreams, but it doesn't matter because my brain is determined to stay in them. Rose holds my hand and we sit on the beach, our toes in the sand.

"I met a guy," she tells me.

"Me too," I say, and her fingers are warm against mine. "He's amazing. The most wonderful guy I've ever met."

"How?" she asks. "What does he do that's so great?"

"He's protective and kind and funny. He's sexy and he's got a big dick."

"Big dicks are important."

"But so is being kind. And he's treated me so good. Better than I've ever been treated." I think about Rafe and the way he touches me, like I'm gold. Then I add, "He gives me good orgasms. That's important, too."

"It is important," Rose says solemnly. "You should marry him."

I laugh, high and wild, because in my dream, apparently I have a crazy laugh. "He doesn't want to marry me. He doesn't even think we should have sex." This makes me sad, and I begin to cry. I love Rafe, and he doesn't want me.

"Everyone should have sex," Rose says, her voice dreamlike. "It's how we connect."

"Sometimes I think he doesn't want to connect to me." I stare unhappily out at the ocean. In the distance, a gigantic dinosaur— no, Godzilla—stomps past, moving through the waves. "There he goes."

"Is that your boyfriend?"

"Yeah."

"He seems nice," Rose says, and she squeezes my hand again. "The guy I met isn't so nice."

"What are you going to do?" I ask, because it worries me to hear her say that. Her eyes are filling with tears and she looks so sad.

"Oh, Ava," she says, and gives my hand a little shake. "Ava. Ava. Ava. Wake up. I've always done what I wanted."

And then she's leaving, walking out into the water, and Godzilla's getting more and more distant. Everyone's leaving me, and I cry harder. My hand keeps shaking.

"Ava. Ava, baby." My hand shakes again, and I look down to see a crab's gotten ahold of it. I shake it again. "Wake up," the crab tells me, and it's got Rafe's voice.

My eyes flutter open, and I blink slowly. The room is dark, and the bed underneath me is soft. There's a window and mini-blinds off to one side, and sunlight filters through. Someone's holding my hand off to the side of the bed. I turn and look, and see Rafe's gorgeous face. I lick my lips. "Hey."

"You were having a nightmare, baby," he says, and squeezes my hand. "I'm sorry I woke you up, but you were crying."

"You were leaving me," I murmur, still groggy. "Everyone's leaving me."

"It's the morphine. You're just having crazy dreams."

"Don't leave me, too," I tell him.

"I won't, baby. You're mine."

"I like that," I tell him sleepily. "I'm going back to bed now."

He chuckles softly. "Okay, Ava. I'll be right here." He gives my hand another squeeze, and I slide back into unconsciousness.

When I wake up again some time later, I have to pee, my shoulder is killing me, and my mouth feels like the desert. My hand is gently held in Rafe's, and his head's resting against my leg, dozing in his chair as he holds on to me. His dark curls are everywhere, jaw unshaven, and it looks like he hasn't left my bedside. It's a good look for him, and I just stare with a sigh of pleasure. I could look at him forever.

But then my bladder insists otherwise. I squeeze his hand to wake him up, and he jumps to alertness, jerking upright. "Hi," I say softly.

His eyes warm as he looks at me. "Hey, baby."

I get goose bumps just with how he says the casual nickname. "I need to use the bathroom."

He helps me get out of bed and I shrug him off to go take care of things, and when I leave the bathroom, he insists I get back into bed. I do, though I'm mostly feeling fine, just tired and achy. Well, that and my shoulder is crap. It doesn't feel right to relax, though. Something's wrong. "Where are we?"

"My island. Tears of God." He moves to my side and tucks the blanket gently around me. "How do you feel?"

"Poopy," I tell him. As if he can sense my thirst, he gets a pitcher from the bedside, pours me a glass of water, and then holds it to my mouth. I reach for it, only to notice that my bad wrist is now wrapped in a bandage, and my pinky has been given an official splint. He helps me drink and I lie back on the pillows again, feeling weak. Memories flick through my mind, of Duval and Rose. "I guess I fucked things up, huh?" I'm trying to be all casual about it, but to my horror, tears flood my eyes.

"Oh, baby, no," he murmurs. His hand touches my good one and he strokes it, caressing me, rubbing my arm. Just touching me everywhere he can. "You did great. Things just went wrong. It happens."

Things went wrong, and now Rose is dead. I went through hell to try to save her. I risked my life for hers, and all the while, she had no clue I was in danger. She was only truly at risk when I showed up. I remember her scream and her falling over me as Duval shot her.

"I couldn't save her," I whisper. My face crumples and I begin to sob.

"I know, baby. I know." He sits on the bed and pulls me against him gently.

Of course he knows. His best friend died, too. I cling to him, weeping. I'm an ugly crier, and I blubber against his chest for what feels like forever, wetting it with miserable tears and snot and unhappiness.

I killed my best friend. I let her die.

"You couldn't protect her, baby. She chose her path." His hands smooth up and down my back, soothing me. "You did your best. We all do our best. Sometimes it's just not enough."

There's pain in his voice, too, and I know he's feeling what I do. He's thinking about Garcia even as I cry over Rose. Eventually, my sobs turn into hiccups, and Rafe holds me against his chest, rocking me, soothing me.

I feel so safe with him. I never want to leave the circle of his arms, ever.

I fall asleep again in Rafe's arms and wake up later that night. They've stopped giving me morphine and switched it to some heavy-duty Tylenol, which means I'm hurting and cranky, but at least I'm not having weird dreams. Rafe insists on me staying in bed and spoon-feeds me soup like I'm an invalid. I'm torn between thinking it's sweet and wanting to knock the spoon out of his hand.

But then after dinner, he climbs into bed with me and we cuddle, and I forgive everything. His hand trails through my hair and his fingers move down my arm, and we don't talk. We just touch and enjoy each other. He's got me cradled at the perfect spot, tucked under his chin, and if it makes my wounded shoulder hurt a little, I don't care.

Eventually, though, life intrudes. It always does. "I have to go to Virginia," Rafe tells me in a low voice. "To deliver the information and get my man back."

I knew this was coming, but I still cling to Rafe, unhappy at the thought of him leaving me. "When?"

He hesitates. "Soon. I wanted to make sure you were okay first."

Which means he's probably overdue and everyone's antsy. My stomach knots with worry. "What happens now?"

Rafe's silent. He's silent for so long that tears prick my eyes again. I'm just a weepy, blubbery mess lately. I know he's trying to think of the best way to get rid of me, though. I think of his words before I went into the bungalow. *Let's just get through today.*

Well, that day's over and we're out the other side. Not a lot of use for a hand model with ugly hands. I bury my face against his neck and start crying again.

"I know," he says, and his hands stroke down my arm again. "Bennito . . . he'll take you home. You just let him know when you're ready and he'll charter the plane for you, okay?"

"Sure," I say in a wobbly voice.

"There's no place for you here, Ava." He sounds desperate for me to understand. "The island's not like life in the city. You'd be bored in a month."

"No, it's fine," I tell him, trying to blink away my tears. I know what he's saying. *There's no place for you at my side.* I've been broken up with lots of times, but it's never hurt like Rafe's pushing me away does. I thought he was different. I thought we had a real connection.

I thought he loved me like I loved him.

I guess that's just me being gullible all over again. I thought I could save my best friend. I thought I could get the guy.

Turns out I don't get anything.


Rafe leaves that night, and our kiss good-bye seems to last for an hour. His mouth is possessive over mine, devouring, and fills me with aching sadness knowing that this is going to be our last one. When he finally gives my nose a gentle kiss and then leaves, this time for good, I hold it together until he leaves the room. Then, I curl up in my sorry bed and cry my eyes out.

They're puffy and itchy the next morning, but I've never been prized for my eyes anyhow. I force myself to get out of bed and shower. There are a few stitches in my shoulder and some on my back. The wound doesn't look nearly as awful as it feels. It's all bruised to hell, though. I wash carefully, which reminds me of Rafe and the sponge bath I gave him, and I start crying all over again.

I dress in an old shirt and cargo shorts that are too big for me and peer out the window of my room. I haven't been anywhere since I got to the island. The room I'm in looks kind of like a hotel room, and I have a view of the beach not too far away. It's gorgeous, and I want to see it before I leave. I figure I might as well.

Bennito flags me down and offers me a few slices of what looks and smells like banana bread. "*Cuca de banana*," he tells me with a grin. "We're not in Brazil anymore, but we still eat like we are." He gives me a cup of something called *pingado* that tastes like extra-milky latte. I wolf the food down and sit with him in the little kitchenette.

"What is this place?" I ask him.

"It's an old hotel. Was a cover for a gunrunner paradise back in the day, but now we just use it as base and let people set up shop here for a few until they can make a home on the island for themselves."

I nod, not really caring. I won't be here to see Rafe again, so it doesn't matter. "I want to go to the beach."

"You sure?" His brows draw together and he crosses his arms. "Rafe says you're still weak."

I dust off my sleeve with my good hand, freeing crumbs. "Rafe's not here and I want to see the ocean before I leave."

"Fair enough, you just lemme know."

I nod and leave the kitchenette, heading for the ocean in the distance. I know he's watching me still—and will probably report back to Rafe, but I don't care.

I remember the ocean from my dream with Rose, and I need to go sit in the sand and think.

It takes forever for me to make it the couple of hundred yards to the shore, and by the time I do, I'm exhausted. I stagger weakly to the sand and sit at the edge of the waves. I tuck my cast against my chest to keep it from getting wet, and I stare out at the ocean as the water moves over my feet.

Rose is gone.

I think of going back to New York and our apartment. Our friends, who are more her friends than mine. Our jobs, which are more her jobs than mine. I spread my fingers and stare down at my hands. They look like hell. There are bug bites and dark red stains from burns. Scratches cover my skin, and my nails are ragged and still have rings of dirt under them. My pinky is splinted and my wrist is in a cast. Hand modeling's an iffy job, and I'll be out of it for a long time. I'm not a jet-setter like Rose was. She'd go off to Paris and Milan to walk the runways. I'd go to the QVC headquarters and hold a shoe for six hours.

I'm lost. Not just because Rose is gone and my hands are shit. I'm lost without Rafe. I need him to tell me everything's going to be okay and to kiss my worries away. I think maybe that's one reason why I thought we were so good for each other. I'm confident in all the ways that he's not, and he's take-charge where I hesitate.

I wish he could see that we belong together.

The stupid tears start again, and I wipe my eyes, then groan because I'm getting salt water in them. I grab the corner of my shirt and dab at my stinging eyeballs, mentally cussing.

When I look up, a woman's coming down the beach toward me.

I think about getting up and leaving, but I'm so tired. I just want to sit here for a while longer and let the water relax me. So I wiggle my toes in the sand and pretend I don't see her. I'm not here to bother anyone. I just want to be left alone until I have to leave.

To my surprise, she comes and sits next to me. "You the boss's lady?" she asks me in accented English.

I look over at her. She's beautiful with the gorgeous Brazilian coloring I admire. Dark hair, bronze skin, and hazel eyes. She's also got a wicked scar slashing across one cheek to the next, as if someone cut her mouth open lengthwise and it was sewn up again.

"Who's the boss?" I ask.

"Mendoza. I heard his lady was brought to the island." She nods at me and crosses her legs, her feet not quite hitting the surf. "You her?"

"I don't know. Why?" What's this woman want?

She looks at me. "My daughter's pregnant. She's thirteen. Couple of other girls are pregnant, too. We need a midwife here."

My eyes widen and I raise my hands. "Wait, hold up, I'm not a midwife—"

She laughs and gives a slight roll of her eyes. "I know. But you're his lady. He'll listen to you. We want you to go talk to him for us."

"Why . . ." I lick my lips, thinking carefully. This seems important and I don't want to mess it up. "Why don't you go to him yourself and ask?"

This time, she's the one that doesn't make eye contact. When she answers, her voice is small. "We're safe here, but we're still scared. It's hard to go to a man and ask for things. There's no woman we can come to and talk to."

Oh. It dawns on me. This is an island run by mercenaries, trying to make a better living for everyone that comes to them, but there are some things you can't ask a guy when you're a girl. Especially if you're a girl that's been abused in the past. "Is there . . . no midwife here? At all? No woman in charge? No female medical doctor?"

"No. And we need things. Pills. Diapers." She eyes me. "Better tampons."

I wince. "Let me guess. They're men, so they buy what's cheapest and not the stuff with the good applicators."

She gestures at me as if to say *now you get it*. "You ever try to have a tampon conversation with a soldier?"

A reluctant giggle escapes me. "I guess that's difficult."

"Real difficult when you're someone like me." Her mouth trembles. "It was hard to come out here. To see you. I had to wait until you were alone."

I soften. "Rafe's a good guy. He would listen. I promise."

"I know," she says simply. "But sometimes it's easier to come to a woman."

We talk for another hour or two, sitting in the sand. Her name is Fernanda, and she worked at a brothel for over ten years before the men shut it down and rescued everyone and took them to the Tears of God favela. I look at her, and she has to be a year or two younger than me, which is horrifying to think about. That she's been a whore since childhood and has a child that's thirteen. God.

She says there are a lot of teen girls on the island that used to live in brothels. Several of them are mothers, and all of them have been abused. Most of them are terrified of men.

"In the favela, it wasn't so bad," she says. "We could wear our Tears of God symbols and no one would touch us. We could go get things we needed. We could see a midwife that wasn't in the favela or bring her to us. But here on the island, we're isolated. And we're not sure how to ask." She smiles. "That's why we're happy that you're here. That the boss has a lady now. Because we can come to you and talk."

I give Fernanda a soft smile and then look out at the ocean again. "I would stay if he wanted me here. But he doesn't."

"Did he say that?" She looks skeptical. "These men, they're good with guns, but they're not good with women. Maybe you need to tell him why he needs you. Show him what he'd be missing if he let you go."

I think of my dream again. Of Godzilla, pounding away in the distant surf. Not the penis, but the monster from the Japanese movies. I think of my conversation with Rose.

*Oh, Ava. I've always done what I wanted.*

*You should marry him. He seems nice.*

Even in death, Rose is trying to prod me in the right direction. Maybe . . . maybe Rafe's not good with feelings, like he wasn't good with sex. Maybe I do need to show him that he needs me.

Not just because the women on this island need someone to talk to, but because he needs me and I need him.

I lift my chin and look over at Fernanda. "You know what? I think I'm going to stay after all."

"Good," she says. "Tell 'em we need real tampons. Not that cheap cardboard shit."

# CHAPTER THIRTY-TWO

## RAFAEL

Virginia is cold. Living on an island in the Bahamas and traipsing through a Peruvian jungle don't prepare you for the ball-freezing weather of Northern Virginia in October.

"Fucking winter, man," Norse complains as we watch the tourists take pictures of the remnants of the docked Apollo Command Module. The chrome is polished to a mirror finish, but I don't see anything in the surface that tips me off to Davidson's arrival. "I would've joined your little band of mercenaries just to get out of this damn cold."

"Aren't your bones supposed to be made out of ice?"

"If they were, it's all been melted away and replaced with sand and margaritas."

"Sounds uncomfortable." I check my watch. The exchange is

supposed to be happening right now and my government contact is late. "Has Rodrigo checked in yet?" I sent Rodrigo back for what was left of Garcia's body. If it was safe, he could pick up Rose—for Ava's sake. After Duval's death, it looked like Pucallpa emptied out pretty damn quick.

"Not since you asked me five minutes ago," Norse replies with deceptive laziness. He's just as keyed up as I am. The death of Garcia has hit us all hard. I'm anxious and Norse is cracking jokes about his balls, but it's all a disguise for our gut-sick feelings of loss.

A lot of the men that come to the island are there because they want to forget. In the sand and sun, it's easy to pretend that there aren't any worries. Make that *easier.* You can't ever fully let go of the past. All those gaps in your life are carved out by a rough, dull blade, and they don't ever heal over properly.

Norse knows that as well as any. His perfect Viking visage and easy smile masks a hell of a past.

But I keep his secrets as I keep the secrets of everyone who is on the island. It's why Ava doesn't belong there. Her life is wide open, full of pretty things and pretty smiles. She doesn't need— or want—to be surrounded by a bunch of hard-ass mercenaries and run-down whores.

"How do you think Davidson is going to take the news?" Norse asks.

"About Garcia?" Davidson's handler had given us a couple of choices—the National Mall, a coffeehouse near the Pentagon, and an airport hangar. All of those seemed like a perfect place for them to execute us and run off with the goods. I told them the exchange would happen in broad daylight at the Air and Space Museum. We might not have been able to bring in our weapons, but there's no way that they can kill us here without creating a massive unexplainable incident. "About as well as you think."

"Right." He grimaces.

"That's why he doesn't get a gun until we are on our way back."

"Right. You going to tell him about Ava?"

I pin Norse's ears back with a glare. "Not her fault, man. She is responsible for getting us this information. Without it we wouldn't have a donkey's chance in hell of getting Davidson back."

There is no question in my mind that had we failed, Davidson would've gotten a bullet to his brain. Garcia's death is mine alone to own. He was my man and those blows are mine to take, but we'll all mourn him.

"Maybe we should stop in Miami? Get him laid, liquored up before we let him loose on the island."

"Your call." If Ava was waiting for me, I would've said fuck that noise and been on the first plane home. But she's not waiting. I've given Bennito instructions to charter her out of there at her first request—whenever she feels ready. I'm not sure whether I want her to be gone when I get back.

"Don't want to get back home?" Norse eyes me appraisingly.

"Nothing there for me," I manage to lie with a straight face. Truth is, if Ava's gone, I might have to head to New York City. Even if she doesn't want me there, it'd be enough just to be near her. To see her on the street. To watch her from afar and know that she's safe.

She's it for me, even if I'm not it for her.

Norse's raised eyebrow indicates that he doesn't believe me for a second, but the time for more questions is over. "Incoming," I murmur.

Norse straightens and his hand goes into his jacket. We share a grimace when he comes up empty. Not being armed is hard on us.

Davidson looks good. Pale, as if he hasn't seen the sun in three weeks, but he's walking without a limp and has no visible wounds.

On either side of him walk a pair of khaki-clad goons wearing windbreakers. I don't make the mistake of believing that they are unarmed like Norse and me. "The guy on the left is wearing a Nationals hat. He's my contact," I mention quietly to Norse. He nods and slips to the side, making sure that Davidson's two guards have to split up to keep an eye on us.

"Rafe, good to see you." Agent Parker holds out his hand and flashes a wide, fake grin. Parker is a hair under six feet, the top of his head coming up to my eyes. He's a wiry guy—more wrestler than bruiser. He'd be no match for either Davidson or me.

"Good to see you too, *Parker*." His eyes widen in surprise that I know his name. "Yeah, I know your name, the blonde you like seeing on Tuesdays that your wife doesn't know about, and the woman you took to bed last night who is neither blond nor your wife. I might hate spy shit, but you should know that your government came to me because there isn't a mission that exists that I can't carry out, including finding out everything about your punk-ass self down to the fact you like to eat ice cream with a fork."

"That shit is weird," Davidson pipes up from beside Parker.

I grip his outstretched hand and pull him toward me. A couple of hard slaps on the back reveals the holster hanging under his left arm. With a strong arm around his back, I hold him tight against me with one hand and slip the gun out of the holster with the other. Davidson steps close and takes the weapon from me, slipping it under his shirt. I stick the receiver, USB sticks, and the roll of papers into the holster. Davidson steps back, does the hand-off to Parker, and then we're done.

Almost.

When we turn to leave, I don't. I shove Agent Parker backward, a hard steel-booted toe on his soft leather one. He doesn't go far.

"We're going now," I inform him. He gasps like a beached fish, his mouth opening and closing without saying any real words. "You've got what you wanted."

With a nod to Davidson, we start toward the entrance, when Parker grabs my arm. "Did you read the information?"

"We're not paid for that, are we?" He shakes his head. I give him a little pat on the side of his face, the anger toward Garcia's death making me a little reckless. "Then take your motherfucking hand off me before I rip it off."

Davidson waits until we are clear of the museum and at the edge of the National Mall before he asks, "Where's Garcia?"

The bleak expression in his eyes shows he knows already. He is just waiting for confirmation.

"Didn't make it out of Peru," I say brusquely. "We took gunfire in the middle of the night. Sniper had night-vision goggles. We had none." Garcia had planned for every contingency but that one.

"What were you chasing after?"

"A hit list. It's a list of people that heads of state have had killed for the last few years."

"Jesus." Davidson shakes his head. He turns away to stare out at the glass-like surface of the reflection pool. "Don't suppose you'd be okay with me going back and beating the ever-loving shit out of those federal agents?"

"Nope." I wonder what memories Davidson is seeing in the water. The three of us getting shitfaced in Berlin after taking out a terrorist cell or the time when we were in Thailand dragging Garcia out of a lady-boy brothel. Or maybe it was all the way back when we were prisoners in the desert, left to die and determined that if we ever made it to safety, we were going to be the captains of our own destinies. I roll around the last memory I have of Garcia—the one where he tells me of his lost love and that he's ready to be with her again. I offer that small solace to Davidson. "He told me he was ready to go. That the Tears of God held no comfort for him."

Still seemingly mesmerized by the water, Davidson answers, "The girl, right?"

I nod in confirmation but Norse, who doesn't know Garcia's story, interjects, "What girl? Ava?"

"Who's Ava?" Davidson is confused.

"His Ava?" Norse jerks a thumb in my direction.

"Your Ava," he says in disbelief. "Since when do you have an Ava?"

"Picked her up in the jungle," Norse explains. "Old man here can't keep his hands off her."

To my surprise I feel heat on my cheeks at Davidson's sudden inspection. "It's time to go." I start walking toward the Metro stop to flag a cab.

"I'm going to need to know a lot more about this Ava girl," Davidson says as he catches up to me.

"They treat you okay?" I ask, trying desperately to change the subject. "I don't see any wounds."

"It was just boring as hell."

"How'd you get caught anyway?"

"Honeypot." His lips press together. "I was in Georgetown checking out a situation. Coed there seemed like she needed help. I helped her."

"With your dick?" Norse interrupts.

Davidson cups himself crudely. "The best kind of comfort there is. Gets 'em inside and out."

Norse musters up a small laugh. I don't even give a courtesy one, because there's a shitload of pain in Davidson's voice.

A cab pulls up and I direct the driver to Dulles. Norse climbs into the front seat, allowing Davidson and me the back one.

"Where is she now?" I ask quietly as we move out.

"Don't know."

"You going back for her?"

He stares at me. "Maybe."

"To kill her or kidnap her?"

"Can it be both?"

That makes me laugh. "Yeah, shit, why not?"

Davidson gives a weak chuckle. "What's this about Ava? I thought you gave up women in some kind of eternal Lent sacrifice."

Only Garcia and Davidson knew I'd never had sex. The rest of the men thought I was just very choosy and discreet. Worked for me. Of course, now that I've practically banged Ava on top of them, it's hard for them to square that with my past. And since I'm a fucking mess, it's hard to clarify things for anyone when I haven't worked it all out in my own mind. I want Ava. I need her but I can't keep her. "I'm still cursed if that's what you're asking. After all, Garcia's dead."

"That's some kind of bullshit," Davidson snorts. "Garcia

would be the first to congratulate you on busting a nut on some girl. And if it's more than that, all the better."

"I don't know what it is."

I lean my head against the door of the cab and close my eyes to signal that I'm done with the conversation. Davidson leaves me to my thoughts.

I tell myself I have people. I have Davidson back. We lost Garcia but mercenaries have short life spans. We're all on borrowed time. We should have died back in the desert. Even before then, outside the wire, some IED or enemy fire should have killed us. I've been on any number of missions and hits that could have seen me dead, but I survived. Maybe it was me who should have died in the jungle and not Garcia.

But I'm alive.

And Ava's back at the island. Healing. Getting ready to leave, if she's not already gone. In a desperate time, she laid her hands on me. She wanted me to save Rose. She wanted me to save her. I got half of that right but it's not enough.

## CHAPTER **THIRTY-THREE**

**AVA**

I don't wait to get started on my new, self-appointed job here on the island. I figure someone will pull me aside if I'm fucking with things that shouldn't be fucked with. I hunt down Fernanda and she gets a few other women, and we make a list of immediate needs and then not so immediate. I'm sad to hear what the immediate needs are: tampons, decent underwear, bras, birth control, medication for STIs since several of the girls came from brothels and have recurring issues, feminine hygiene products, even deodorant. It's clear they don't feel comfortable asking for more than the basics, not when their lives have been saved by these men and they'd feel guilty asking for more. That's all right. I'll ask for more on their behalf. It makes me feel good to help them.

I couldn't help Rose, but maybe her death can propel me into helping a lot of others. It's far more rewarding than hand modeling, at the very least. I feel good about this. I can help Rafe really make his island a refuge and a home, instead of just a place for these women to hide.

And most of all, I can help make them less afraid. After what I've been through in the last few weeks, this is important to me.

Because I'm staying, I put a few things on the list for me, too.

After I get the list, I head to Bennito. "I need you or some of your guys to go to the mainland and go shopping for this stuff."

"I can go," he says, then his brows draw together. "When did you want to leave?"

"I'm not going. I'm staying."

He grins like a naughty boy. "Uh-huh."

"What?"

"You're dickmatized. Boss must be good."

"It's none of your business," I say primly, but I'm smiling. I might be a bit dickmatized. So what? I happen to love the rest of the package, too.

He gestures at the list. "Seriously, though, tampons? Panties? Are you fucking with me?"

"I'm not, and I want those specific brands." I point at the paper. I've taken time to write down very specific brands, sizes, and types. "I don't care how long it takes to gather up, this is the stuff we need. It's very important to the women on the island."

"You speaking for them now?"

"I am," I say, and lift my chin. "A lot of them have been abused in the past and they're afraid to ask for basic stuff or to tell you that you're buying a crap brand. They feel more comfortable coming to someone like me."

He snorts but scans the list again. "I can head out and get this shit today, I guess. You want to come with?"

"Not this time." I'm afraid if I leave the island, I won't come back again. Like he'll dump me on the shore with a mention of "boss's orders" and then I'll never see Rafe again. I'm keeping my ass planted here until I get to talk to Rafe. Then, if he really wants me to go, I'll tuck my tail between my legs and head home to figure out what to do as a hand model that has ugly hands.

Bennito checks over the list again. "Extremely sexy lace bra, size 34DD? Matching garters and stockings in black? Red stilettos, size nine? Lubricant? Handcuffs? You sure this is all for the ladies on the island?"

There's no point in lying. "No, that shit is for me. It's a welcome home present for your boss." I plan on seducing Rafe until he's so lost that he won't possibly think it's a good idea for us to split up again. "Any other questions?"

He grins. "Just one. Can I watch?"

"Not on your life."

Bennito and two of the men return late that night with the stuff I've asked for, and I spend the next morning with Fernanda, distributing it and setting up a central "supply closet" in the old hotel. Two other women and I have keys to it, and we discuss setting up regular distributions and what we should ask the men to get next. It's sad to see the light shining in a sixteen-year-old ex-prostitute's eyes when she gets underwear with decent elastic or her baby gets a new blanket. It all makes me more determined that these ladies should have a better life. The island is gorgeous and safe, but the men won't know what they need if the women are too scared to ask for anything.

I get hugged by woman after woman, who exclaim their excitement in Portuguese, and I make a mental note to ask for some Rosetta Stone disks the next time Bennito heads out, so I can learn the basics. Fernanda looks happy, though, so it's a start.

Buzz is that the men are returning home that afternoon, so I take off to make myself pretty. Everything has to be perfect for my seduction tonight. I shave every inch of my body, even my pussy, because I remember he likes that I'm bare. I lotion up my limbs with my favorite sweet-scented body lotion, and take time curling my hair until it's big and bouncy. I put on light makeup—mostly mascara and eyeliner—so my eyes look big and luminous.

I put on the bra and adjust the straps. It's a push-up bra (Bennito's such a horndog) and my tits look even bigger than normal and jiggle as if they're about to fall out of the fabric. That's all right, because I don't plan on wearing this for long. I put on the garters and stockings, deliberately without panties, because I want to blow Rafe's mind. Last comes a pair of red stilettos and matching red lipstick.

There's no making my wrist bandage sexy, so I tie a bit of lacy ribbon on it. My bullet wound is two spots bandaged on my front and my back, and a lot of bruises. There's nothing I can do about that except hope that it doesn't detract from the overall picture.

I've also invaded Mendoza's room. The bed has newly washed sheets, and I've straightened the place up since there was laundry everywhere. It's obvious it's a guy's room, because there's almost nothing on the walls except for a shelf that holds a bunch of sports video games. I fix up the bed and dust it with rose petals, then set a few strategic candles in the room and light them. I turn on soft, sexy music.

Then I recline on the bed and wait.

According to Bennito, the men should be home any minute now, and I'm a bit nervous. Is Rafe going to think I'm too presumptuous? Too forward? I eye the handcuffs I've put on one corner of the bed. They're part of my plan. If he doesn't want to listen to all the reasons I think I should stay, I'm going to tie him down (sexily) and show him (also sexily) how good it will be if I stay.

The door opens, and I fluff my hair, waiting for Rafe to get a look at me.

The man that walks in is . . . not Rafe. He's tall, blond, and surprised to see me. Behind him is another man, good-looking, pale . . . also not Rafe.

I squeal and rip the blankets up, covering myself just as Rafe steps in behind the guys. Their eyes are wide.

The blond grins. "You must be Ava."

Rafe looks shocked to see me.

That's all right, I'm pretty freaking shocked myself. I hold the blankets over my pelvis (God, I am totally shaved and they've seen everything) and try to think of something to say. "Um . . . yes."

"I thought you'd be gone," Rafe says in a low voice. He's staring at the rise of my tits as they spill out of the bra. I probably should have covered them.

Nah, he can look his fill. His friends can, too, so they can see what he's getting in his bed.

I arch and fling my hair back over my shoulders, recovering

my groove. "I decided I was going to stay, and I thought I'd try and convince you why it was a good idea." I wiggle my eyebrows at him and hope he's not noticing my bullet wound, and staring at my sexiness instead.

He adjusts himself and nudges both the blond guy and the new guy. "Quit fucking staring at my girl."

"You're nailing that?" the new guy says. "Damn."

I tilt my head at Rafe. "He can if he wants to." I pat the bed, ignoring the fact that I've probably strewn rose petals everywhere. "Wanna come and talk about it?"

"Rafe, my man, those are handcuffs on the bed," one of them whispers. "If you pass this up, you're a goddamn idiot."

"You guys get the fuck out of here already," Rafe growls. He moves forward and tugs the sheets over my breasts. "Quit goddamn staring."

The blond grins. "We just came to get the new Madden game." He moves to the wall and plucks a few of the games off the shelf. "Though we'll stick around if—"

"Go," Rafe snarls.

They laugh, elbow each other like a pair of frat boys, and exit the room. Rafe shuts the door behind them quickly and then locks it.

He turns to me. "Ava."

"Rafe," I say, swinging my legs over the side of the bed and standing upright. I'm at my full height now, and he can see my bra, my garters, my lack of panties, and my freshly bare everything. I strut across the room in my red heels toward him. "You and I need to talk."

"That's what this is about?" he asks. "Talking?"

"Nope," I say, and grab him by the front of his shirt. I tug him toward the bed and he follows willingly. "This is about me saying that I missed you." I direct him to the edge of the bed and he sits down with a thump. I unbutton his shirt, revealing a wife-beater undershirt and lots and lots of hard, brown muscle. I sigh with pleasure at the sight. Man, I've missed looking at him. He's gorgeous. I even dig the scars. I strip off his shirt, and his gaze flicks down to my bare pussy, inches away from his mouth. His hands move to my ass, to cup me and drag me forward, but I shake my head. "Lie back."

He does, and I crawl over his body to retrieve the handcuffs, then take one wrist and cuff it to a bedpost. This causes my wound to twinge with pain, but I'm more interested in seduction than a few aches and pains. Besides, Rafe's not putting up a lick of protest as I crawl all over him, which excites me. Instead, he's gazing up at me. "What's all this for, Ava?"

"Persuasion," I tell him. Then I move down his chest and start kissing skin. "I need to convince you of all the reasons why I need to stay here on the island."

He groans. "Baby. I failed you."

I sit up straight, just before I'm about to lick his belly button. Is that what all this is about? "How did you fail me?"

His gaze is hungry as it feasts on my body. He looks me up and down, as if he doesn't know where to rest his gaze. It's probably a sensory overload for him, which makes me proud. He's not talking, so I straddle him and rub my pussy on his bare stomach. I'm wet already, because seducing him turns me on.

"Talk and I'll let you touch me," I say, reaching between my legs and beginning to play with my clit as I sit on top of him. He reaches for me with his free hand and I slap it away. "Nope. You haven't earned that yet. Talk to me. Tell me why you keep trying to send me away."

"Rose," he says gruffly. "I know you were with me because you wanted to save her. And I failed you."

I sigh and shake my head at him. "Rose got herself into trouble, and I'm the one that failed her. And if you think I slept with you because of bribery, you're an asshole." I lean forward and jab a finger into his chest. "I slept with you because I thought you were sexy and I wanted to. Because I'm crazy about you. Still am."

"And Rose?" he asks.

Boy, he's so sure that he's impossible to love, isn't he? My jabbing finger trails down his chest, and my other hand is sliding up and down against my clit. "I'm still processing her death, you know? It doesn't feel real to me. Like I might turn the corner and there's Rose, flirting with some old businessman." My breath catches and I have to stop for a moment. Crying over my best friend while I'm sexily straddling my guy is not the look I'm trying to achieve. "I just . . . I'm torn between being devastated that I lost my best friend and furious that she was such an idiot. And I do feel a bit lost without her, and it doesn't help that you keep pushing me away when I need you the most."

The look on his face is stricken. "I'm sorry, baby." He reaches for me again. "I just . . . you don't belong here. You'd be miserable and feel trapped."

"Are you kidding? I love you." The words choke from my mouth. "Wherever you are, I want to be there. Even if it's back in the jungle. Say the word and I'll go there with you. I just want to be at your side. Showing you that you're worthy of being loved." I lean forward again and press a kiss to his mouth. "Because I love you, Rafe Mendoza. All the bullshit aside, all the people and the bargains and the islands and the jungles and jobs and whatever other crap you think might stand in our way, I love you, and without you, I'm just sad, lonely Ava. And I'm tired of being her when Rafe's Ava is so much better."

## CHAPTER **THIRTY-FOUR**

RAFAEL

I stare wordlessly at her because she's struck me mute and dumb. I press her face into my neck because I can't look at her and say what I need to.

"There are no nightclubs here. You can't want to stay. What about the city? And parties? And fancy restaurants? There's very little shopping here. You're a model. Your hands will heal and you can go and model again."

"And I can't do that from the island?" She pushes away from my embrace. "Did Bennito not get on a plane today and get me all of this?" Her hand cups her satin-covered breast.

"That plane is two screws away from falling apart. I'm not putting you in that." I scowl.

"Baby, it doesn't matter. I wanted to live in New York because that's where Rose lived. She's not there anymore."

"The fact that I couldn't save her is even more reason you should be leaving," I growl harshly.

Her lips quiver. "I don't know why Rose was there but no one could save her."

I feel myself weakening. My desire for her is overcoming every honorable instinct. Insidious parts of me whisper that I can afford a better plane with the money the government deposited in my account after I delivered the goods. Davidson was just extra security for them. There are plenty of men coming and going from the island, undertaking different trips. Even if she wants to take up modeling again, there'd be transportation available. And as for keeping her safe, there is no place on Earth safer for Ava than this island, this room, and my bed. "Even if I believe you, what is there for you here?"

She gives me a small, secretive smile and unlocks the handcuff.

Disappointed, I rub my wrist as I watch her walk over to the French doors, admiring the flex of her bubble-shaped ass. I could watch her endlessly.

With a flick of her wrist, she throws the doors open and turns to me, gesturing. "What do you see?"

I rise to stand behind her, looking at the grove of palm trees separating us from the beach and then the ocean. The sun is setting and the water looks as if it's been painted by a master artist in golds and blues and silvers. "Sand. The ocean. Stars." *You. Your beautiful body, your amazing spirit. I see all the hope I've never had but wanted . . . in you.*

She laughs. "No, over there."

I follow the line of her pointed finger where a few of the women that we have brought with us from the favela are taking down laundry that they hung earlier in the day. Their colorful dresses wave like flags in the light breeze, and a couple of the children run in and out of the women's legs, playing tag.

"People?" I don't know where she's going with this.

"No, baby, this is a family. Rose was my family. She loved me. Maybe she had shit taste in men, but she had the hugest heart. She never backstabbed or gossiped about the other girls. She was the first one to congratulate you when you got a job, even if the job was the one that she had wanted. She would genuinely be happy for you. I miss her so much. I miss my family."

"And I took her away from you."

"No, Louis Duval took her away. You tried to save her. And then you brought me here where I'm needed. You've made a family here, Rafe. You have your brothers and sisters. You have children. But you don't have someone to sit by your side, hold your hand, and tell you that you're doing a good job. You don't have someone who can talk to the women and help ease their transition. You wanted to build a community and you've done it. You've laid the first bricks, but you need help. I want to be that help. It's so much better than holding bananas for three hours for a fruit ad." Her words tumble out in a passion I didn't realize she felt. And I can't keep turning her away if she wants to stay. I need her because she is the oxygen in my lungs, the blood that keeps my heart pumping, the spirit that fills my soul. I need her more than I need anything. I *burn* for her.

"You're right," I tell her, cupping my palms around her smooth, rounded shoulders. She's a vision of ripe curves and shadowed valleys. "But you've forgotten one thing. I kill people for a living. That's how I pay for all of this. My men and I? We're killers. The hands that you want on you are stained with blood. I might not have pulled the trigger on Rose, but I've made that shot a hundred times before."

She has to know the depravity we deal with to keep the heart of this community running before I fold her into my arms and accept whatever gifts she's giving me. She turns away from the doorway to press a finger against my lips.

"No. You've saved people. Me. Those folks out there. All of us."

"Oh, Ava," I mutter and crush my mouth against hers. For some reason she has chosen to look at me and my life through rose-tinted glasses. And no matter how many times I tried to tear them off, she remains steadfast to her own vision of it. So be it.

I have given her every opportunity to leave. I have confessed the worst of my sins to her. She still remains. And I do realize that the gift of her acceptance and her love can only be turned away so many times before it is withdrawn completely.

I kiss her with all the passion I've been holding back. My desire is strong enough to stir the water into a hurricane. Her mouth mates with mine with equal ferocity. I grip her to me and stride over to the bed.

The only thing I've ever thought I could offer to anyone is safety. I couldn't provide that to Ava but she still wants me. Still *loves* me. I don't understand it, not fully.

Laying her gently on the mattress, I tear at the lace and satin and cotton that she so carefully chose for her seduction, until she is adorned with nothing but scraps.

In the dim light of the room, her eyes glitter as she delves one provocative hand between her legs. I watch with unfettered hunger as her fingers dip inside her honey.

"Want some?" The offering sets me ablaze.

I grab her fingers and suck every pearl of juice from her digits, and then I push her hand aside to go to the source. Her cunt smells like the tropics—full of sunshine and pleasure. I place reverent kisses all over her smooth skin and inside her thighs that are wet with her arousal. Even I know that this can't be faked.

I lay the flat of my broad tongue against her warm core and drink. This is the fountain of life, I think. If I die tomorrow, it will be all right because tonight I have taken from the goddess herself. As I suck, kiss, and lick every pink-flushed inch of her, I feel invincible, nearly immortal.

Because no mere man should be allowed to touch flesh as exquisite as this and taste nectar as delicious as she produces. She begs for me to make her come, to shove my *huge dick* inside her until she screams. But I'm going to make her scream now, just from my tongue. I want the juice to flood my face. I want her to shake and quiver into my mouth so that when I'm standing around tomorrow I can still feel the pressure of her thighs as she squeezes my head and tugs at my hair. I want her to come so hard that with every swallow I still taste her.

"Fuck, you taste good," I moan as I lick her over and over.

"More," she pleads. "I need more."

I work two fingers inside her, the passage tight even around my fingers and I marvel that she can stretch to accommodate my fat cock. I worship her pussy, jacking her with my fingers, tonguing her firm, aroused clit until her nails dig into my scalp and I feel her tighten and then explode under my touch. And it's everything I hoped for, everything I imagined. She screams as she comes, a loud, long wail that the sirens probably use to lure sailors to their doom. Her whole body lifts off the mattress, pressing into my tongue, clutching at my fingers. And I drink it all down.

Every last drop until the aftershocks stop and her shakes turn to tiny trembles.

"Oh, baby," she whimpers when I withdraw. "That was too much."

"No way. There's no way you can have too much good in your life. You deserve it all. All these orgasms, every day of your life. I want to give that to you. I want to love you."

"You do. I can feel it." She reaches for me, but I move away.

With shaking hands, I grab the discarded handcuffs at the side of the table. "You're moving too much," I whisper hoarsely.

"Am I?" Her voice is coquettish and challenging. "What are you going to do about it?"

"This." In one quick move, I tenderly grasp her wrist and latch the handcuff onto one of them—on the side opposite of her hurt shoulder, and then hook it to the bedpost. "I've spent a lot of years going without, but that doesn't mean I haven't had fantasies."

I run my hands across her collarbones and down along the ridges of her rib cage. She feels like the most expensive silk the East has ever produced. "You okay? This isn't hurting you?" Her shoulder is still tender.

"Oh yeah," she breathes out. I smooth my hands down her arms, testing to make sure that she's comfortable. My hands move up to cup her tits, and my thumbs rub her nipples, which have hardened into tight points. "Pinch them," she says.

I do as she tells me and she shudders. "More?" I ask. She nods and I pinch harder. Her legs squeeze together and then release. No fantasy has ever been this good.

"I want to suck on those tits and fuck you with my cock while you're handcuffed to the bed. You good with that?"

"Yes, please." Her sweet cunt clenches again in anticipation.

I palm her ass in one hand and grip myself in the other. She widens her legs and we share a gasp as I position the broad head of my shaft at her wet entrance. She's always so wet for me, so ready.

"Now?" I ask.

She nods, lip caught between two rows of perfect teeth. I slide into her carefully, pausing at each juncture to make sure she's comfortable, that this is the right side of pleasure for her.

"Keep going, baby. I have to have you in me *now*!" Her demands cut through the straining tether of my self-control. I slam the rest of the way in until my balls are slapping her ass. She cries out but by now I recognize that high keening noise as one of utter fucking delight. "God, I feel everything with you. Everything. Hurry now," she orders and then pushes up, grinding her hips against mine.

I let her fuck me, using me as I latch onto one nipple. Lightly restrained, with my big paws clamped around her hips and my mouth devouring her tit, she owns me completely. She rides me with abandon, grinding her clit against my pubic bone, shafting herself on my cock until her head lolls back because it's too heavy for her to hold it up. I take over then.

I thrust into her, jacking her until her tits are bouncing, her hair is swinging, and her entire body is one jagged erotic motion. I fuck her until there are stars in my eyes and the whole of my heart detonates like a bomb. She's not the last hope in the world; she's the only hope for me.

# EPILOGUE

## AVA

It's been a month now, and I'm still coming to terms with Rose's death. I catch myself wanting to call her to tell her a funny joke, or I see a dress on one of the island ladies and think, oh, that would look great on Rose. Then I remember that my best friend is dead, and there's no getting past the pain. Maybe there's never a way past the pain.

Rose is in my dreams, though. She visits from time to time, and she's always smiling and happy. Maybe because that's how I saw her in life, that's how I choose to see her in death. It's all right, though. Someday, those dreams are going to disappear, so I cherish them while I have them.

I've been on the island for a few weeks, and every day feels like . . . well, to be cliché, it's paradise. I wake up to freshly made, delicious food and the scent of the ocean on the air. I wake up in the hard, muscled arms of the man who fucked me six ways from Sunday the night before. He kisses my brow and touches me all over, and we usually have sex before we start the day, because we can't get enough of each other.

One month isn't enough time to get tired of Rafe Mendoza. One year, one lifetime—it'll never be enough. He's like an addiction to me, and one I find I crave more as the hours pass. His smile is better than any narcotic, and when he holds me under him and pushes so deep inside me, I feel . . . everything.

I've come to love life here on the island. It's weird. When I was in New York City, I was the den mother to a bunch of skinny models who wanted to smoke all day and talk about the food they wouldn't eat. I didn't think twice about it; I just stepped into the role and took care of them.

Here on the island, I'm the den mother to dozens of ladies who have been used hard in life. They come to me for all kinds of things, from small complaints about laundry soap to bigger issues like sickness and babies and romantic advice. Because I'm Mendoza's "lady," I'm the leader of the women here. I'm den mother all over again, except instead of herding a bunch of skinny chain-smoking models, I'm herding a bunch of young women with tired eyes who have seen too much life. I'm handed babies and asked advice about cooking, laundry, nutrition, and a million things I've never considered before, but which are now of grave importance. These women on the island are bringing themselves up from nothing. They are starting over, or trying to, and they need help.

It's become my new goal to bring joy to their faces. To make the world a safer place for them. To give them hope.

Because that's what Rafe Mendoza has done for me. He's given me a new world to live for, and new hope every day. He's given me a new family that welcomes me with open arms. They don't care that I had the world's silliest job in the past. What's important is that I'm here now, and I want to help.

And Rafe? Rafe is amazing. He's the best man in the world. I don't care that he's a contract killer and that's how these men make a living. I don't care that sometimes Rafe has to leave in the middle of the night to mete out justice. That's how they make the money to save these women and men that are in hiding here. I like to believe that the good that they're doing far outweighs the bad, and when I'm handed a crying child that was born to a once-crack-addicted mother from a whorehouse? When I look into that baby's eyes, I see the life we can give it. The hope we can give it. This child isn't going to grow up on the streets selling itself to pedophiles to make its mother enough money for a drug hit. It's going to grow up here in an island paradise made safe by men who risk their lives to make their new family one worth coming home to.

Because the Tears of God is all about hope. And to me, Rafe is about hope. He's my life, and my love. I look into his eyes and see the hungry way he looks at me, and I know I'm looking at him the same way. And I can't regret a single moment, a single hour, a single minute of our time together.

Rafe's my life, and I'm his. May we go on forever this way.

# Don't let this Hitman novel be your last— read all of the books in this thrilling series!

## From bestselling authors
## JESSICA CLARE and JEN FREDERICK

## ON SALE NOW

"Sexy, thrilling romantic suspense."
—Smexy Books

"Phenomenal."
—*New York Times* bestselling author Sara Fawkes

"Everything you could ask for."
—All Romance Reviews

**jillmyles.com**
**jenfrederick.com**
**penguin.com**

Penguin
Random
House
BERKLEY